A HALFWAY *decent* GIRL

A HALFWAY *decent* GIRL
A NOVEL

RHONDA TALBOT

CREATIVE ARTS BOOK COMPANY
BERKELEY • CALIFORNIA

A *Halfway Decent Girl* is published by Donald S. Ellis
and distributed by Creative Arts Book Company

For information contact:
Creative Arts Book Company
833 Bancroft Way
Berkeley, California 94710
1-800-848-7789

ISBN 0-88739-333-0
Library of Congress Catalog Number 99-069688
Printed in the United States of America

for Judy

A HALFWAY *decent* GIRL

CHAPTER ONE

MY MOTHER MADE PROMISES. "IT WILL GET BETTER," SHE WOULD SAY. "Good things are just around the corner. Our luck is about to change." Next month, next summer, next year. We'd be happy, eventually, later on, sometime in the future, in some other place. Her promises swarmed wild and weightless, rising and settling with her moods. Dust.

We were watching *Play Misty for Me* on our fossilized black-and-white television set, sprawled out, hot and swollen, on her floppy waterbed, munching Wheat Thins and swilling Tabs.

"That's where we belong, Sugarsnap," my mother said. Clint Eastwood was holding her captive, his face etched with determination and secret knowledge. Clint knew the answers, racing his sexy convertible along a beachfront highway. Mom vaulted forward causing the waterbed to hiccup and slosh, and followed the darting image with her finger.

"Right there on the coast," she pointed, charting a trail of static.

I rolled my eyes, too heat-stunned to protest—summer's cruel humidity robbing my good senses. Just as Clint was about to get scissored through his manly chest by psycho-girl, Mom fell to her knees like an obedient church girl and embraced the set as though she might crawl inside.

1

"Christ, I even look like his girlfriend! I mean, not Miss Beelzebub, but the petite blonde. Don't I?"

I raised an eyebrow, used to my mother comparing herself to fashion models, actresses, first ladies. "Not really," I grunted.

Reluctantly releasing her grip, Mom collapsed back on the bed, generating more waves and ripples, rocking me something sick. "C'est la vie," she said with a romantic sigh. "You know, I can't think of a single person I would miss."

This kind of talk made me nervous. I straightened up.

"Well, I have friends here, Mom. I actually made some friends. I'm liked. Loved," I whined, stretching it. "I almost have a boyfriend. Let's not move for a change."

"What friends?" she smirked, reaching under a pile of *Cosmopolitans* for her cigarettes. "Who, Jeannie, who, for example? Give me a name." She lit what seemed like her hundredth smoke, forcing any remaining oxygen out of the room.

"Bill," I blurted, regretting the word as soon as it came out of my mouth.

"Bill?" She made him sound like a contagious disease. "The hippie with the rat-infested hairdo? Reach higher, Jeannie! Reach higher! Have I taught you nothing? Doesn't he have six fingers?"

I bit into a Wheat Thin and thought about Sandy Duncan's glass eye. What happened to it anyway? "That's a rumor, Mom."

She jumped up and shook out her rigged-up mane, jeweled stickpins exploding like blasting caps, then arranged the wispy strands into an unruly mass. "Hoods," she said. "All of them. They give me an itch. Except Lara. Her I like."

"You like anybody who's rich," I said.

Clint was making torrid, seaside love to the petite blonde, waves lapping at their sandals.

"Lara has class. That's what intrigues me."

"What's so classy about California?" I challenged.

My mother squatted down on the wood-framed edge of the bed, again transfixed, holding one hand in the air like a stop signal. "Jeannie," she said, her voice dropping a few octaves like she was possessed. "If you can't be quiet, I'd rather watch this alone. And quit making waves in the bed."

A few weeks later Mom's hair was stylishly layered and dyed the color of the sun—an expensive, start-packing gesture. By now, there were no farther points west for us in Michigan. We had already exhausted half a dozen suburbs, each one supposedly filled with promise and salvation—a superior school system, provocative employment opportunities, more desirable men. But none of them had come through. Keego Bay, nestled miles outside Detroit, in the midst of so many polluted lakes, had been our last shot at redemption and it too had failed us. California beckoned, the next logical step, my mother's latest daydream.

❧ ❧ ❧ ❧

I needed to see Bill. I had to lose my virginity before I entered Eden.

"Think he'll be in the lot?" Lara shouted. She was all cheekbones, lips and legs; painted, powdered and photograph-perfect. Being friends with her gave me an enviable though wholly undeserved "foxy" status.

"Get movin', you old bag!" Lara eased the car right up to the old bag's bumper, then honked.

"Bill lives at that place," I shouted to be heard over the music. The very mention of Bill's name caused my stomach to flutter.

We were aiming to get the Cutlass up to eighty miles an hour on Woodward Avenue, Detroit's main artery, the lifeline of culture. Woodward began at the Detroit River, or One Mile Road, and dead-ended at the suburban lakes at Nineteen Mile Road. We knew where it was still safe to cruise and where it might get dicey. For example, girls could get raped south of Eight Mile. Going the other direction, things got pretty dull once you were beyond Fourteen Mile, so we teetered between Nine and Twelve Mile, looking for trouble at the Burger Kings, shopping malls, roller-skating rinks.

The sun was setting, headlamps and streetlights popped on in all directions as we whipped past familiar neighborhoods. Local news broadcasts and the smell of meat loaf filled the air. I was getting anxious about the whole sex idea.

"What if I get crabs or vd?" I yelled.

"Just have him pull out before the flood," Lara recommended, rocking back and forth to the music. She glimmered and tinkled, both arms layered in bracelets, hands gloved in mood rings, ears dangling golden triangles—a human percussion instrument.

"God, girl, I'm so bummed out!" she whined, pounding the wheel dramatically, shooting sparks. "I want to go to California with you. Imagine working on your tan all year long!"

But I was thinking only about Bill and the sex, afraid of the actual act. I'd never met anyone who I'd want to be naked with or even be that physically close to. At fifteen, I was an "old" virgin, a spinster. The very thought of the male anatomy revolted me. Boys were muscled and furry; beast-like. They were pimpled, had bad breath and were always playing in the dirt. I rolled down my window and let the cool breeze flatten my face.

Someone dared to honk at us. "Fuck you," we yelled in unison, then flipped the rude driver the bird. I always had more nerve when I was with Lara.

We fired up smokes, pulled into our parking lot destination, and idled.

"I already told my parents I plan to visit for Christmas." Lara's long black hair was carefully plaited, topped off with an elaborately beaded headband she wore like a tiara.

"Cool," I nodded, searching the lot for signs of our group.

Lara dumped the contents of her hulking suede purse onto the seat. Assorted lipstick tubes, eye shadows, charm bracelets, and crumpled Kabbala literature clacked into a pile. Lara's braids were so tight they looked fake, like store-bought clip-ons. Sometimes I wanted to yank them.

"Tell me the truth, Jeannie," Lara said, looking directly at me. "Do you think I look like a Navajo?"

"Totally," I guessed, having never really seen a Navajo. Having recently grown tired of being Jewish, Lara was telling anyone who mattered (well, boys) that she was adopted from a reservation in Arizona, a tribe so mystical they glowed in the dark.

"Give me your face," Lara demanded, gliding soapy lipstick over my mouth. "Guys go nuts over this stuff."

Lara jerked the gear stick and we rolled a few more feet toward the shopping center, the Thirteen Mile intersection, our hangout.

"Okay," she said, turning off the radio. We needed to concentrate. "Let's scan the crowd."

The mall parking lot was void of regular traffic, civilians

abandoning any further shopping after dark—show time for the rest of us. Twenty or so junked-up cars were parked irregularly around the lot, several gleaming motorcycles grouped together, a few customized vans with their back doors spilled open—a tailgate party without a game, a drive-in theater without the screen.

Dozens of young hoods milled about, grouped together by drug preference—potheads sat huddled in one smoky circle-jerk, pill heads in another, and the heroin addicts were banished to the edge of the lot like contagion. Beer-guzzling bikers pretty much kept to themselves, standing guard around their Harleys, hurling insults at everyone. Bad Neil Young guitar riffs were provided by the potheads.

"God," Lara sighed, checking out the scene. "I've got like at least ten bathing suits for you to take, plus ankle straps, and some mules." I grabbed Lara's arm and shushed her. "There he is." My stomach churned and shimmied its way into my throat. Bill had a paralyzing effect on me. Leaning against his Pontiac, drinking a Molson, Bill was a dead-ringer for Jesus—the unkempt chestnut hair, frowning mustache, hang-dog expression. To complete the look, a red-and-white bandanna crowned his head like thorns. His best pal, Dandy Dave, blew high notes on a harmonica.

"All right!" Lara cheered, pushing open her door. "Dave's here. He always has good pot."

Dave was the most noteworthy among us, the one we revered, the walking pharmaceutical textbook who claimed to have double-Dutched with Mick Jagger at Studio 54. He was forever flaunting an exhausted-looking silk ascot as a reminder.

Lara spritzed me with her Shiseido Sport spray.

"Just fuck him, Jeannie," she urged.

I took a deep drag off her cigarette, hoping to inhale some of her courage.

"I don't know what you're waiting for," she said, spritzing her wrists, neck, and inner thighs. "You're like the oldest virgin I know. I would've fucked him a long time ago. But he never wanted me."

She gave me a soft punch in the arm, and I thanked her for the pep talk. It was puzzling, this idea that Bill didn't want Lara, my friend with all the curves, a succulent, dangling pear easily plucked. It seemed wrong, slightly irrational that he chose me, a know-nothing, a hard, green banana. Maybe he was gay.

Lara sashayed through the parking lot, hips swaying under her tiny swatch of buckskin skirt.

It struck me that maybe her sexual spunk was inherited from her father, the o.b. In Lara's family, reproductive organs surely held no mystery—discussed at the dinner table, where a vagina might be polite table conversation, the word "penis" passed around like a stick of butter.

I waded through the crowd, nodding and waving to the regulars. "When's Clara getting back?" "How's her tan coming along?" the stoners gaily inquired, like she was vacationing in Aruba, though everyone knew she was lodged at Juvenile Hall. Clara was missed, mourned by some on account of her being the parking-lot dope supplier. Lara flashed me an encouraging smile and disappeared into a van.

I sauntered up to Bill and let out a long breath, not realizing I had been holding it in, then blurted, "Should we have sex?"

Faster than he could say "free-balling," we were parked near the junkies on the edge of the lot, slipping around, frantic fish in the backseat of the Pontiac.

"Dreams come true out in California, baby," he whispered to me with garlic breath. "Anything's possible. Look at Morrison, Jefferson Airplane. Mama Cass, Gidget. You've got it made in the lazy shade, my friend."

In my nervous state, I suddenly remembered something.

"Did you know that Mama Cass's real name was Ellen Cohen?"

"Well, there you go," Bill continued. "Before she went to Cal she was just another fat Jewish girl."

Bill's hands were fast, unpredictable. Somehow they were cupping my ass, ramming our groins together.

"Did you know my friend Lara's real name is Laura? She dropped the u in middle school. After she saw Dr. Zhivago."

"No shit?"

During the talking and groping, Bill had managed to get my pants down around my knees. He paused to see how I might react, or if I had changed my mind, but I hadn't. I think he was a bit stunned at his good fortune.

I cringed, remembering I hadn't shaved my legs in a couple

days. Then there were my flapjack tits. Bill would soon learn that I was flat-chested and prickly, a rolled-out strip of cheap industrial carpet, not at all worthy of his love.

I lay on the vinyl seat in a state of increasing panic, moving my arms around, not really knowing where to put them, desperate, on the brink of tears.

Bill breathed heavily into my ear. I imagined how we looked to someone walking by, wondered if the passerby could tell I was useless, pitifully inexperienced. Maybe someone could give me good, solid instructions. Stroke here, caress that, say this. Then I had a strange thought. Maybe it was possible to deflower yourself with a tampon and I wasn't a virgin after all!

Bill held my feverish face with both hands, then ran one finger across my filmy lips. Suddenly I was so terrified that I began to laugh.

"Bill, this seems so goofy. Is this really what people do?" He looked at me in a serious, adult way. He was experienced, a man.

"I have such a mongoose in my pants," he explained, grinding me into the seat with his hips. As he moved with urgency, gasping and yelling and carrying on, I tried to keep up, move in rhythm with him, but my breathing was all wrong. I sounded ridiculous, huffing and panting, a thirsty dog. We had trouble getting Bill's "mongoose" inside me but after some effort we succeeded. This was followed by a sharp pain, a forced cramming with what felt like a thick, knotted rope. I had been anticipating something smooth, perhaps sheathed sausage. I continued the huffing, my head inflated with white static, my ears ringing. The in-and-out motion went on for a few seconds—then I was seeing stars and maybe even heard music and I wondered if I was having good sex, or if I was just hyperventilating. Bill screamed something unintelligible and collapsed on top of me. Dead and heavy. It was over.

We lay motionless, Bill struggling for breath as if he had been laboring for hours, like it was so much hard work.

The world came rushing back inside my head. Lights, horns, city noise. Finally, I had sexed it up, gone all the way, taken the salami. I wondered if I was glowing. Bill had not warned me about the flood, hadn't said anything at all, millions of little sperm, swimming, flailing, lost. Bill leaned close to me and whispered, "Do you want a beer?"

The feeling was coming back into my limbs and I wondered if I'd had an orgasm. Clara had told me it was like a tiny bomb going off. A cherry bomb—a fast pop. I had not felt this. I wondered if I was bleeding.

"Sure," I said, becoming aware of a dull soreness between my legs. With a giant thirst, I chugged half the can of beer.

"You know what I've always wanted to do?" Bill said. "Take the Coors Beer factory tour." He was scrunched up on the floorboard, fumbling with the snaps on his jeans.

Bill snatched my beer can, drained the remains, then tossed it out the window. It landed with a loud clink among the others. He belched freely, without reservation.

"Those fools out in Colorado let you walk through for free and to top it off, they give you a complimentary brew."

He shook his head in disbelief. I was only half listening to him, my mind still experiencing the sex, going over every detail, trying to figure out exactly what it had felt like, if I had missed something.

"The beer itself is made from Rocky Mountain snow," Bill said, then winked.

"Wow," I said, trying to sound involved. Bill didn't seem to notice that I had just lost my virginity. But then again, maybe I hadn't. I wriggled around in the backseat and felt between my legs. No blood.

"That's where I'm headed just as soon as I can," he continued, oblivious to my scrambling. "I'm going to start working double shifts at the Tool and Die, save up my dough. Hey, that way you won't be such a far drive."

He twirled some of my hair around a finger and climbed back on top of me. "That's always been a big dream of mine," he said with a sexy moan. "Walking through that factory, seeing those big vats of hops being pumped and pumped." I wondered if we were going to fuck again.

"So what's your dream, babe?"

I felt caught, I had no answer, so I went with something my mother might say.

"Paul Newman. I mean I've always wanted him to be my dad."

"Cool."

How stupid. My cheeks burned. Bill lit a cigarette, little halos sprung from his mouth. A siren blared in the distance.

"I mean that's just a joke, Bill. About Paul Newman. I have some dreams," I boasted, thinking quickly. "Big dreams. Like discovering life on Polaris, for example."

Outside the window, the moon was a dangling orb, a pockmarked pearl, below it a pulsing, glass star.

"Whoa. Heavy."

"Bill, do you think it's true that once you lose your virginity you never get it back again? Like the dissolving cherry idea?"

"That is so fucking bogus. You can get your virginity back whenever you want it. It's like faith."

He leaned forward and pulled his coveted Swiss Army knife from the inside of a decaying work boot.

"Here. Don't lose this. I've had it since the eighth grade. It's original, with the little cross and shit. It'll bring you good luck."

I ran my finger along the smooth, silver edge, then pulled out a miniature can opener.

"This doesn't seem like it would be useful in a battlefield," I said.

"You'd be surprised. That thing can do mucho damage. Anyway, thought it might come in handy. You might want a beer when you're blowing across the country with your mama."

"Wow, Bill. Wow."

I wanted to tell him that I loved him, but I couldn't risk it. I took comfort in knowing we had reached some new level in our relationship. The sex, the after-sex period of smoking cigarettes, discussing dreams, a gift-exchange. It wasn't a cliché after all. It was evidence of love.

"You know, I usually shave my legs every day and also I generally have more orgasms. It's just the crowded space we're in. I'm just usually a lot better at this." I clutched the knife in one hand and chugged more beer with the other. Lies came out of my mouth more naturally than the truth. Then I wondered if that was true for everyone.

"I love your legs," he whispered, then sucked on my neck. My heart raced. I looked at him longingly, full of expectation.

"Hey. I gave you my knife, babe. You're my girl."

I was his girl.

He licked my face, then jumped into the front seat.

"What happens now?" I asked, searching for answers.

"Nothing," Bill said, turning up the radio.

"Right."

"Dominique" was playing. Bill lit up a joint, whoofed in the smoke and held it there, slowly pulling in his words as he spoke.

"So . . . what's . . . going . . . to . . . happen . . . to . . . Clara . . . anyway?"

"Probably go live with my dad. She'll hate it."

"Bummer. Clara used to be such a fox."

He exploded with pot smoke, his whole body bucking and deflating, then held the joint up in the air as if to admit defeat. "Whoa." He found his breath, then helped me roll over onto the front seat, our legs touching, his sperm gooey between my thighs. I was his girl.

"Listen to this crap. Do you think those nuns were even fucking French?"

He shoved a Deep Purple tape into the cassette player.

"Yeah. They're like from Paris. My mom knows all the words. She played this album all the time when I was small. Now she even speaks some French."

I saw Mom reclining on our front lawn, strumming an old guitar, singing, dreaming of some other life, doves cooing at her feet.

"Christ. Your mom probably likes The Flying Nun."

"No way," I lied. "My mom's way cooler than that." But she loved the show, and so did I. We both caught the afternoon rerun whenever we could. I took another hit from the joint.

"And who the fuck was crazy enough to give these evil penguins a record contract?" Bill said. He cranked the volume full throttle. "Hey. Here comes the good part. Dah dah dah dah dah dee dah, dah dah dah dee dah."

"Babe," I whispered, having never called him this before, testing my new role as his lover. Sex was supposed to bring you closer, perhaps give you courage. Lara suggested post-coital ownership. But I felt none of this.

"I really should be getting home," I suggested, pocketing the knife.

CHAPTER TWO

BILL DROPPED ME OFF A BLOCK FROM MY HOUSE, A ROUTINE WE started, given my mother's opinion of him.

At first I thought I was hallucinating from bad pot, but as I stumbled farther down the gravel road the blur that was my home became clearer, less deniable. All of our furniture and belongings, some bagged, some boxed, had been basically dumped onto the front lawn of our condominium—a year-end clearance sale of everything we owned. Draped across the front window was a banner reading, "Everything Is Free!" Positioned in the middle of this heap, knee-deep in soft cushions and sharp corners, my mother was already dressed for the beach, cigarette in one hand, staple gun in the other.

The cheap lantern-like porch light illuminated her, along with two bright floodlights that she had rigged to cast a glare over the front of the condo, giving a kind of opening-night feel to the whole affair.

I stopped in the middle of the road and rubbed my sore, pot-stung eyes, suddenly craving a bowl of Raisin Bran, some buttery toast, an apple. I wondered if my mother had already tossed out the food.

Our bed mattresses, yellowed with age, leaned up against each other like a teepee; box springs lay in a heap along the front wall; packing boxes were stacked on top of tables; dressers leaned on their sides; drawers gaped open, their contents spilling out. My attention was drawn toward the gleaming white refrigerator that blocked our front door. It wasn't even ours; it had come with the place. But that hadn't stopped my mother. There it was, ready for a buyer, decorative magnets and all. A few family photographs were still tacked onto the freezer section.

My mother saw me and waved her staple gun.

"Hey, hey!" she yelled. "Jean, you're home. Well, guess what?" She lifted both arms up in the air. "Clint Eastwood isn't just a fantasy! Donna Mills, move over!"

I pulled my jean jacket tighter around me and felt the color rise in my cheeks. Looking down the deserted block, I was ever so grateful that we lived on a dead-end street.

"Did you hear me, Jeannie?" she shouted.

She was wearing a Budweiser T-shirt and blue-jean cutoffs— a college kid ready for a round of beach volleyball. Autumn leaves sat in crackling stacks all around us, the clouds bloated with snow not quite ready to fall. Mom winked at me, then leaned over and stapled a price tag into the wood of our dining room table.

"What do you think? Twenty bucks?"

"I thought everything was free?"

"People with a conscience won't pay any attention to that."

I wondered what lucky owner would have the privilege of discovering the years of wadded-up bubble gum and other assorted garbage stuck to the underside of this contemporary antique.

"Did we get evicted?" I asked, wearily.

My mother smoked, whistled, and stapled. "Does it matter?"

"Mom, I just started school. Shouldn't we take some time to think about it? Maybe we should wait until next semester or something."

She stopped whistling, put one hand on her hip, the other still working the staple gun. Click . . . click . . . click it went, spewing out small pieces of steel wire. The thing looked lethal. With a Stetson hat and cowboy boots, she'd come in first-place if there were such a thing as an Annie Oakley look-a-like contest.

"Jeannie, love," she said, her trigger finger taking a rest. "We're out of time. My babe years are rapidly dwindling." She struggled to take puffs off her cigarette without removing it from her lips, resumed firing.

"Where've you been anyway? I could've used your help," she said, studying me, her face veiled in smoke. I was suddenly afraid she'd be able to sense Bill's presence, smell his sperm, which, by now, had dripped down to my socks.

"Just out with Lara," I mumbled, walking away, thankful for once to smell like cigarettes and pot. I buried my face inside my jacket and waded through the maze of household stuff: empty coffee cans stuffed with stiff-bristled paint brushes, piles of pot holders and throw pillows, a potato masher, a milk crate. I plopped onto our metallic gray sofa, nappy and uncommon, our Siamese cat. The seat was stained with wren poop, dating back to when mom was in her "save the wounded creatures" phase. We also had taken in a horny stray poodle, a grounded robin, and once a lost Canadian goose. I ran my fingers through the soft fabric and yanked out some tufts, shoved them between the cushions, then, out of habit, used my purse to hide the stain that was normally hidden by a throw pillow.

"When are we leaving exactly?" I asked.

My mother spat her cigarette on the grass and snubbed it out with a beat-up clog. "You want a Tab, sweetie?"

She sauntered over to the disconnected refrigerator and opened the door—a stick of margarine and a faded box of baking soda.

"God, we've got a lot of junk," she complained, giving herself a quick temple massage.

It occurred to me that she must've dragged all of our possessions outside by herself. She had probably waited for me to leave, then began dismantling our home—at it all day and into the night. That's how it was with my mother. Balls up high, juggle, juggle—whoops. A green hose snaked down from the second-floor window, draining the waterbed, irrigating our neighbor's lawn.

"Maybe I should just kill myself, Mom," I said.

"Oh, rats," she said, snapping her fingers. "We're out of Tab."

She was pulling things from a Hefty bag, arranging them on top of the dining room table. A rusted curling iron, a scummy toilet bowl plunger. Like, who's going to buy that?

"Did you hear me, Mom?" I said. "I'll just slit my wrists. Then you can do what you want, go anywhere you want."

She looked at me and sighed. "Look, if you still hate it once we're there, we'll reconsider. Okay? There's always Hawaii."

"Or Japan," I mumbled, closing my eyes and staring into the insides of my lids.

"Besides," she said, unable to resist. "All we have are those cheap disposable blades. That would be a tough trick."

I threw her a smart-alecky smile, but it let her know it was all okay. Could you eventually shave down to that important vein?

Rambling around the lawn, I peered into boxes, wincing, horrified at the remnants of our life so far. I found a faded papier mâche' bluebird Clara had made in the fifth grade, when her life still seemed hopeful. Now the bird's eyes were plucked out, its tail chipped—another wounded creature.

"Hi, Jean. You must be splitting a spleen with excitement!"

I pretended to not hear the comment, yanking yellow thongs from a box. Leslie, our scary next-door neighbor was also dressed for summer, wearing a man's white dress shirt and high-heeled bedroom slippers with red fuzzy balls on the tips.

"Can you imagine this, Leslie!" my mother yelled. "The only teenager in Michigan who doesn't want to go to California!"

"I didn't say that, Mom!" But before I could clarify my position, my mother and Leslie had begun a conversation about policemen as potential lovers. They were laughing and whispering, not wanting me to hear. As if I gave a damn. It wasn't their conversation I found disturbing, but my mother's sudden friendliness toward Leslie. Under normal circumstances, we both avoided the woman. Leslie had worn us down over the past year with her incredible stories, her award-winning dramas. With a voice that reminded me of Hitchcock's violins, she'd go on and on about the fisticuffs she'd had with her brutal ex-husband, her three hyperactive children, the failed job interviews, her ability to fit into a perfect size six.

"But does he wear the gun to bed?" I heard my mother ask, followed by Leslie's piercing laugh. Like my mom actually cared! Apparently, Leslie was dating a cop now. That made sense. The police had been to her house often enough, to arrest her door-banging ex-husband. What a rabble-rouser. The dutiful officer had probably seen Leslie in nothing but a flimsy nightgown, her slender legs turned in at the knee, saucer-eyed, hot tears running down her distraught face. I could almost imagine, in that situation, in the soft moonlight, how Leslie could be pretty.

But tonight, all lit up by our yard sale floodlights, I had to shade my eyes. Her hair was bleached white and stood straight up like toothbrush bristles. Leslie took a drag off my mother's cigarette, then wiped a laugh's tear from her eye. My mother handed her an oversized black-and-white portrait of John Wayne. John had hung above my mother's bed since the beginning of time. He would not be coming to California with us.

"This is super, Daisy," Leslie said. "Now there's a real man for you." They laughed and began digging through a box of books.

"You know," Leslie said, pointing at me with a bony finger. "When my ex dumped me here in this god-forsaken armpit, I thought, what will Leslie do? How will Leslie survive this? But I did. Right? You're gonna be fine, Jeannie."

Shut up, psycho, I thought.

"You'll love it out there," she squealed. "It's the Golden Coast. Eureka! Get it?" She was flipping through The Female Eunuch searching for pictures. "You've got real pioneers out there. And there's a brand of touchy-love not associated with the Midwest. Why, you see it all the time on the TV. Right, Daisy?"

"Leslie, do you have any more Ativan?"

I stared up at the sky. For a moment thought I saw a UFO, but no such luck. A small plane sputtered overhead. Searching the skies for any suspicious activity, I was suddenly hit by a small shower of seed casings shaped like miniature whirlybirds, fluttering down from the trees, landing at my feet.

"Are you going to leave this stuff out here all night, Mom?"

A baby shrieked from inside Leslie's townhouse. She rolled her eyes and tossed The Female Eunuch back into the box, grabbed the portrait and our ironing board, balancing them under each arm, and jogged up to her porch.

"Did you hear me, Mom?" Then in a stage whisper: "How can you stand talking to her?"

"Oh, honey. She's not that bad. Anyway, we'll never see her again, so what the hell."

My mother was sorting through her albums: Tom Jones Live in Vegas, The Singing Nun's Greatest Ever Hits, Joan Baez—music we maligned at school. She was whistling a popular Roberta Flack tune, then it became a hum, then finally she was belting out the lyrics. "He was strumming my face!"

I told myself to lighten up, go with the flow. Maybe it wouldn't be so bad "out west." Lara would visit, maybe Bill. My friends all spazzed out when it came to California, a place they all wanted to be. But the idea of being there alone with my mom depressed me. I took a deep breath and tried to shake it off.

I glimpsed Clara's old beat-up black jacket sticking out of a box marked "Salvation Army." Jerking it free, I sank my face into it, breathing in Clara smells of broken-in leather, stale cigarette smoke, White Castle burgers, and Jungle Gardenia perfume. I thought of her locked down in Juvenile Hall, where she had been for over two months. I regretted not having formally visited her and wondered when I'd see her again. Sighing heavily into the jacket, I told myself she would be better off there.

Clara was just one year older than me, but lived in another time zone, having slipped off some invisible ledge shortly after puberty. In that abyss she had discovered intravenous drugs, crime, ex-cons, and motel sex, followed by ambulance rides, emergency rooms, the backseats of police cars, and detention halls. My friends and I used to be in awe of Clara's toughness, her rebellion, but over time we lost respect. She had turned into a thieving junkie, a loser, an example of what we vowed never to become. By the time Clara was sent to Juvenile Hall, all of the veins in her arms had collapsed.

I decided to take ownership of the jacket.

A large, heavy cloud arrived like a spacecraft, blotting out the moon and stealing our shadows. I looked down the row of identically built brown brick townhouses to see if any other neighbors had gotten wind of our sale. Not a soul. An even line of waxy black crows sat perched like evil omens on top of the telephone wires. Black magic, I thought. A shiver ran through me like an electrical current.

My mother stood on the front lawn, arms akimbo, surveying the merchandise then began to rearrange some of her slutty bartending outfits. She placed a wide gold belt across the middle of a tiny red cocktail dress, then positioned a pair of high heels at its hem to give it a finished look.

"Look at this, honey," she said. "I should be in the fashion biz. I've got an eye for this sort of thing."

"Mom, who the hell is going to come to this stupid yard sale? It's night time!" I held back tears of frustration. "There are no signs. You're supposed to plan these things. What about my school? What about Clara? When do we tell her?"

My mother lit a cigarette and looked at me with something like sympathy, or maybe fury. But I couldn't look at her so I stared into the ground, clutching a pair of old thongs to my chest.

She came over and stood next to me; her legs were muscular and smooth, slightly tanned. Rich blue varicose veins ran down them like thick bulbous roots spreading beneath a tree, veins she hated, blamed on her pregnancies, and planned to have removed as soon as she had extra money. She sighed and put her arms around me.

"Honey, give me a break here," she said, bending her face toward mine, trying to get me to look at her. "Come on, look at me." But I wouldn't. I really wanted to punch her. "I know what I'm doing, Jeannie," she said. "I planned it all out."

I jerked away from her. She pointed her cigarette at me, jabbing the air.

"Listen, Jeannie. Clara does not need a trip across the country, okay? She needs a regular home, that middle-class condition your father's got down so well. He'll put her in a strict school, keep her in saddle shoes and off the streets." As my mother spoke, smoke trailed dragon-like out of her nose. "He's got that whole, you know, family out there in Bumfuck. Hoosier Molly, with the teeth. They have church potlucks, all that fabulous provincial stuff."

She rubbed my shoulders. I let her.

"Mom, Clara doesn't want those things. She's going to hate it. I'm sure. Saddle shoes?"

"You think I don't know that?" she said, eyes wide with exasperation. "You think I'm some idiot? She needs the consistency, Jeannie. It'll be good. I just know it."

She was starting to convince me.

"Just work with me here, Jeannie. I promise it'll all be perfect. We'll send for her. Later. After we're settled." She handed me an industrial-sized roll of masking tape and we began to close up boxes. The ever-present cigarette dangled from her mouth as she continued with her rant.

"I can't go around anymore saying, 'This is my eldest, Clara, the dope fiend.' Forget it! Not anymore. You and me. We still have a chance."

"Okay, Mom," I said, relenting. Sometimes my mother actually sounded like she knew what she was talking about. Sometimes she tricked me into believing she was a good parent.

"Gosh, don't be such a worrywart," she said, shaking my shoulders like a pal. "Always the worrywart. By the way, did you know that your new high school sits on top of a mountain? Can you imagine? It'll be like going to school at the Taj Mahal! It's one of the best high schools in the country. That's one of the reasons we're going there. I'm always thinking of you, Jeannie! Always thinking of my girls!"

She tousled my hair. I pulled away, wondering if she even knew where the Taj Majal was. I tried to picture the beach; I imagined swooping seagulls and flying Frisbees. Finally I would have my mother all to myself. We were going far away to a land of envy and dreams.

I searched through the album box, pulling out Janis Joplin and Lou Reed, people I felt understood me, travel companions.

"I'm going to take some design courses as soon as we get settled out there," she said, fiddling again with the hot pants and miniskirts. I wondered if she even bothered to have this stuff cleaned before trying to sell it.

I remembered something my father had told me a few years ago, the day of his wedding to the new pot-luck wife: "Living with your mother was like being strapped inside an airplane that was about to crash. Best you could do was hope for divine intervention." My father had been in the Air Force and knew something about planes.

As I turned to go inside the house, some actual customers pulled up in a brand-new cream-colored Monte Carlo.

"See that, oh ye of little faith!" my mother yelled to me. A well-dressed couple around my mother's age walked hand-in-hand up to our lawn, looking professional—real estate agents, maybe psychiatrists; clearly not from Keego. I looked at our humble junk sale and winced. My mother lit a cigarette, trying to appear natural as she first watched, then stalked the couple.

They studied her artwork—a dozen of Mom's oil paintings were lined up against the front window like needy, wide-eyed orphans. The tableaus on display were the ones she considered her best, most personal work. Masterpieces. A flock of golden unicorns having animated sex, cherubic babies lolling around on a dollar bill—paintings I hid whenever my friends visited. My mother came up behind the couple and started to talk, to lie. She went on and on about how Degas and Picasso had been her inspiration and how these paintings had once hung in a gallery in Birmingham. "Je ne sais quoi," she tossed off, before sickeningly complimenting the woman on her ensemble, a well-tailored dress suit, sensible pumps, and a crisp white blouse. Clothes my mother and I knew nothing about. Mom continued: How ever did she stay so slim? Were they passing through or did they live in Keego?

I kind of marveled at my mother's ability to talk to people, any people. Within seconds, they would appear to be best friends, family.

My mother unearthed other oil paintings, pulling out Reluctant Uterus and Sheepish Beauties, paintings that had followed us everywhere. They would hang above our beds, sit stacked in closets, haunting me. As if this wasn't enough, sometimes my mother would paint similarly themed murals right on the living room walls. There was nowhere to hide.

Our only customer looked genuinely interested in the paintings, fixing her stare on the sad orphans. I inhaled her sweet perfume from across the yard. Surely, she'd never been evicted from anywhere.

The man, however, was impatient to leave, jostling the pretty woman by the arm, checking his watch, whispering into her ear. He glanced in my direction and smiled, clearly bored, showing a large row of picket fence teeth. I decided they were having an office affair. They were being sneaky, hiding their tryst, so they came to witless Keego. Normal, lucky people with intriguing lives. I wanted to do things like that when I was older, have illicit office affairs, go slumming after dinner.

The woman laughed, affectionately tugging at the man's arm, smiling up at him the way actresses do in some TV ads—saintly and sexy at the same time. I suddenly felt great love for this woman who seemed to like my mother and appreciate her artwork. The woman caught me staring. I must've looked like an idiot, choked with envy, love-struck. I burned with shame and hugged my albums closer to my chest.

Finally, the man pulled her back to his car. "Don't leave," I wanted to yell. "Save us. You could save us! Become friends with my mother. Show her how to dress, how to treat men, how to act!"

My mother pitched her cigarette into the street and watched them drive off. "Fuck 'em," she grunted. "Spoiled rich brats, what the fuck do they know about art, anyway? They wouldn't know a Degas if it bit them on the ass."

Small flecks of gravel and sand skittered on our street as the car disappeared around the corner. Gold dust, I thought. Perfect people leave long trails of gold dust.

My mother rewrapped her paintings in newspaper, preparing the orphans for the long trip ahead.

"So when did you say we were leaving?" I asked.

"Before the stroke of midnight. Go pack."

"What!"

"Go!"

I charged past the refrigerator and into the house, jumping over miscellaneous boxes, piles of old magazines, and heaps of clothing. Scrambling for the telephone, I noticed through our small kitchen window, a brand-new white Cadillac sitting in the parking stall that normally housed our shabby old Vega. Even in the dark, the chrome and steel of the Caddy was blinding to the eye—a fistful of silver dollars.

I grabbed the phone, surprised to get a dial tone, then punched in Lara's number.

"Lara!" I shouted. "I'm totally freaking out. We're leaving tonight! I need to see Clara!"

To pack, I had to first unpack my old blue vinyl suitcase. The original stuff had remained since previous moves: a faded Christmas photograph of my family when we were still together, my growing collection of rocks (which I thought would become valuable with time, like comic books), a mayonnaise jar filled with dead bumblebees, a small red diary that I never opened. Each time we'd move, I'd take these items out, examine them, and redeposit them safely inside the vinyl case. I could no longer remember why I had been saving them, but they were important. I added to this collection a bundle of blue jeans, albums, and Clara's leather jacket. With some difficulty, I snapped the suitcase shut, then dragged it to the bottom of the stairs.

I took one last look around the room (a basement, really, masquerading as our bedroom) and decided to leave everything else. My mother had pretty much cleaned it out, except for a few melted candles, fading rock posters, wadded-up pantyhose, and other debris. Cleaning had never been a priority in the scheme of our hasty departures.

I stepped up on a box marked "girls' merde" and hoisted myself up to the window, where Clara kept a stash of cigarettes and pot. Pressed between the shattered window and the ripped screen was a pack of Kools, its cellophane squashed and faded. I lit up and blew rings of smoke out the tiny portal, Clara's escape hatch the day she was taken to Juvenile Hall. Having scraped her skin down to the bone trying to get free, Clara was found bleeding in the local Laundromat, passed out from huffing too much liquid Clorox.

Now she was locked behind some other tiny window, soon to realize she was going to go live with my dad. I could see her teacup eyes pooling with tears, peering through a rusted gridiron, the second-story window of a harsh, cement building. She would be wispy and ghost-like, like she might pour right down and splash onto the sidewalk.

Next to Juvenile Hall, living with Dad was Clara's biggest dread. Neither Clara nor I saw much of our father. After spending time away from him, we had both decided we hated him, found him guilty of child abuse—belts, paddles, tree switches, a plastic baseball bat. Once Clara and I tried to count all of his instruments of discipline, but our numbers didn't match. Clara's figure was much higher. He had given us moronic nicknames— Porkfat and Clap.

My mother encouraged us go to Dad's wedding; that was when we discovered another side to him—he, like his bride Molly, had become some kind of Jesus-freak, a World Order Christian, an idea Clara and I found peculiar given his earlier contempt for anything religious. "Church is a coffee klatch for gimps," he had convinced us. My father was supposedly another kind of man now, mellow and kind, not a supporter of violence. After they married, he moved his new family (Molly had a flock of children from a previous marriage) into a much fancier neighborhood. He suddenly made more money, belonged to a country club, and took his new kids on exotic summer vacations to places like Niagara Falls and Lake Okeechobee. All of this, of course, made us hate him even more. Why couldn't he have found God earlier?

Lara blared the horn and I wondered how I would break this California news to Clara.

"Be quick with your goodbyes, Jeannie," Mom yelled as I ran to Lara's revving Olds. "Love to Lara."

CHAPTER THREE

WE EXITED THE CHRYSLER FREEWAY INTO THE HEART OF DOWNTOWN Detroit, creepy, pitch black, and eerily quiet. The thick moldy breeze from the river wafted over us.

Lara turned the car behind an abandoned warehouse and we parked on a patch of decaying grass. Beyond a towering fence and a large open field was a two-story flat-topped structure, the only lighted building in the area.

"That's it," Dave said, getting out of the car. Lara, Bill, and I floated behind him, using his star-kissed ascot as our guide. The fence grew taller and more foreboding as we approached, the top of it garnished with thick coils of razor wire. Dave pulled from his pocket a serious pair of hedge clippers and started ripping into the fence.

"I've cut this section of the fence like ten times," he chuckled, struggling with the clippers, "and they keep trying to patch it. Really lame."

"Dave, are you sure it's not electric?" Lara blurted.

She and I linked arms, both of us giddy with fear and excitement. We were doing what we liked best, venturing out with big people, committing the crimes they liked to commit. But this time I was filled with dread, some inner-sickness. I wasn't sure I wanted to be running around in the dark anymore with daredevils. But I needed to check on Clara.

"So, did you do it?" Lara whispered. "I mean, you won't be dragging your virginity all the way to California. Right?"

"Right," I squeaked. I wasn't quite prepared to answer this, but I decided to stay casual. Bill and Dave were within earshot.

"All right!" Lara squealed, throwing a fist up in the air. "How was it?"

I put my hand over her mouth and shushed her. "Good, I *think*." We giggled and yelped.

"Isn't it like losing ten pounds?"

"Sort of. I guess," though I did not feel any lighter. "Why? Do I really look different now?"

"Fuck yes," she said. "You look all twinkly like a Hollywood star. Modelish."

Lara's excitement for me was contagious and I kept laughing, maybe out of relief, maybe excitement. Suddenly I felt that I could go to California ready for anything.

"Hey, keep it down," Dave warned, making one last snip in the fence. Bill came up from behind Lara and me and embraced us. "What are you girls talking about?" He was holding up a fat joint. "Why are girls always giggling, anyway?"

"Blow-jobs, loser. You wish," Lara teased. She took a big hit off the joint, then pulled away from us and strutted toward Dave.

"Make that hole bigger, okay Dave? I don't want to rip my jacket. This is genuine rabbit fur," Lara said.

"Just come on," Dave said, finishing up. He grabbed Lara's hand and held open the slit he'd made. "Christ, man. Girls." One by one we slithered our way through the hole, then began our trek across a weedy field.

"Look, you guys, nobody mention to Clara that I'm going away," I said. "She doesn't know. Okay? I'm not going to tell her just yet."

All at once they declared, "Cool."

As the building came into clearer view, I could see windows criss-crossed with solid iron bars and cinder blocks outlined with thick gray cement. The whole place was a sewer-grille framework of harsh, fixed lines.

The bad feeling in my stomach grew worse, my spine felt crooked, and my face went numb. I didn't want to see the place up close. I didn't want to believe Clara was inside.

I tried to shake off the feeling, playfully grabbing on to Bill. He hoisted me up, piggyback-style.

The building was surrounded with lots of tall maple trees, countless grainy birches and umbrella-like elms, like it was pretending to be a nature center. The dead foliage crunched beneath our feet. We tried to tiptoe around the leaves and birch rods as if they were land mines, maneuvering our way around high piles of yard trash.

"Boy, I can't imagine anything worse than losing your freedom," Dave sighed, nursing a roach.

"Clara didn't do so well with her freedom," Bill said for my benefit and I was glad he did.

"One word. Castaneda. Now there's a guy who could handle both freedom and lots of drugs," Dave said, waving us around a corner.

Across the way a brightly lit parking lot was populated with a few police cruisers, ambulances, and other state-issue vehicles — signs of authority. My stomach tightened.

"We should get out of here," I said.

No one seemed to share my growing panic. Lara shushed me, enjoying herself. But, then she would never end up in a place like this, and I could. My mother could get that official call and say, "Keep her, what the fuck." She could give up on me.

I whispered to Bill, "I'm starting to freak out. Can we go?"

"Just hang on," he said.

"Here it is," Dave announced, already chucking rocks up at a second-story window.

"Christ, how do you know that's the right window?" I screeched, my heart pounding wildly.

"Jeannie, relax. I've been here," Dave said. "Nothing's ever happened. I've never been handcuffed on this soil." He gave me a comforting, grown-up smile. I relaxed a little, my queasiness subsiding, then tried to hide behind my hair, thinking it would somehow protect me.

Lara passed me her hot-boxed cigarette, its browning filter covered with gummy lipstick. We shared it down to the Kool letters.

"Boy, I'd never survive a place like this." Lara shuddered. "Poor Clara. I think my biggest fear next to like, suddenly waking up fat would be to wake up in a prison cell."

Bill rolled his eyes. "What would you do if you found out your Navajo tribe was a bunch of fat asses?"

"Very funny," Lara smirked, "and fuck you too."

"Look you guys, the rocks aren't working," I said. "Let's just go. I'll send her a letter."

But they ignored me. Though I was more afraid of walking away and being alone than staying with them, there was the time issue. My mother wanted to leave at exactly midnight and she had meant it. I picked up a beer bottle and flung it at the bars.

"Clara! Oh Cla-ra!" Dave sang, then Bill chimed in like they were going to start to harmonize. A dark-skinned girl appeared at the window, her Afro stabbed with dozens of combs.

"What's going on?" she hollered, adjusting a comb.

We all shushed her in low voices, then called again for Clara.

"Clara?" the girl hissed. "Your asses are gonna sizzle like fucking bacon if you get caught!"

Clara pushed her way to the front of the bars. "Who is it?" she demanded, looking down. "Oh my God!" She struggled to fit her entire face through the middle square of the corroded bars. I could see her big round eyes—clear, alive.

"Jeannie, is that you? Fuckin' *a*, girl!" she yelled, her voice solid. She wasn't swaying, slouching, or drifting. She was clean. My heart swelled.

"I just wanted to say hi," I called out.

I thought of the many times I had to shuffle Clara around our townhouse to keep her from passing out, shoving her rubbery gray face under the cold-water faucet to get some kind of reaction.

"Wow. Dave, what's happening, man? I hate this fucking place," Clara screamed. She managed to get an arm through the rusty square; her skin was still punctured and gashed from needles.

"Hey, I'm so happy you all came to see me," she gushed. "You better have a party waiting, goddamn it, Jeannie. I hope you got a party waiting or I'll kick your ass. Tell Mo I still love him. I miss that little fucker," she whined. "He better not have fucked around on me or I'll kill him. You know I will," she said, gripping the bars. Her fellow inmates grew impatient, shushing her threateningly. By their pissed-off, snotty tones, I figured they knew how to hide razor blades beneath their tongues, were incarcerated for more menacing reasons than running away. But Clara, technically arrested as a "status offender," certainly qualified as a criminal, and knew how to intimidate. She could hold her own.

"You guys get going," the Afro girl huffed. "They'll put us all on restriction, no TV and shit."

Clara ignored her. "Jeannie, how come you and Mom haven't visited? I miss you." She was wiping tears from her face. When Clara wasn't acting tough, she was weepy and childlike. "I'm actually starting to miss her. Can you fucking believe it? Tell her I want to come home."

"Don't be sad, Clara. You'll be getting out soon." I wanted to change the subject. I was a traitor and a liar.

"Give me some drugs, Jeannie," Clara whined. "Come on, babe. Dave. Bill. Come on." Her reedy arms were reaching out. I didn't want her to have any drugs, but it was too late. Dave and Bill were already tossing up a colorful assortment of tablets and pills.

"All right!" Clara cheered. She was practically dancing, the other inmates right behind her, getting in on the giveaway, trying to catch the drugs. But the pills fluttered back down. Lara was on all fours collecting them, eating them.

"You guys, this isn't working," Lara observed.

"Keep trying!" Clara yelled. Then she used her puny body to push back the other girls. "Stop *crowding* me!" she yelled to them, followed by shoving and slapping.

"Cat-fight!" Dave hollered.

"Is that Dandy Dave down there? With that cat Bill?" one of the inmates shouted. A gaggle of girls were at the window, reaching hands, painted dagger-nails, groping for life outside. "Oh yeah, I fucked that dude. Send up a doobie, bro."

Bill was tossing up joints, shamelessly flirting with the girls. Someone tossed down a fuzzy-soled sock, then a padded bra, panties. "Bill! I'm so horny! Come penetrate me with some of your fine dick," someone yelled, thrusting her pelvis against the bars.

"Fuck," the Afro girl said. "I think somebody's coming."

"Take off, Jeannie!" Clara called out. "And don't be hanging out with these losers. They're dogs. Now get your ass home before you end up in here!"

"Uh-oh," another girl screamed. "It's the pigs!"

Bill gripped my arm, pulling me into the field. "We gotta hide," he said. I could hear the brush and scurry of approaching footsteps, floodlights clanked on.

Bill pulled me down between two maple trees and lay on top of me, motionless, waiting for the danger to pass. I wasn't sure how to feel. I felt horrible about Clara, about leaving her here. And then there was Bill, the thrusting. Had I given myself to a dog, a horny toad? We stayed prone for what seemed like an hour, but no one came after us.

"Get off of me," I huffed, making sure he knew I was pissed.

Bill rolled off. We lay side by side staring into the night sky.

"Hey. See Polaris?" Bill said. His voice was tender and misty and I knew he was trying to be nice, to show me he was a decent guy, but Clara could be very convincing. And the flirting. Dogs and losers were much worse than hoods.

"I could care less about some dumb star," I spat.

"Well, maybe you'll go up there some day," he said. "You now, walk on the moon."

"God, Bill. Just shut up. Okay?" I sat up and hugged my knees. "I mean, are you a dog? Why did you wait around so long for me? I'm not exactly, you know, Joey Heatherton."

"Jeannie," he whispered in my ear, "I meant what I said in the car. You're my girl."

"Plus there's no life on the moon. We already know." I yanked myself away from him and lit up a cigarette. "I mean if you just wanted to get laid, you could've just had Lara. She wants to. I really feel sick about all of this."

He gently took the cigarette out of my mouth and held my face, forcing me to look into his doleful eyes.

"Jeannie," he said. "Come on. I was just fooling around with those girls, and your sister's full of shit. She thinks every guy is out to fuck her. What the fuck does she know? And I don't want to fuck Lara."

I still wasn't buying it.

"We weren't just screwing, okay?" Bill yelled this to the open field. "We were makin' love! All right? *Making love!*" Then he flicked his cigarette into the inky sky and said softly, "Now we're like connected in a real deep way."

I sighed and breathed in the spicy birch smells. Maybe he was telling me the truth. What *did* Clara know, anyway? She was always stoned.

"Really, Bill? You really mean that?"

"Yeah. Yeah. Totally." He looked down at his groin. "Look, the mongoose is back. See? It's love."

He was back on top of me and I let him kiss me. His hands moved urgently through my hair, up my shirt, down my pants. I didn't want it to end.

"You really do love me, Bill? You couldn't do this otherwise, right?"

"Of course," he said, his voice smooth and easy.

"My mom says that most guys would screw a piece of cold liver."

"Not me."

We laughed and kissed, the burning image of Polaris filled my head, and I was thinking the closest I would ever get to a star was a constellation map.

From beyond the trees came a high-pitched scream, the horror-movie variety. My heart raced as I sprang to my feet thinking Lara had been robbed, stabbed, raped or maybe stuck on some part of the fence that *was* electric. I found her standing outside of her car, crying—no blood, no rapists, no deviants. Dave was trying to calm her, ease her into the car.

"What's going on? What's wrong, Lara?"

She had tears smeared all over her face, snuffling and shivering.

"Lara, tell me." I looked at Dave, who looked at Bill, who looked at me. They shrugged.

Lara sniveled into her muddy coat, its shoulder torn and tattered. I had never seen her like this. Then she started in.

"I was getting into the car. I saw my reflection in the window. But it wasn't me—it was a different horrible face, a face so fat and ugly that I thought it was some witch, some escaped mental patient that had gotten inside my car. We just stared at each other, and then I froze and waited for something to happen and that's when I realized it was me, my own face. The witch was me. My fucking reflection! My eyes were black holes. My face was a skeleton face like at my Aunt Tanti's funeral. Do I look like that, Jeannie?"

"No, Lara, no."

"Then it all just melted, but now I keep seeing it."

"It's the dope," Dave said. "The THC."

"That's it, man," Bill agreed.

"Oh, fuck," I sighed. I was tired. I wanted to go home. Pretty soon I'd be five states away. Dave manned the wheel; Lara and I huddled in the backseat. I held her close to me. "Lara, you're beautiful. You just have makeup under your eyes, mascara, and the pot was really bad. Really shitty."

"I looked like Keith Richards," Lara whimpered.

"It was just a hallucination," I assured her. "You'll be okay once you're home."

She rested her swollen eggplant face on my shoulder and continued weeping out the bad drugs, as I groomed her coat.

The rest of the drive home was silent. We smoked cigarettes and stared out the window. Occasionally Bill, Dave, and I would share a knowing look—Lara did not belong downtown, really didn't belong anywhere outside of Birmingham.

As we coasted along the freeway I noted the familiar exit signs—directional signs to the Detroit Zoo, Ann Arbor, Rouge Park. I wondered if Clara would ever get away from here. I kept seeing those iron bars, her thin arms, her milky face and high hopes. I wondered if I would stop worrying about her once my mother and I were in California, if distance could do that.

CHAPTER FOUR

⁂ ⁂ ⁂ ⁂

WE HAD BEEN DRIVING FOR TWELVE HOURS STRAIGHT THROUGH THREE states and we still hadn't gotten out of the morbid Midwest. Except for gas, coffee refills and pee breaks, we made no stops. Mom didn't want to break her momentum; she needed to get to California while she was still attractive.

"It's easy to go fast in this car," mom had bragged back near Chicago. "Like driving on ice. Imagine taking this trip in that old Vega. We got lucky there, that's for sure."

Mom had gotten the pimpmobile from a drive-away ad in the *Detroit News,* a Cadillac gangster ride we were to deliver to some crook named Cappy who had relocated to San Francisco.

"I think he's an investment banker or stockbroker," she had said. "His secretary was really chummy on the phone." Then she gave me a wink, high-browed and full of hope.

Nebraska should be burned down it's that boring. The initial excitement of hitting the interstate had faded long ago with my favorite radio stations. I pecked at the dial like it was a type-writer. The Nebraska landscape was made up of endless acres of swaying corn, a few rickety farmhouses, billboards announcing jackpots in Reno, the odd silo.

Mom was in a driver's stupor, her forefinger manning the wheel. In her coma-state, unmasked, her despair and grief were undeniable.

"Mom!" I shouted, unnerved, needing back her enthusiasm, forced or otherwise. "Check out all the corn. Acres of it. Does summer heat ever cause it to suddenly pop? Also, how does it get in those frozen packages back home?" I asked with an urgent need to know.

With that, she swerved off the road and right into a towering curtain of sunburned, brittle corn, the stalks scraping along side the car. We plowed deep into the field, the Caddy bouncing and hopping, wedging our way in.

"Wake up," I shouted, fearing for my life. Then the car stopped and we lurched forward, enveloped in tall corn, their yellow cobs gamely poking out of the husks, saying hello.

"Sugarsnap, I have to have some of this corn and I don't want to be seen."

"What! I thought you were asleep! Are you insane?"

She shoved open her door, slapping at the corn, yanking out whole cobs. I sank into the seat, getting itchy, my stomach caterwauling with hunger.

"In case you haven't noticed, we haven't eaten since flippin' Chicago and I have to piss! Let's go."

All I could see of Mom was the top of her blonde head, a golden tassel, the rest of her sucked up by the twitching corn.

"Oh, honey, come on!" she yelled. "Help me!"

"We could get shot by a farmer! They'll think you're a giant crow. C'mon! Plus I don't want any raw corn."

My mother emerged from the stalks, weighed down by vegetation, her manner deadly serious.

Tossing her loamy bounty into the back seat, she slid behind the wheel and pressed down hard on the gas pedal. We raked through the field and fishtailed back onto the highway, trailing a cloud of dry dust.

"Look," she said. "I'm hungry too, okay? And I wouldn't mind a shower. But that ain't gonna happen until we're out of this fucking ghost town!"

"Well," I pouted, "I'm not waiting until we get to damn California to take a piss. I can't hold it anymore. I'm starting to feel sick."

The car careened back onto the shoulder and came to a fast stop.

"Fine. You're driving me crazy. Sending me into a blue funk.

Go in the corn. Just hurry it up."

I was so surprised that I just sat there, mute. My mother rarely got this angry at me and when she did I usually thought she was kidding. Fuck it, I thought. How dare she drag me across the country and not feed me? I was tired of rolling with the punches.

I pushed against the door, slipped out, and slammed it shut. I hated Mom at that moment—furious that she wasn't together enough to move us across the country properly. Where was our big moving van, nutritious snacks, silly car games? And then there was Clara! How come nothing was ever planned? Boy, Mom had it coming to her. I stomped off, back toward Michigan. I'd call Lara and live with her, become Jewish, learn Yiddish. Her parents were *parents!*

Crunching gravel under my tennis shoes, I looked into the traffic as it whipped past. Who would dare stop, pick me up, take me away? C'mon. A junky pickup flew by, a large dog's head sticking out the passenger window, barking and howling, jowls flapping, wet and loose.

"Get back here," my mother brayed. Then, "Honey! *Come on!*" Pleading, now. She was probably figuring that a fight wasn't worth the time it took; in a month, she would be thirty-five. "We'll order big, fat steaks at the next exit!" she lied.

I could hear her getting closer; backing up the Cadillac, running down cornstalks, pulverizing the crop. I picked up my pace, almost running.

"I'll call the police!" she hollered. "I can have you put away!"

How dare she give me a hard time, I thought. I was her only good daughter, and by choice.

"I'm doing all this for you!" she shouted. "There was nothing for us in Michigan."

I stopped and turned toward her.

"For *you*, Mom. There was nothing for you! Just like every place. We left Dad because there was nothing for you! At least with him we had a home!"

I huffed and puffed, knowing I had gone too far, but I couldn't stop the words from coming. An old photograph of my father popped up in my brain like a slide. He was in his twenties, smiling, movie-star handsome, wearing his Air Force uniform.

"He wasn't that bad," I ventured, like I was guessing. "We had a home."

She jumped out of the Caddy, looked up at the sky and shook her head with great melodrama.

"Boy, how we forget!" She was really screaming now. "That wasn't a home! I've kindly spared you the *real* truth. It was a prison. Now cut this shit out. We had no freedom!"

"I didn't *need* freedom, Mom. I was ten."

"Fine, then. Go to jail with your sister."

She stood next to the car, hands on her hips, pinched face hidden behind her oversized sunglasses. Cars and trucks blew by, their gusts of wind making the corn stalks chatter—leafy pod people stealing my air! I couldn't get a breath. I stepped closer to the road but then remembered that freeway shoulders could be perilous—hapless pedestrians flattened without warning, gone missing in the Nebraska wasteland.

Emboldened by her new curse on me, my mother repeated herself with real venom in her voice.

"That's it—go be like your sister. How perfect. Forgive me if I wanted something *better* for you."

She got in the car, slammed the door, and idled. Briefly, I considered running back to the refuge of the creamy white leather seats, but I needed to scare her, so I stuck out my thumb. A truck the size of an apartment complex pulled over without hesitation.

I galloped toward it, catching a glimpse of my mother from the corner of my eye as I climbed inside the cab.

Hopping onto the high seat, pulling the heavy door closed behind me, I did a quick check in the side mirror to make sure Mom had witnessed my actions. She pulled onto the freeway behind us. I took in a breath and felt a bit of satisfaction. The cab smelled like cigar smoke, rotten vegetables, and body odor. I'd never been up so high above the road; everything dwarfed below us. Soon we were up to speed, moving ahead. This is how shit happens, I thought. You get pulled in, pushed forward. Life was a series of whims.

"Where you heading?" the driver asked in an inhuman voice. I looked hard at his shiny, oversized forehead, made more prominent by his lack of eyebrows—his features were bunched together toward the middle of his face like a bouquet of dead flowers. He was trying to grow a Fu Manchu, but he didn't have enough hair.

"Um, next town." I wasn't sure how far I wanted to go with this guy. There was something wrong with him, something genetic. An elephant man, hunched and crouched, willing himself to fit inside an 18-wheeler. A silhouette of a naked showgirl hung from his rearview mirror, making me nervous.

"You heading for Lincoln?" he reverbed.

I bounced up and down on the seat like I was weightless, grabbing hold of the door handle to steady myself. The jostling made having to pee worse.

"Michigan, actually," I shouted to be heard over the Godzilla roar of the engine. My driver laughed a *Fee Fi Fo Fum*. What a freak. I searched for something good in his face—he may have had a congenital deformity but that didn't mean he had to be a maniac. His teeth were irregular, tobacco-stained brown pegs, his neck a Michelin tire. I had wanted to be comfortable in this truck cab, to enjoy my vengeful ride. I had wanted my driver to be jolly but no such luck. I got the driver that ate Englishmen. My body began to knot up.

His tree-trunk arm pulled a tape out of the glove box.

"Name's Buck, by the way. Buck from Lubbock. You like Streisand?"

"Who?"

"Barbra. She relaxes me."

He rammed in the tape and Streisand's melodic voice floated out of the speakers, soothing him—a golden harp.

"You don't look like the Streisand type," I observed.

He snorted and pawed at his crotch like an ape picking gnats. *Gross.* All was forgiven with Mom. I needed this ride to end.

The CB radio crackled, then a voice boomed out: "Galahad Chaste to Big Gawain. Galahad to Gawain. How she blowing?" Big Gawain snapped off the radio.

"So, what's in the truck?" I asked, hoping to sound my age, curious and stupid.

"Pussy," he said, patting my thigh. I smashed myself up against my door, straining to get a glimpse of Mom. It was over. I was doomed.

"What's a pretty thing like you doing traveling all by your-self?" He winked.

My heart dropped into my empty stomach, my face burned.

"Wanna steer?" he offered, then began to sing along with Barbra, a regular baritone.

"Oh, look. The windmill," I announced with a lilt. "That's my house. Could you please stop the truck?"

"Fee Fi Fo Fum," he roared. "I want some pussy!"

I rolled down my window, searching for Mom. We would have a grand life sunbathing, cracking coconuts, snorkeling.

In my peripheral vision, the giant's arm was moving in quick up and down jerks like he was cleaning a gun.

My upper body was stretched outside the truck searching the skies like a baby bird looking for its morning worm. *Where the hell are you?* The truck cannon-blasted, lurching us forward from a backfire, my head bouncing off the dash like a basketball.

"Damn, old girl. She often somotizes my moods," the giant explained mysteriously, patting the dashboard.

"You should calm down too, sister. I ain't going rape you on our first date or anything."

Date? Practically throwing myself out the window, I finally caught sight of the Caddie, hovering behind us like a fallen cloud.

"Mom!"

She was honking like a true maniac, smiling and waving us over.

"You better pull over," I ordered, turning toward the psycho, having momentarily forgotten about the slithering python in his pants. The very sight of the gripped, swollen flesh made my stomach buckle, the taste of bitter saliva rushed up my throat. The giant's mouth gaped opened like a garbage pit and as he was about to let out another double-bassed *Fee-Fi*, I heaved all over the seat—hot regurgitated coffee from three different states splashed on Buck and all his equipment. Miraculously, none of it got on me.

"Good Christ almighty!" he roared, slamming on the hydraulic breaks, screeching us to a halt. Heart racing, I threw myself against the door, forcing it open, then clambered down the steel steps until safely planted on gravel. "You big perverted twink!" I shouted, then ran through the corn, punching it with my fists until I found a spot to relieve myself.

"Jean, honey, stop being so glum. You're starting to depress me."

I pressed my face up against the backseat and breathed in the cool leather. My mother had followed me and Buck down the freeway—had let the truck pull her along, a freeway gravitational secret she had read about somewhere. She revealed that she'd saved quite a bit of gas.

"You're lucky some freak didn't pick you up. Next time I won't even care; I'll just let you go. Don't think I won't."

"He *was* a freak," I protested.

"I knew you were safe, though," Mom interrupted. "He was driving a truck from Wrigley's. They are very reputable. One of the richest and most prominent families in America. I wasn't even worried."

"The truck was filled with chewing gum?"

"In any case, honey miss, you will be a lot happier in California. You'll meet new friends. Oh, and the boys! You'll thank me later, I can promise you that. Well-educated types. Athletic, sophisticated, studious. Families that own vineyards, shipping yards. Think trust funds. Let's not fight anymore, okay, lemon drop?"

I could already tell from her description that I wouldn't like the boys in California. I missed Bill. I liked hoods.

"In order to have new things in your life," she said, "you have to get rid of the old. You know, *le petite mal.* Let's pretend we're French." She threw an arm over the seat and squeezed my knee. "Sil vous plait?"

I held my fingers to my temples.

"Mom, can you just be quiet for a minute? I've got a headache. I'm starting to feel crazy."

"Oh, enjoy yourself. Sheesh!"

She was laughing, smoking, having a great time. As usual, she missed the severity of my comment. Her tune would change when she started getting monthly bills from the loony bin. *Hears voices, talks to the walls, slices her arms. We keep her in a straitjacket, in a padded cell, in a locked facility.* That's what the reports would say.

Insanity was sneaky, arrived unannounced. Dementia attacked randomly and frequently. The very idea kept me in a state of perpetual anxiety. Having learned that headaches preceded bouts of schizophrenic activity, I began logging my headaches on the inside flap of my Psych One workbook. If anything unusual happened to me, I'd have a record. This had put me at ease for a while, but too many headaches later I stopped keeping track. It was simply too much work.

Cold air blasted in through the window; night had fallen. The emptiness around us was stark and infinite.

"Mom, come on. I'm freezing. How about a little heat?" My mother was spastic from caffeine overload, flogging the steering wheel while she sang "When the Saints Go Marching In." We still hadn't eaten. She kept her window down but turned on the heat.

Insects of every size and shape thumped against the windshield, beating out an erratic rhythm. Each set of passing headlights created a glare on the window, illuminating the bloody mess.

"Guess we'd better stop at a motel soon, huh?" I asked.

My mother was back in her trance. Lying across the backseat, I felt the car slow down, make a turn, then another turn. I was a bloated, stiff body lying in a coffin as the hearse approached the cemetery. Creeped-out, I popped up, hoping to see a motel. Instead, I saw more nothing. I felt like blowing up Nebraska. My mother crept up a gravel road, then turned off the ignition.

"What are you doing?"

"This looks like a good spot for some sleep."

"Mom! We can't stop here. You're giving me a heart attack. This is how people get axed to death."

"Oh, honey. The doors are all locked. Don't worry."

I considered scaring my mother by telling her the whole story of Buck, but I knew this would really upset her, and she'd blame the entire episode on me. She plumped her purse against the window and began to snore. I searched the darkness for the gnarled hand, the bloody ax, Buck's dick. I thought I heard slurping sounds.

"Mom. I'll drive. Mom!"

How could she sleep? We had slept in the car once before, right after our first eviction. Clara and I had lain tangled together in the back seat of the shabby Vega in the middle of a supermarket parking lot. Mom had stayed awake *all* night, armed with a baseball bat and a can of Raid—back in the days when she exhibited a kind of motherly concern. I had actually slept that night, knowing my mother was standing guard. But not tonight. Someone had to keep an eye out.

Mom sawed major logs. I wanted to tell her things—that I

had slept with Bill, ingested questionable narcotics, skipped school, stolen countless dollars from her purse. That I had seen Buck's penis and he was deformed, maybe even a hunchback. I wondered if I'd ever tell my mom anything important.

"Mom," I whispered. The word drifted upward, small and whiny, making me feel useless, pathetic.

I was boxed in, suffocating, yet terrified to venture outdoors. I wondered if you could be claustrophobic and agoraphobic at the same time.

Searching the sky for Polaris, the star that burned brighter than the rest, I saw it radiating down on us like a spotlight. Relief. Maybe Bill had loved me. Maybe he would come for me in California. I lay back down and let the star's beam cover me, holding it against my chest like a handful of lilies.

CHAPTER FIVE

THE FIRST TIME MOM HAD A BIG PLAN, I WAS TEN, COMFORTABLE IN OUR home, a real home, the last place I remember where no one questioned our being there. For a while, we belonged, ensconced in the red brick house that was dependable and solid like the sturdy Ford that was planted in the garage. The moat of green lawn, clipped hedges that enclosed the house—a suit of living armor; the iron swing set and its feet of cement—we were secured by these small defenses—distinctions that made homes permanent and steady. My identity was fixed there like the initial "W" my father had attached to the front screen door. We lived in a suburban pocket of Detroit, miles from the rioting city, where fires often raged and flecks of white ash fell from the sky as a reminder.

Our life had an order, symmetry. We had schedules, routines, daily chores, habits. My father ran the house with charts, budgets, calendars, and belt straps. It was there that Dad branded me and Clara "Porkfat" and "Clap," *pet* names that would cut a groove into my brain, a troubling mantra for years to come. *Porkfat and Clap.* He referred to Mom as "That Woman," "Her" and "Hey."

Looking back, it's impossible to see how my mother fit into such a world, obediently following rules and neighborhood rituals, putting up with my tormented Dad. But like the frenzied puppet in a jack-in-the-box, she was destined to spring loose.

While Mom was biding her time, she attempted adding color to our ordinary lives by sewing bright, snappy outfits Dad wouldn't allow her to wear. Each spring, Mom planted scads of flowerbeds—pansies so rich in violet they seemed hand-painted. Ours was the only house on the block boasting six-foot sunflowers—rising suns growing outside the window, she would say. To my father, they were vulgar, faceless men hooded in *faggy* sunbonnets, laughing at him. Every summer, he'd plow them down to their sad little nubs.

During our last year in the Plainview house, Mom started oil painting and the orphan collection began—clumsy stacks, the sheer bulk of canvas. Dad banished Mom to the back porch, where turpentine fumes rose up like steam. It was there Clara discovered her first "high."

Mom was not allowed to venture off the block with anyone my father labeled "suspicious," essentially women who left their houses for any reasons besides errands or attending school and church functions. I sensed the end was drawing near when Mom starting taking big risks visiting girlfriends only to chat while neglecting laundry. Once she bussed Clara and me downtown, where we helped restore a giant mural of Martin Luther King. We also bought love beads and incense sticks that we kept hidden in sock drawers and under mattresses. We were keeping secrets from Dad, and it was exciting.

Even so, the days limped along, our lives interchangeable with the rest of the neighborhood. But this was the year I noticed our Dad was slightly different, a bit askew. Perhaps Dad had always been peculiar and I had been too young to notice before, or perhaps he was suddenly going berserk.

After pulling up in the Ford honking his arrival for the whole neighborhood to hear, he swept through the house as if looking for something of vital importance, peering in closets, behind curtains. "Did you lose something, Dad?" I would ask. "Could've sworn that lamp was on the end table when I left this morning," he'd grumble, moving the lamp from table to table until it felt "in its place." Then Dad would unlock the telephone (no one, including my mother, was allowed to make outgoing calls unless he was present), drill my mother about her day—how was it spent, what had she done, why was there was a thin layer of dirt on top of the Fridgidaire! He'd hold up one dusty finger, sigh, and shake his head. Sometimes he'd bark. The finale to this routine was Dad throwing open the water closet as if Count Dracula might be hiding, then yanking out his coveted Eureka. While he burrowed into the carpet, Dad would rant about the "crazy niggers destroying the city" and how "all the whores want a say in things these days" and finally "*that woman* doesn't even know how to run a proper vacuum!"

The familiar order of our lives was ending; hairline cracks were becoming notable fractures. Our predictable world collapsed. Dad stopped going to work, Mom started sealing herself in her bedroom listening to rock-n-roll, Clara began her descent into drugs and boys, and I stopped sleeping.

"Christ," my mother said. "Your father is just so stubborn. I thought he would come around, change, reach higher. But this is it for him."

I was helping Mom hang laundry on a dull summer morning, our bare feet slippery from dew.

"Plainview Avenue. He's arrived. There are no tomorrows. I can't believe I stayed in this Jello mold for twelve years, but you know the damn Catholic Church. *Thy husband shall rule over thee!* Not anymore, baby. He followed me on a bike yesterday when I went to Joan's! I outran the son-of-a-bitch. I need to chase my dreams, Jeannie, even if I'm only running in circles. And I can't run very far with your maniac dad around."

I winced at her words while handing her clothespins.

She went on. "I think he's trying to *kill* me," she whispered, then looked at me with pleading eyes as she clamped a clothespin on the line. "Death by smothering," she added mysteriously. "If I hadn't gotten pregnant, I would have never stayed with him. I just know it. Now he doesn't want me to leave. But Jeannie, I had such huge visions, glamorous ones. Where I was headed was a much grander place." She sighed.

"Your Dad's a bully, but how could I have known?" Her movements were swift and exaggerated as she called my father names.

"He's getting worse. A regular Simon Legree!"

She shot nervous glances at our back porch as she talked,

keeping an eye out for the overseer, her mouth pulled into a tight line, blue veins pulsing under the skin of her stretched-thin neck.

Even in her wrought-up state, Mom's beauty was vivid and obvious, with her loose, blonde curls, creamy skin, and flinty eyes. People commented plenty, all sorts from relatives to clergymen. "You mom is pretty as a summer blossom," they'd say. Dad often called her saucy, but they fought regularly over lipstick shades and skirt length.

"People with vision have a light inside. It's always there, a flashlight beaming them forward. It doesn't just snap on in someone dark—the deceased can no longer be illuminated," she lectured, taking a clothespin from her mouth. "Don't you ever forget that, Jeannie," she went on, shaking it at me. "After meeting your father, I readjusted things, set my sights too low. My dreams were too small."

A cool breeze passed by, flapping a damp sheet into our face, the air thick with bleach. Summer was ending.

"Thank God you're finally old enough to understand this stuff." Wiping her hands down along the sides of her housecoat, Mom fished a cigarette out of her pocket. This was a new habit, indulged only when my father was not watching.

She lit up and drew in a long, deep drag, closed her eyes, then slowly exhaled, smiling, enjoying something that had nothing to do with me. The next puff seemed even more private, and I contemplated leaving or at least looking away, but instead I did nothing. Finally she opened her eyes and looked at me, and in my reflection, I felt a stir of relief.

"Can you keep a secret, Jeannie?"

My heart raced, a clothespin dangling from each hand. "Sure, Mom." We squinted at each other. The sun had fully risen and everything around us started to sparkle.

"Looks like your hair got a little blonder this summer," she said between quick hits off the smoke. I handed her the wooden pin. I'd have to wait. She wasn't ready, but I knew she would tell me eventually. She always told me her secrets—the sneaking around, the incense, how she'd once written a fan letter, sealed with a lipstick kiss, to John Wayne.

Just then our next door neighbors, Mr. and Mrs. Kapinsky, burst out of their back door, laughing and grasping at each other, making their way toward their small silver car. My mother and I stopped what we were doing and watched them. We always watched them.

Mrs. Kapinsky was exotic, the talk of our block, nicknamed Lady Godiva. She was outfitted in suede hip-huggers and a sheer top, her wispy blonde hair fell around her shoulders like a satin shawl. I could see the outline of her breasts, her nipples. For sure she was going to hell, but we stared at her anyway. Her parents were originally from Sweden—a country, according to Dad, where clothing was optional, where everyone sinned in broad daylight.

Mr. Kapinsky worked in television advertising, subscribed to *The New York Times,* and drove a foreign car (which was practically a cardinal sin on our block.) He was going to hell too. The couple had lively, outdoor summer parties blaring rock music— my parents were never invited. Mom, Clara, and I secretly loved this couple, certain they knew something we didn't. We spied on them during their parties, dancing in our socks and underwear, excited by the music, the possibilities. My father sat alone in his vinyl chair, protected by waxy earplugs and a game show, hurling insults.

"Hello, Jane! Hi, Brian!" Mom shouted, throwing them her jazziest smile, waving with both hands like she was sending a distress signal to a passing ship. She always waved and smiled at them, but the Kapinskys pretty much ignored her.

"Well, there they go, off to some interesting brunch. I'll bet they know Bobby Bonds." Bonds was Detroit's most popular news anchor and the closest thing we had to a local celebrity.

Again my mother's face contorted. The anger was back, but now it centered mostly in her eyes, dulled and black, my reflection gone.

"What does she know anyway? No kids, clever husband. See, more proof. You know, if I hadn't gotten pregnant I could've been the next Jane Powell." I had heard this before, countless times. Jane Powell, like my mother, had been born in Oregon. *That is their only connection!* To make up for her missed calling, she named her children after dead movie stars. I was named after Jean Harlow. Clara, after Clara Bow. Neither one of us knew who these actresses were. Whenever anyone asked I said my middle name was Faye as in Dunaway, who was in my opinion much more exciting then someone dead.

My parents met at a USO dance in San Francisco, during a weekend pass the Air Force handed to my father. The story went that Mom pursued Dad until he got her pregnant; he married her and dragged her back to Michigan.

I still can't imagine my mother clinging to my father like that—hounding and pleading. "She used me to get away from her crazy mother, the lounge singer, the sailor harpy," my dad had said, setting the record straight.

"As far as I'm concerned, you kids do not have a maternal grandmother. Let's leave it at that," Mom would say, ending the conversation.

"Mom, what's the secret?" I was hoping to bring her around, get her mind off Mrs. Kapinsky. She managed one more drag off the cigarette, then buried the smoking butt beneath the Kapinsky's imported rose bush.

"You can't even tell Clara," she warned. "Soon we'll be free of your father. Gals on our own, going places, grabbing at dreams. Like princesses. It will be paradise."

My mother tousled my hair, drifted away, and disappeared into the back porch, screen door banging. I stood in place holding clothespins, unsure of what to feel. Then the music drifted toward me, causing me to wobble. Yesterday it was *Midnight Confessions*, today the Rolling Stones. "Hey, hey, you, you, get off of my cloud," Mom wailed, her voice scratchy and hoarse. These sing-alongs made me nervous, dizzy. I needed Mom to act normal and listen to Lawrence Welk, maybe hum along while she dusted. But of course I hated Lawrence Welk and after a few minutes I'd join in with Mick too.

⁙ ⁘ ⁙ ⁘

"Be prepared for anything," Clara warned. We were loitering and acting defiant in the alley behind our chipped and peeling garage, smoking discarded cigarette butts. I was struggling to inhale, hadn't yet learned. Trashcans brimming with week-old garbage lined the alley; the air smelled of decaying meat and burnt bacon. Buzzing flies orbited our heads and occasionally flew into the side of the garage, kamikaze style.

"Mom's flipped out. Dad says she's in some kind of white-magic trance. He's says top forty music is going to bring down the family." Clara waited for a reply, and I wondered how many days she had gone without washing off her mascara, eyelashes hardened and brittle—her sun-streaked hair was the same—ratted high and sprayed to the point of breaking.

Clara ran with the local adolescent hooligans. Maintaining membership required scowling, cussing, ingesting deadly chemicals, and listening exclusively to Motown. More than once, Clara caught me unawares as I hummed along to a blander beat. "Davey Smegma Jones," Clara would spit, then kick me hard in the thigh.

"Dad's thinking of calling a head shrinker," Clara threatened, the same way a child might say "You're gonna get it!" She lived to scare me, but I had learned to hold my ground, not react, give nothing away.

"Big deal," I replied, but later in bed, I would lie awake for hours, agonized. *Head shrinker!*

"Mom's okay," I murmured, swallowing more fumes, tendrils of smoke escaping through my nose. My lungs were ablaze, smoldering down to black ash, but I diligently puffed on. The sun was blurry behind a white sky, but our shadows remained. For a second I thought I smelled snow, although impossible since it was August.

"You'll be sorry when *your mother's* in a special institution for freaked-out Moms getting electrical shocks," Clara went on. "Who will make your toast and eggs then? Huh? "

Your mother and *your father* as if Clara didn't have or need any. I would be the only one facing such a loss. Ignoring Clara, I thought about Mom's secret plan—she'd been thinking, calculating, reaching conclusions. Something was about to happen. *Princesses and paradises.* Excitement exploded in my stomach like a little firecracker.

"Mom's okay," I repeated.

"You're pathetic," Clara shrugged, extinguishing the hot tip of her cigarette with her finger. She jammed the remaining butt into the back pocket of her short-as-possible cutoffs.

"Let's get the hose," she suggested.

Clara led the way, her spry breasts directional points, and proud of it—breasts that had recently started to develop, now stuffed into a Dixie Cup bra, little shaved-ice cones. At night, a pack of boys would pant in front of our house, circling on their bikes and skateboards, whistling for Clara, hoping for a glimpse. My father charged at them, fists in the air, yelling and shooing them away, Clara dangling from our bedroom window—a smutty Rapunzel.

But she messed around plenty with those boys on other occasions—in the school bathroom, the local park, huffing liquid cement, giggling and humping, French-kissing. Sometimes I tagged along, secretly terrified she would burst into pieces, her head just explode—gummy fragments, bone chips. I'd coax her back home, only to worry my father would smell the potent chemicals. Finally I stopped going anywhere with her. I didn't want to know what she was up to.

Along the side of the house we examined the empty flowerbed, the remnants of the maligned sunflowers, wilted yellow petals, dead stems.

Turning on the garden hose, we washed away all cigarette evidence, Clara doing extra turpentine removal duty. Then she fullthrottled the water, turned the hose toward the sky, water cascading, our private rainstorm.

"Remember how Dad used to chase us, pretend to be the creature from the black lagoon?"

Clara chased me through the peonies and tulips, mascara running down her cheeks like spilled tar, her nest of hair a sticky clump of Dippity-Do. We fought over the hose for a while, dousing each other until Clara abruptly grew bored and flung the rubber tube into the shrubbery, a dead field mouse she had just stumbled across.

"You're such a kid," she scoffed, shoving moistened gum into her mouth.

"A few more years and I'm out of this crap hole," she added, cracking gum, adjusting her Dixie Cups. We wandered toward the back porch, our clothes heavy with water, hair dripping.

"I've decided I'm definitely going to be a nurse," Clara announced, grasping my wrist and feeling for a pulse. She had recently taught herself to count pulses. "You are calm, Jeannie. Always so damn calm."

❖   ❖   ❖   ❖

I wouldn't sleep that night, lying frigid in a state of panic, garroted by my thoughts, heinous images of destruction playing themselves out against my dark bedroom wall. Turning away, the figures arranged themselves in mid-air, a silent horror film projected from the moon. The relentless characters performed under the covers and across the curtains, beneath my eyelids. My mother, strapped down, being jolted by electrical branding irons, grotesque doctors shouting orders, grasping sharp instruments to carve out pieces of her mind. My father being bludgeoned with his vacuum, cordoned and flogged; a masked burglar stealing our appliances, our big-screen TV; my unknowing parents burning to death, curling flesh trapped in by airtight storm windows, wisps of smoke escaping from under their door, bodies flaming rotisserie chickens.

I jolted forward, muscles tense, my skin wet and tacky with fear. Times like these I thought I might be possessed by the devil. I hadn't prayed enough, confessed often enough. And my lack of pagan babies! I was weak, and Satan had exploited the opportunity!

Leaning forward, I needed to hear a normal, reassuring sound—my father's gravelly cough or the click of his toothbrush against porcelain. I strained but heard not a sound, the silence pressing on top of me like a dental blanket, forcing me into hell. Covered with sweat, I mumbled simple prayers but the images persisted. Gathering some inner strength, I leapt off the bed and tumbled to the floor with a loud thud.

"Get the hell to bed!" My father's voice lashed out, a leather strap climbing up the stairs. I froze, then relaxed a little. He was alive after all. I crawled back into my bed and worked hard to forge better images in my head: the mysterious beauty of Mary Magdalene, a bowl of buttered popcorn, Steve McQueen's "bedroom" eyes—imagery my mother suggested in times of terror. "Turn the monster into a movie star!" my mother would offer. Then it occurred to me that my father didn't know what he was yelling at. It could have been an actual thief falling in through a window, desperate, unpredictable, possibly unhinged, maybe with a group, one among many, a den of thieves. Anything seemed possible. It wasn't safe anymore, anywhere.

The next morning I would confront him, demand to know why he so quickly assumed loud thuds were just his children. Why didn't he check on us? It was Sunday, so I'd have to wait until after Mass.

During the hymn singing, my mother stood tall, erect, looking directly into the tortured eyes of Jesus, the butchered figure whose slaughter we celebrated week after week. Although Mom was just over five feet, she stood above the crowd, the music blowing out of her, sharp and urgent, causing fellow church members to turn around, raise eyebrows. Mom ignored them and continued with gusto, as if she was the only one there, personally auditioning for God.

Leaving church, my mother walked ahead of Clara and me, smoking a cigarette freely, not caring who saw her, whistling "Galveston."

I caught up with her.

"Mom, did you know that God can hear us even if we whisper? I mean you could even pretend to be singing and he would hear you."

She looked down at me with suspicion.

"Yeah, okay. So?"

"Well, I just wondered if you knew."

"Passion is a good thing, Jeannie. That's what God recognizes."

"Listen," she said abruptly, grabbing my arm. "Can you hear that? It's so quiet you can hear the trees chatting. They love you Jeannie. They're saying they love you," she sighed, dropping my arm.

I had hoped the conversation would have gone in a different way, with Mom's understanding that I was trying to help her be less strange. I let her walk on ahead of me.

I had paid attention in church that day, forcing myself not to daydream. I looked directly into those statues of hope, the miserable Jesus with his concerned and supposedly helpful parents, and I challenged them with my fears, worries. *Save my family*, I commanded them, then immediately felt embarrassed and ashamed. Who was I to ask such a thing? But I had never asked the holy triad for anything, not once. Not in any specific way. Now it was time to trade in on all those hours spent in rancid confessionals, the memorization of litanies, Latin hymns, all that stale communion. In my ten-year-old mind God was a mean old bastard, still angry about what happened to his beloved son. But I appealed to him anyway, scared as I was, then blessed myself with holy water and ran out of the church.

The afternoon seemed long, slow, and without end. Sunday minutes always took on the length of hours, the day threatened death by boredom. Our house grew claustrophobic, the walls seemed to pulse inward, their whiteness blinding. Swarms of termites chewed their way through wooden beams, sewage sluiced along in rusted pipes. I became overly aware of my physical self, wondering why elbows only bent in one direction, where were our gills?

I sat at my father's feet wearing itchy polyester play clothes and watched him absorb a football game.

"I think we had a burglar last night, Dad," I announced ominously.

As usual, he was entranced by the game, yelling at the muddy football players, drumming out a rhythm on the rickety plastic television tray, his tall bottle of Squirt threatening to topple over. Maybe he didn't know I was there. Perched in his vinyl easy chair, wearing plaid shorts and black socks, Dad acted out the most exciting plays, poised with an imaginary football. He was athletic with a wide chest and rounded calves the size of my head. Small lines fanned out around his eyes, suggesting a pleasant demeanor that he didn't fulfill.

"Did you hear me?"

I leaned against Dad's prickly leg, and wondered where my mother was. Out of loyalty to her, I didn't want to show too much affection toward my father. *No longer under his thumb,* I thought, pulling away from his leg.

"I think I heard a *burglar* last night, Dad."

He squinted at me and tilted his head like he was deaf.

"I heard noises. Big thumps."

"You're imagining things, Porkfat."

"I swear, Dad. I thought I saw a face in the window!"

My father was picking his teeth with the edge of a matchbook. "You know, you got that crazy imagination like your mother," he *tsked,* shaking his head. I pulled myself under the sofa and poked at the thin layer of fabric that encased the stuffing. I wanted to rip through it, let everything fall out, allow the insides to flood through our house, bringing down the roof.

"How was the sermon?" Dad asked, reaching under the sofa to knuckle the top of my head, something he had picked up from the Stooges. Suddenly I felt too old for it.

"Stop it." I slapped his hand and pulled away.

My mother leaned around a corner, investigating, then disappeared. She was in the kitchen, still in her dressy church clothes, peeling potatoes, grinding meat, opening fruit cocktail cans. She would cook tonight. Maybe things were back to normal.

"Hey," my father whispered.

He glanced toward the kitchen and winked at me, as if to say, *let's keep her out of this.*

"Did your mother visit anybody after the mass?"

"No," I said, unable to hide my disgust. I was annoyed by all the questions he'd been asking about Mom lately.

"What about that Father John? The young, ugly one."

I sighed and rolled my eyes. "No."

"Hey." He leaned back in his chair, thinking, then leaned forward again and whispered, "Want to come for a drive with me? Let's go get a custard."

"Really? You mean without Mom or Clara?"

"Yeah. Let's go."

I was shocked. My father rarely took us out on Sundays, never for ice cream, and certainly never just me. I was excited, guilty, and afraid all at once. We didn't bother to tell anyone. We just left.

"Do any of these houses look familiar? You must have gone with her when she meets her friends!"

We were in the Ford, driving under the warm sun, going in loops around our neighborhood. We weren't anywhere near the Dairy Queen. I slumped against the car door, trying my best to look confused, which wasn't that hard because I was getting dizzy from driving around in circles.

"I don't know, Dad," I said, annoyed. "I don't go anywhere with Mom after school. She's usually home. She's always sewing. I don't know."

Such lies came easily to me. They felt natural. That's why people told me their secrets.

My father slowed down in front of a two-story colonial brick, an election sign planted on the front lawn said VOTE YES ON EVERYTHING. The house belonged to the neighborhood's only feminist, Joan—unmarried, a social worker.

"Is this where the communist lives?"

"Nope. I've never been there."

As I lied, I pictured the truth. I had sat for hours on Joan's cushy sofa drinking sodas, watching reruns of *Flipper* while Mom and Joan guzzled coffee, talking about things I didn't understand, making long-distance phone calls to Amsterdam and Chicago. When John married Yoko, Mom and Joan wept, held each other and sang "Strawberry Fields Forever" at the piano.

My father leaned into the steering wheel, a maniacal look on his face as he eyeballed the house. We crept along as he looked at some other suspicious addresses, gripping the wheel as if it might try to escape.

"What about *this* house?" he quizzed. "I know it's nearby. What does she do over here?"

I shook my head no until it rattled. "She's mostly home, Dad. She gardens and cleans and . . ." He jammed on the brakes; I flew forward, my head thumping the dashboard.

"Oh, c'mon. I'm not stupid, little girl. She's got you lying to your own father now." I froze, every muscle in my body clenched, staring into the well-vacuumed floorboard.

"Look at me, young lady, and tell me where she goes."

He cupped my face, confronting me with his cold blue stare, his hot breath pressing into my face like a poisonous vapor. My heart was making so much racket in my ears I thought I had gone deaf and then I stopped breathing.

"She goes to Joan's," I squeezed out. "But I can't remember where she lives. They just talk, that's all. And drink coffee."

Dad dropped my face, but the imprint of his big thumbs would last forever. I took in quick, shallow breaths as though the air was too thin.

Shoving the gear stick into drive, we continued our creep up the street.

"I knew she was still talking to that whore," he said, pounding the wheel. "Goddamn. Are there ever any men over there? Huh? That faggot Father John."

I ignored him. We turned up another block. He studied the mailbox numbers and tried to x-ray the houses by squinting hard at them. Some kids were tossing a football in the street; my father honked until they ran up onto the curb. A redheaded boy my age looked me right in the eyes and we stared at each other until he was out of range. I imagined the boy could sense my fear, my danger. I imagined he understood because maybe he'd been on similar rides with his own father.

"Are you looking? Keep looking," he demanded. "You'll recognize something soon."

"Stop it, Dad, I want to go home. I don't know where she lives." Then I added under my breath, "This is so stupid."

He yanked the back of my long ponytail, my neck snapped backward until I was looking straight into the vinyl ceiling.

"Watch your mouth," he seethed.

I nodded with my entire upper-body.

He let me go and I curled up against the door, covering my face with my arm. *We got big plans, fucker, big plans, and they don't include you!*

"You're all on her side. Why?" he whined, then hit the dash so hard I jumped, buried my face between my knees, and waited for the punch. He had never hit me with his fist, but everything was changing. I squeezed my eyes closed as tight as I could. In that darkness, I was being pulled into the sky by a handful of bright red balloons. Off in the distance a church bell rang out three times. My body vibrated as I waited.

My father let out a long sigh. "Am I such an evil man?" Then he started to chuckle. I peeked over at him from under my arm; he was shaking his head back and forth, smiling. Then he laughed much bigger, loosening his grip on the steering wheel. The laughter came in bursts until his whole body began to shake. Even the car seat shook. Wiping a tear from his eye, he then reached over and squeezed the funny bone just above my knee. I started to laugh too, first fake, then for real.

"I'm sorry. C'mon, Jeannie, I'm sorry. Your silly old dad."

My muscles relaxed all at once and I slipped lower on the seat. He wasn't going to punch me after all. Thousands of tiny needles pricked my sleeping skin. I started massaging my thighs with my sweaty palms.

"I'm a man of my word. Right? That's one thing you can always say about your old dad," he said as we pulled into the Dairy Queen. The familiar white building, no larger than a tool shed, brought me great relief. Its blue aluminum roof, the two sliding windows, big steel machines that produced such white creamy magic—all these were symbols of hope. The Dairy Queen was a fun place, a pocket of joy.

We sat across from each other on a sticky picnic bench, shaded by an awning like a giant bird wing. My father was calmer now, resigned. Sad, really. We looked over each other's shoulders without speaking. There were no other customers. We listened to the slow and easy Sunday traffic.

My father, a civil engineer, had inspected the Dairy Queen, like many of the business establishments in the area. His job was to make sure certain buildings were "up to snuff," as he put it. He prided himself on never taking a bribe. But we were always welcomed at these businesses and often served gratis.

My root beer float made fizzing noises like radio static. Listening for a message, trying to think of something brilliant to say, I wanted to forget about what had just happened, wanted our family life to be the way it used to be.

"How about some badminton doubles after dinner," I suggested gamely.

Dad stirred his melting vanilla custard, his eyes watery and vacant, small blue oceans.

"There's something wrong with her," he sighed, rotating his slender gold wedding band. "Our whole block is changing. I think she's fucking Father John, Jean."

I straightened up, not to the fucking part, but to the sound of my name. Dad speaking my name was some kind of signal, however vague.

"The whole goddamn church changed since that prick got there with his folky guitar. Guy's a queer."

Tears stung my eyes. I felt nauseated, my float a puddle of curdled milk.

"Jean," my father blurted, "you're losing your daddy!" he said, reaching out for me like he hadn't seen me in years. "Your mom wants me gone. She wants to file for divorce."

A robin swooped down and hopped across our empty picnic, jerking its head to and fro, watching us, like we were a tennis match. Under different circumstances, my father and I would be fascinated by the bird, study its movements, hypothesize where its nest is located. But now, if the ignorant bird inched any closer, my dad might reach out and squeeze the life right out of it.

"I wanted to tell you this without Clap," he added. "She doesn't seem to care much about anything anymore."

I blinked hot tears, shooing away the robin.

I don't remember much of the ride home. I tried to imagine happier scenes, like carnival rides, but one idea kept strong-arming its way into my head—I would soon be fatherless. Was this my mother's idea of paradise?

As we turned onto our block I thought of the Hogan family. A perfectly fine set of neighbors in every respect, until the day Mr. Hogan choked to death on beef jerky. After his funeral, Clara and I we were not allowed to play with the Hogan kids for reasons we never understood. Fatherless families were whispered about and sealed off like infectious disease.

"You're not really going to leave, are you, Dad?" I cried, throwing myself against him like a bad actress. I didn't want to be a freak, a leper, alone. In spite of my better judgment, I let the tears stream down my face, spilling onto my dad's thighs, dissolve into his skin.

We rolled into our driveway and he gently pushed me upright.

"Get yourself together, girl. I don't want your mother to know we talked." Pulling out his handkerchief, he wiped tears from my face. "I'm sorry again for back there. I'm just afraid of losing my family. Afraid of losing my girls. If I just knew what she was doing, maybe I could get things back to normal." He shoved the handkerchief back into his pocket, then patted my shoulder.

"Maybe if you and I stick together, we can get your mother to change her mind. Okay?"

I nodded my head in agreement.

My mother was waiting for us when we walked in through the back door, leaning against the refrigerator, arms folded. Upon seeing her, I noisily burst into tears and flung myself into her arms. Holding me tight, her skin was warm, soft, like fresh bread.

"What did you do to her!"

My father grunted and walked past us, creating a breeze that made me blink.

"Jack! I want you out of this house! I want you out now!" She pulled off a highheel and aimed it at him like a gun. He kept walking, his heavy steps leaving imprints in the fluffy living room carpet. Then he turned and raised his hands into the air.

"You're out of your goddamn mind, you know that? I took her out for ice cream. That a goddamn crime? Is everything I do a goddamn crime?" He kicked the TV tray. It flew across the room, crashing against a wall, causing my mother's painting to fall to the ground. I gripped her and shuddered.

"You think you're so high and goddamn mighty!" he yelled, "You and your hippie-dippie friends!"

My father's next movements were so fast that when the painting hit my mother in the head, it seemed to have dropped down from the sky. She shielded the two of us as best she could, but the wood frame clipped her near the eye.

"Get out!" she yelled again. Dad spun around to face us, his big hands clenching at his side. "Traitors! All of you!"

His words crawled beneath my skin and menaced my heart. My mother trembled; a small trickle of blood fell from her temple like a tear. We stood there entwined, stunned, waiting for what would happen next. My father took large strides away from us, cursing God and my mother as he stormed out the front door. I ran to the window and watched him walk away, to some unknown place, defeated, hands in his pockets. I wanted to run after him, stop him, bring him back. Instead I put my hands around my neck and pressed until my eyes watered. I was the traitor. I would punish myself, save God the trouble.

"He's gone, Mom," I said, easing my grip.

She stood in front of the screen door, her weight shifted onto one hip, tapping the screen with the heel of her shoe, mumbling. She didn't look like she was about to change her mind.

Like magic, Clara was suddenly next to me and both of us looked into the street.

"God, Clara, you missed it," I said.

"Nah," Clara said, bored. "I was sitting at the bottom of the stairs. Look." She held up two finely sharpened Popsicle sticks, poking her finger with one to demonstrate its effectiveness. The sight of her blood made me turn away. "See?" she kept saying, "See?" She proudly held up her bloody finger to the bright afternoon light.

❖ ❖ ❖ ❖

The next few days were gauzy, dreamlike. My father stayed away, though he seemed to be lurking nearby, behind a piece of furniture or under a bed. He was no longer my father, but a symbol of danger. My mother called him "our greatest enemy" and began referring to him as "Thor."

Clara and I were not to ask questions, to *work* with Mom, mimic her actions—checking window locks, standing guard—a household of edgy women. School was about to start, but no one seemed to care. We had bigger issues, life-threatening. There was a crazy, unpredictable man on the loose, though I wasn't certain exactly how dangerous. Mom was caught up in the nervous energy of her big plan; Clara was secretly thrilled at the prospect of less supervision. I followed orders, dusting, taping boxes, searching.

One day, while Mom and Clara were at the hardware store, I slouched into Dad's vinyl chair and settled into a rerun of *The Fugitive*. For the umpteenth time, David Janssen was about to run down the one-armed man, when Dad walked in. Just like that, right through the front door like he had never left. I froze, following him with my eyes as he breezed past me, disappearing into the bedroom, completely ignoring me. I gripped the arms of the chair; if David Janssen snagged the one-armed man, I had missed it.

I launched myself from the chair and hesitantly walked over to the bedroom. I thought I'd ask my dad how his day was going. Act normal. Maybe it had all just been a dream.

"Hi, Dad," I squeaked, then the rest of the words got caught in my throat.

He was scraping coins off his dresser and shoving them into his pocket.

"Judas," he sneered, then looked at me with such hatred I thought I would dissolve on the spot. "Get the fuck away from me," he hissed. I ran into the bathroom, locking the door behind me, afraid for my life, afraid of *Thor!* Dad stomped through the house, drawers opened, chairs scraped against the kitchen linoleum. A girlish chorus was chirping about aftershave on TV. I took in a breath and recalled his vicious expression, his narrowed hateful eyes telling me I was no longer his daughter. I was vile and maybe even contagious. My legs wobbled and I slid down the door, weak, thinking of St. Dymphna, who had earned her sainthood by standing up to her father, scorning him until he drew his dagger and sliced off her head. I imagined my own head rolling down the hall and landing at my father's feet.

The front door slammed and I pushed myself up, blood began

to flow back into my legs.

When Mom returned, she knew immediately that Thor had been home. Slicing through the house, Mom barricaded doors and windows, made phone calls, filled out forms, smoked.

I woke up the next morning to the sound of my mother's laughter, along with others, Joan and some strangers. Rhythm and blues blared.

Clara wasn't in her bed. I flew down the stairs.

"That bastard's never going to leave," Mom wailed, stuffing candlesticks into a pillowcase. Clara, in her nightshirt, sat on the kitchen counter, drinking a cup of instant coffee, household items in her lap—a flour sifter, coasters. My mouth fell open when I saw Father John, the hip preacher, shirtless, in carpenter pants, packing boxes. Mrs. Kapinsky, plaited, wearing overalls was unhooking our front window curtains. All of them were singing along with the Staple Sisters: "Mercy, mercy me! I'll take you there!"

"Pack your clothes, girls! We're leaving," my mother called out. "We are going to the end of the rainbow."

By noon, everything we owned was compressed into an unfamiliar white VW van. My mother left behind a child's bed, the vinyl chair, an old beach towel, and the New Testament.

Clara and I sat in the back of the van on top of bulging packing boxes and Hefty bags; my mother up front with Joan. Father John and some solemn-looking nuns followed us in their nondescript black car like FBI agents.

"The shit done hit the fan," Clara remarked as we watched our home recede in the distance.

"You okay?" she asked, tapping me with her foot.

I put my hands to my mouth to stop my lower lip from quivering.

"I keep seeing Dad come home," I said. "Wandering around the empty house. Looking for us. I know we're not supposed to like him anymore but I just feel bad. That's all." Tears plopped from my eyes like fat raindrops. Clara looked away. Though her hardened face revealed not a trace of sadness, I knew her heart was aching too—blinky eyes belied her indifference. Clara had absorbed most of Dad's abuse—she would eventually take the fall. I sniffled back the rest of my tears, knowing it was time to close up my heart, stash it inside a jar like the dead bumblebees Clara and I sometimes trapped on hot summer afternoons.

My mother's cheery voice floated indistinctly between boxes and furniture, her words absorbed by high-pitched rock music and the wavy noises of traffic.

We drove through strange towns, past schools and neighborhoods I hadn't even imagined. We made a loop around the local park, then beyond to areas I knew nothing about. Home seemed impossibly far away.

A few years later, my father would explain that a number of housewives in the neighborhood had followed my mother's example—up and left their husbands, filed for divorce, ran away. The sad men would go to my father, by then considered an expert, for advice and consolation. He would tell them, "Good riddance. Now all the whores are off the block. Maybe we can finally get a little peace and quiet around here." Even Mrs. Kapinsky left.

We pulled the VW bus up a steep hill and parked. Clara and I jumped out and took in the surroundings. Four towering tan-colored structures, still in the process of being built, were lined up on the hill; their windows reflected the mid-morning sun. The buildings were only three stories high, but to us they were skyscrapers, the kind of monuments to civilization that were usually found in big cities. Carefully arranged flowers and exotic plants were placed strategically around each building like the outside of an art museum. Tall, thick evergreen trees lay in flat beds waiting to be planted, an army of Christmas trees in August!

All around us were tractors and trailers, fresh dirt piled in pyramids, workmen with metal hats. Clara nudged me and pointed to a sign that read Moulin Rouge, a prestigious experience in living-ADULTS ONLY. We weren't even allowed here. A surge of excitement shot up my spine.

We helped carry boxes, bags, and furniture up three flights of stairs into our new two-bedroom apartment.

The place smelled of fresh paint and brand-new carpet. Everything was white or beige, the kitchen filled with chrome and mirrors. New appliances and squared-off rooms, clean and perfect, waited before us, a newly stretched canvas.

Clara and I set out to explore the grounds and find good places to smoke. "You're visiting an aunt," my mother instructed, a dodge we'd get used to over the years.

Recognizing the familiar smell of fresh trash, we soon found ourselves leaning against a garbage dumpster, lit up smokes. Beyond the wall was our new neighborhood, similar to the old, brick homes, Fords, and Schwinns—only this time, partitioned. We already didn't belong. There would be no Welcome Wagons.

Upon further inspection, we came upon a huge crater between the buildings, kicking dirt clods into the hole. A few years ago this giant's grave would have provided us with endless hours of entertainment, employing Tonka trucks and water buckets. Now this pit meant something else entirely—a symbol of new hope. A built-in pool! Mom had our best interests at heart all along. She was thinking ahead. We'd be fine. I was just about to share this with Clara when she muttered, "Big fucking deal. I hate to swim anyway."

But I imagined myself diving into an expanse of blue with the grace of Esther Williams, floating under the stars in a lacy two-piece, sharing secrets with my new friends. I peered into the muddy hole and felt immensely relieved. I couldn't have possibly known then that we would be evicted long before the pool was completed.

❧   ❧   ❧   ❧

Only a few weeks after settling into Moulin Rouge, Clara was stealing, smoking pot. She eventually fell into the mud pit. She had walked right into the manager's apartment and lifted an entire ounce of marijuana that was hidden inside a Ouija Board. Along with the pot, Clara stole rolling papers, a jar of BacOs, and a Fresca. Clara's victim, a heavy-set George Harrison, was more furious about the dope than the fact that there were innocent children on the premises. Mom paid him back, but we were evicted anyway. So, off we went to Ferndale Gardens—then the Southfield Hillside Estates, Pontiac Parlor, Royal Oak Manor, Telegraph Park and finally Keego Bay. All adults-only complexes, all like minefields for our fractured family. Clara's drug problem grew worse with each move, her crimes more punishable. She hooked up with some older boys, scabby addicts fresh from prison, one being her boyfriend Mo. Together, like drug-addled *Bonnie and Clydes,* they stole cars, broke into homes, fenced hot

goods, and eventually began to sell drugs. Clara was apprehend-
ed during ceramics class for attempting to sell mushroom caps to
a teacher's aide, dragged down the long, echoing hallway into the
principal's office, my friends and I watching in silent horror. To
keep Clara off the streets, my mother locked her in our Keego
basement. But Clara managed to stay stoned, nearing coma
states, me lugging her around, cold water, hot coffee, long nights.

When Clara was taken to Juvenile Hall I was relieved, everyone was. After all our humiliating failures at putting down new
roots, attempts at starting over, the idea of hitting the road with
my mother—and without Clara—sounded smart. Perhaps it
could still work out.

CHAPTER SIX

AFTER WE MANAGED TO GET OUT OF NEBRASKA WITHOUT BEING killed, we sped through boxy Wyoming without making one tourist stop. Though greatness loomed all around, a post card from a Texaco would have to suffice. Needing some evidence that I was near National Monuments, I settled on a photograph of a Great Plains medicine man, complete with headdress and war paint, sun-dancing barefoot in front of a frothing 200-foot geyser. I gushed on, telling Lara how I had shared a hookah full of dried peyote with the big chief, then imagined Lara churning with envy.

"What will we do when the money runs out?" I asked as we crossed the Continental Divide. Rows of dark, pointy mountains pricked up in the distance like Doberman ears.

"That's a hundred dollars away," my mother said. "Let's not get ahead of ourselves."

Mom gussied up in a Texaco bathroom—shaved legs, rouged cheeks, glossied lips. She wore a short skirt, low-cut blouse, high shoes—the works.

Settling on a high-end diner called The Ribcage, we scarfed down animals last seen in the Detroit zoo—elk, buffalo, bison. In

Utah it seemed anything on four legs was game—broiled or braised. The restaurant appeared to be constructed out of bleeding leather—red velvet tapestries, fiery candle domes. After our bloaty meal, Mom searched in vain for men to flirt with, sauntering, traipsing, lingering at the bar.

Staring hard into my gristly plate, I pretended not to notice what she was doing. Over the years, we had relied on the kindness of incidental men to help us through tight places—to pay an overdue utility bill, to stock a bare refrigerator.

More than once, Clara and I had eaten in fancy river-front restaurants, courtesy of such "boyfriends." My mother had many over the years, and if the night went well, Clara took the opportunity to go through their wallet. Clara looked forward to visits from these "generous" suitors and even encouraged the flush ones to return. "My mom makes a mean pot roast!" she would tease.

My mother had been gone from the table over an hour. I thought about calling my dad or checking on Clara, but decided to wait. I really had nothing to say to either of them. Maybe I'd have more to say once I got to California.

Fishing through the ashtray, I picked out a nearly intact cigarette butt and attempted to scrape off the sticky lip-gloss when Mom abruptly walked into my line of vision, swaggering on her bony pumps, exposing a lacy bra. Tipsy and acting girly, she was being shadowed by a big-bellied man wearing a cheap beige suit that looked as though it may have fit back in the stone age. He was sallow-faced and possum-like. A toothpick dangled from his lower lip like an old scab. The pickings in the bar must have been extremely slim.

"Doll, this is Skip," my mother said, speaking in a mock Southern accent, something she recently started to do when she drank. "He's from Chicago. Can you believe it? We were just there. Small world." She pronounced *world* like *wurrelled.* "Isn't that just too goddamn weird. He's joining us for some coffee."

They both squeezed into her side of the booth and immediately began playing footsies, heels clunking on the tiled floor. She leaned over Skip, her neck against his chin, and held up her nearly empty wine glass. "Yoo hoo," she called out. "Need a refill here."

"You must be Jane." Skip peeked around my mother, then

gently pushed her aside like a curtain, tilting his head at me.

"June," I sassed.

I lowered myself into the seat and slowly sank deeper into the vinyl booth, wishing I could disappear. I hated when my mother sprung strangers on me. She continued with the accent: "Egg yolk, mustard, baby shit. All yellow, all different."

Our dinner check sat on the edge of the table, as dangerous and patient as a bear trap.

Skip had his wide head cocked to one side, impressed with my mother's refinement, his eyes shiny from too much beer. I could tell he lived a life of boredom, a compulsive watcher of TV police shows—a real Sunday drive, my mother most likely the biggest challenge he would ever face. Mom leaned back, stretched, exposing more lace.

"I think interstates are tunnel-like, vaginal," she teased. "The *open road*," she explained, doing a breast stroke. "Got to get my baby to the sea before it dries up."

I squirmed and prayed for the end of the world. Skip twiddled his thumbs, then cracked his knuckles, and sucked on the toothpick, squinting. Maybe he was thinking.

"Guess what, Jeannie. Skip's a salesman on his way to Sacramento," she said to me, eyebrows raised, as though trying to impress me with her knowledge of his personal history. "We're both driving Caddies. He sells pharmaceutical products."

I perked up. "Oh, yeah. Have any samples?"

"Jesus, Jeannie." My mother rolled her eyes and puffed on her cigarette.

"Matter of fact, I do," he said. "Got some extra Ortho-Novum."

Skip produced a round white packet from his shirt pocket and tossed it to me. My mother sighed.

"They're contraceptives, Jeannie," she groaned.

"Oh."

"Hey, don't knock it," Skip said. "Our biggest seller. Keeps my beer kegs filled."

Finally, Skip reached for his wallet. My mother lit another cigarette, using the hot tip of the one still burning. She acted cool, then laughed at nothing, making all kinds of noise with her shoes beneath the table.

"Anyway, Skip. Like I said earlier, I don't fake orgasms. *Rully*," she said, breathy, her phony accent vacillating wildly between British and Southern.

Skip had the bill in his pudgy fingers, a look of concentration on his face. I slid deeper into the booth, watching Mom's exposed foot scamper alongside Skip's trouser leg. My mother had sunk so low I simply did not know what to do.

"Porkfat and Clap!" I shouted. They both looked at me like I was a freak, then got back to their conversation.

"You won't be faking no O's with me," Skip said, then made an O shape with his mouth. "Now that I can guarantee," Skip boasted. Then he eyeballed the bill. "Let's see here." Skip examined the numbers while fingering his greenbacks. I guess the seduction had worked; he would pay for the bloody meal.

"I mean," my mother continued, "not that I *haven't*. But I can tell you're a real sharpie, hip Skip. Most men can't read woman very well."

"Holy hayseed, I know I can." Skip put his wormy mouth on her ear and I dry heaved, focusing on the red exit sign across the room. When I was too young to understand the term, I had overheard Mom promising my dad a "mind-altering blow-job" on his birthday if he taught her to drive. We all piled into the Ford that afternoon for Mom's first disastrous lesson. My father threatened to kill Mom if she ever went near the Ford again, so I don't imagine she made good on her promise.

"Hey, sweet-lips, I'm just up the road at the Copperbottom Inn."

My mother tilted her head back and blew smoke into the air as Skip peeled off a five and threw it onto the table.

"This'll cover my beer." He fussed with his zipper, hoisted himself up, then winked at Mom. Her face went flat, her lips hard little cement ledges. Skip twisted his head around in a circle, his neck crackling.

My mother ignored him, her body growing rigid as a Barbie doll's.

"Well, Ms. Michelangelo, you know where I'll be." He formed more O's with his mouth like a suck fish, then chuckled.

"Sure will," she hissed, baring her teeth.

He snorted and walked off into the murky room, swinging his big ass, sucking on that toothpick.

"Damn! What a waste of time *that* was." Her movements were

quick and jerky as she buttoned up her blouse. "Should've stole his wallet when I had the chance. Imagine that fucking idiot thinking I would actually come by his motel room!"

She plastered on more lip gloss and drained her wineglass. "Cheap son of a bitch. Dream on, fat ass!"

She looked at me as if this was somehow all my fault.

"Well, if you weren't so damn hungry all the time. And why do you have to humiliate me so! Porkchop and Clap?" She scanned the bill, then fanned her face with it.

"Well, c'est la fucking vie. People have to eat, don't they?" she said, pulling out her checkbook, which was now a complete work of fiction.

"Rather be dipped in battery acid than fuck that guy anyway." She sighed, exasperated.

"From a distance, he looked a bit like Jack Nicholson, didn't you think?" She ripped the worthless check out of her checkbook and flung it onto the bill tray.

"Mom, I can't believe you were talking to that creep about orgasms. And what the hell were you doing under the table. God, I could die. That's so gross. He didn't look anything like Jack Nicholson."

She stabbed her cigarette out against the wood table and shook her head.

"Come on." She secured her purse strap over her shoulder, hiked up her skirt, and headed for the exit sign.

A few of the waitresses studied us as we walked by—ruddy girls wearing red fluffy dresses. My mother had earlier called them big-boned breeders. In this town, they were probably considered beautiful, voluptuous. Back in Detroit, we'd consider them homely, or just plain fat. Ignoring their stares, I put the packet of birth control pills on top of the bill for a tip.

CHAPTER SEVEN

⠿ ⠿ ⠿ ⠿

WE WOULD PASS BOGUS CHECKS ALL THE WAY TO CALIFORNIA, cheating grocery stores, motor inns, and truck stop diners. Our remaining cash was only spent when absolutely necessary on gas, motor oil, and cigarettes. My mother figured out ways to use checks for whatever else we needed, including coffee, tampons and licorice ropes. In Nevada we splurged and bounced checks for genuine felt cowboy hats, buckskin moccasins and a special suntan lotion made from limestone which strangely smelled like burned fish-sticks. At the cash register, the drill was always the same: mom would lean on one hip, smile, lower her sunglasses. "One of life's unexpected curve balls," she would explain, something about an emergency, a sudden cash shortage, then gesture toward me. The sales clerk would shoot me a glance, shake his/her head knowingly—the troubled teenager. I'd act distant, maybe roll my eyes as if to say, yes it's all true—I'm an expensive pain in my patient mother's ass! Mom would say something witty about single motherhood—they would laugh, share their sorrows, kissing-cousins commiserating. "Merci beaucoup," she would call out, waving, well wishing.

My mother and I never discussed her transcontinental trail of fraud.

"Your father hated California," she commented airily. "Couldn't wait to leave. Too much sun."

We were approaching the border of California, both of us wearing sombreros, tanning our arms through the windows, sucking up licorice. We had passed through Reno without pulling on one slot machine. The city was like the gates of heaven, my mother had explained: a town filled with sin and temptation but only a few miles away from the true Nirvana—cleverly designed to keep the riff-raff out of California. There was no need for us to stop there. We were exhausted, having seen too much dry, menacing desert. The very name "Lake Tahoe" held out the hope of something cool and refreshing. Not to mention, it would be our first real tourist stop.

"He was a handsome pilot, though. He really was, but couldn't wait to be back in Michigan, to his cream of rice world. I was tricked, Jeannie. Don't ever fall for a pretty face."

"I know, Mom," I replied dutifully.

All four car windows were still open as we entered higher altitudes, the air turning wintry-cold. I yanked off my sombrero, bidding a final adieu to the endless plains and breathed in the smell of snow and pine cones.

"Mom, look!" I could see the shimmering, sapphire lake through openings between the enormous, cloud-capped redwoods. We pulled off the road to get a better look. The sun was setting, splashing the sky with painter's shades like tangerine, claret-red, salmon-pink—my mother's latest canvas. The lake rested still as an ice rink—a brilliant jewel reflecting the oversized trees that reached for heights that made my stomach dance, my head spin. The chill factor was as cold as any winter night in Michigan, but neither of us cared. We were caught up in a beauty so large that for a moment there was nothing to say.

We stood on a clump of wet land near the lakeshore, our reflections looking back at us. My mother wore her wide-brimmed hat, red chiffon wrapped around the rim—a cigarette dangled from her mouth, arms crossed against her black turtleneck. Standing along side her in my dark sweater and battered jeans, our unseemly image bounced back—a couple of banditos, faces fixed with big shiny teeth—naïve smiles.

"This is something, huh, Jean? This is the California I remember."

Mom held out her cigarette like a pointer. "This all belongs to you, Jeannie: Lake Tahoe on a silver platter."

I smiled for her benefit but felt myself wilting inside. Although I knew what she meant, it was so far from the truth. In all likelihood, we were trespassing.

Mom dipped her moccasin in the lake. I did a quick search for forest rangers, suddenly frigid cold, the icy wind drilling into my ears.

"Mom, let's go find a town."

"Oh, come down here, Jean, and feel the water. It's the coldest lake in the world. God," she moaned, her entire foot submerged in the lake. "Feel this."

I stepped unwillingly toward her. "It can't be the coldest water in the world, Mom. That can't be possible. What about the Antarctic or the North Pole? That's got to be colder."

She looked at me and sighed. "Just feel the goddamn water, Jean. It's the coldest. Believe me, it used to be a glacier for Christ sakes!"

I knew we would stay there all night unless I felt the water, so I dappled my fingers along the lake's surface.

"Wow. Like ice-water," I agreed. We sat for a while, cupping the melted glacier in our palms, shivering, teeth chattering.

Lake Tahoe really brought out the criminal in my mother. A bona fide crook surfaced. Stealing from Motel Six's and Stop-N-Shop's was one thing—minor, petty—but stealing from vacation resorts seemed rather serious—convict-y, felonious. I knew there was a financial line drawn, an amount you are allowed to steal before it becomes consequential—*grand larceny!* I kept an eye out for flashing reds. Not that I'd know what to do, but at the very least I could alert my mom that the law was on our tail. She'd probably make a run for it. After all, Cadillacs drive like they're on ice.

We checked into a ritzy resort, the rooms individual chateaus, each complete with a storybook loft and hickory- burning fireplace. Floor-to-ceiling windows overlooked tennis courts and flower-filled gardens. Sun-drenched patios stuffed with jungle-like potted plants linked the units. The expansive living room displayed downy sofas and cushy leather chairs. There were stacks of recent fashion magazines, bowls of fresh fruit, a guest book! The last of the sunlight filtered through the window blinds, casting a golden glow. It was the most beautiful room I had ever been in. We each had our own king-size bed with bed-spreads the color of finely whipped butter.

"Fuck me! This is incredible!" My mother jumped on the sofa, then the chair, finally the bed. She bit into an apple, then a pear.

I threw my tired blue suitcase onto the bed, ignoring her. Outside, the sky was darkening, a few stars beginning to poke their way through. I saw Polaris and held its light in my eyes, relieved that it followed us here. Beyond the tennis courts I could see the spark of a dinky town—a village—and therefore people. Tourists, locals, real people in Tahoe by choice—the types who made reservations and planned their itineraries. My mother and I did not belong here. It wasn't right for me to enjoy this.

Mom made an entrance through the bathroom door, wrapped in a fluffy hotel towel, large puffs of steam billowing out from behind her.

"This is a dream, isn't it? They have individually wrapped soap in there—and a heat lamp! Go shower, baby."

She strutted through the spacious room, swinging her arms in grand gestures indicating her good mood. Sliding open the glass doors, unaffected by the cold or her nudity, she shouted, "Look at this sunset! Hey, there's the North Star! Hurry, make a wish."

But I couldn't even look, couldn't stand the idea that we both looked to the stars for some kind of salvation or magic. Instead I looked grimly at the tennis courts, knowing I would never learn to play. Fuck Wimpledon, or was it Wimbledon?

"Oh, honey. Isn't it wonderful?" Mom was starting to get sentimental, and I didn't want to hear her speech about how this was all mine again, how everything would all be perfect, so I disappeared into the shower.

As we strolled down the winding cobblestone path that cut through the village, we peered into windows, peeked at menus. The street was lined with cozy-type restaurants, antique shops, miniature storefronts for tourists to fawn over, like Mom. "Now this is quaint," she sighed, then stopping in her tracks, hand on mouth, "Oh my God, how precious." Then, practically falling through a window, "Sooooo enchanting. Positively bewitching! It's that California imagination."

I let myself imagine that just beyond the snow-covered tree-tops there were pointy houses made out of gingerbread, surging rivers formed from colored sugar, and kind, wealthy witches who loved teenagers and gave them money. Maybe this *was* some freaky, fairy-tale town. Even the air smelled sweet.

None of the shops were open—we were off-season.

"This is what I'll do one day," my mother announced. "Open a junk store, sell crocheted plant hangers, hand-painted chiffons and silk scarves. But I'll stay open all year. Never closed, my sign will say. Come in anytime! Have a coffee. Christ, I'll bring back the wimple!"

An icy breeze passed through my skin and settled into my bones. Harrah's casino was at the end of the street, all lit up with dancing lights like the entrance to an amusement park. Festive and noisy, it seemed out of place given the empty streets and the noticeable lack of consumers. My face grew hot as it occurred to me that we would likely be their big customers for the night.

We walked inside to meet a blast of hot air—and the noise! Bells dinging, machines clanging, elevator music blaring. Having never been inside a casino before, I was amazed by its acreage. It seemed to go on forever, but then with all the flashing colors, spinning lights, and high and low mirrors, it was hard to tell. What struck me the most was the emptiness: the deserted black-jack tables, still roulette wheels, and lonesome crap tables. A few card dealers played solitaire on the green felt tables, slumped into tall chairs without arms. They looked bored, just doing their time, a look I recognized.

But the racket. I wondered if a soundtrack was broadcasting the bustle and clatter of a busy casino, just so the employees wouldn't fall asleep. Then I spotted a ruckus around a craps table. "Look, Mom. Let's go watch them play."

"Forget it, they're fools," she said, striding ahead of me.

I felt the eyes of strangers on us, and I pulled my tattered purse close to my chest. My mother was again gussied up, extra topaz stickpins chaining up her hair.

We found an all-night cafeteria overlooking the casino with a large neon sign—MELLOW YELLOWS—placed above the entry-way. We loaded our plastic yellow trays with fried chicken, potato salad, and red gelatin. We paid cash—down to our last fifty bucks.

As we ate our yellow chicken, seated in the hard yellow vinyl booth, small yellow cloth napkins in our laps, I surveyed the casino. I loved the idea of winning, being lucky, getting money for nothing. I studied a hunched-over Asian woman as she fed quarters into a slot machine. She fed the beast during the entire course of our dinner and well into dessert, working with a mechanical rhythm. Quarter in with the right hand, left hand pulls, one step back, then repeat. Once she broke the pattern by looking anxiously from side to side, gave the machine a good, swift kick, and yanked down the lever; then as if on cue, three cherries lined up! Lights flashed and spun, buzzers blared, sirens whirred, and hundreds of quarters spewed forth and clanked out, a silver landslide. The woman rocked back and forth, stepping on the coins, then made strange hand gestures above her head, like she was swatting bothersome insects. Soon there was an employee at her side, handing her a large white bucket that looked like the bottom half of a Clorox jug.

The woman grabbed the bucket, and began scooping in the quarters. When the bucket was nearly full, she placed it between her feet before resuming her rhythmic ritual, using the quarters that were still in the silver dish beneath the machine.

"Did you see that, Mom!" I was practically jumping out of the booth. But my mother ignored the commotion, concentrating instead on lighting her cigarette. She looked around the room in search of our waitress, holding up a small, nearly empty yellow porcelain coffee cup while doing her "Yoo hoo?" routine.

"She must've won over a hundred bucks." I gripped the edge of our table and leaned in closer. "Maybe we should try."

She blew smoke out the side of her mouth, then shook her head. "That woman's an idiot. Just look how desperate she is. I'll make you a bet. I'll bet she's been here since last freakin' Easter hovered over that machine. All these places are fixed, Jeannie. They keep you here until you go bankrupt. I'll also bet she's an ex-showgirl."

Our waitress appeared, confined inside a tiny yellow cocktail dress, her orange hair puffed out like a pastry shell, gluey eyelashes in danger of falling off. She was in her fifties, buxom, another ex-showgirl. "Refill," she predicted with sarcasm, holding out the yellow coffee pot. I leaned back to let her in and she loaded up mom's cup. We both smiled at her until she left. Then we didn't talk about her, which was unusual. She was the sort of person my mother was anxious to criticize, hold out as an example—an older woman trying too hard or not hard enough.

But the waitress seemed to have made my mother nervous, as she doctored her coffee with creams and sugars. Adjusting her hair pins, she leaned back, slurped, and gave me the eyeball. *Here it comes,* I thought, then looked away, tearing at the edges of a Keno card.

"Herein lies the problem, Jeannie. Miss China doll may very well have won, if you call a few quarters a victory. But . . . she also used up a large portion of her luck. We only get a certain helping in life and we had better use it sparingly. Luck is congenital and finite. One day when she really needs it, surprise, it ain't gonna be there!" My mother looked over at the woman, then tsked.

"Just look at her. Shit, she'll probably get hit by a drunk driver on her way home. Then what'll become of all those lousy coins?"

I considered my mother's "reservoir of luck" theory and if it were true, I had truckloads coming to me. Eighteen-wheelers. Scraping the last of my Jello out from its fluted glass dish, my fingers appeared magnified, fleshy and plump. I flashed on Buck, the giant from Lubbock, singing "People Who Need People," squeezing his purple dick. I coughed up the waxy cubes.

"Jeannie, really. We're not in Detroit anymore."

"Sorry."

My mother stretched and let out a noisy, gaping yawn.

"Well, you sure look tired, honey. Why don't you go back to the room? I'm super awake from all this coffee. I think I'll hang out for a while . . . look for a glass of wine somewhere." I took this as my cue to take off, grateful she would begin her manhunt without me.

I couldn't imagine my mother getting into much trouble with so few people around, so I patted her on the shoulder, and headed toward the exit. When out of her view, I scrambled through my bag for quarters. Standing in front of a long line of sunny machines was the Asian lady. She wore thick, dark glasses, had chapped, bitten lips, and seemed to be looking right at me. When a quarter slipped from her hand she screeched like a hawk and fell onto her knees, moving frantically over the dice-patterned carpet. The coin was directly in front of her, as big as the moon. When I realized the old woman was blind I walked around the machine, picked up the coin, and handed it to her. She grabbed it, spit out words I didn't recognize, then turned back to the machine.

I stood watching for a while, stunned. For some reason I felt embarrassed for her. No way was she an ex-dancer.

I turned away and found another row of quarter slot machines, the "lucky banana" series. Slipping in a coin, I yanked down on the handle: cherry, uneven bar, seven. No bananas. I pulled, tugged, yanked, looked around suspiciously, closed one eye, both eyes, kicked the machine, then did a yank-look-kick-wink combination. Nothing.

"Truckloads!" I shouted to the Wheel of Fortune, stomping out of the casino. "Fucking truckloads!" The sound of my voice startled me as I walked out into the frosty night air.

Shuffling along the passageway of patios, I heard muffled sounds pouring out of the chateaus: talking, canned TV, laughter, arguing, fucking.

It occurred to me that there were more people vacationing than I had thought. We had arrived late, after all. Tourists were partying in their rooms, drinking hot toddies in cavernous bars deep inside the casino—older, wealthy people who owned diamond watches and designer handbags. I realized that I could easily slip inside random condos, seize their cash, wallets, and ruby bracelets. I was just an innocent kid, traveling with my sophisticated mother. No one would suspect me. Excited by this turn of events, I scurried over to our balcony and scoped out the situation. Each unit was equipped with an open patio; fake, cozy porches reached all the way around the property. This is how I would break in. I would have to wait until the drunken guests were asleep, then tiptoe in my socks and make off with some easy loot.

After brushing my teeth I jumped onto my king-size bed and pulled the covers up to my chin. The plan was to take a nap, be awakened by my mother, wait for her wine-sloppy snore, then sneak out into the night. It was perfect, a far less risky plan than, say, stealing from the five-and-dime. There were no security shills or narcs hanging around the balconies.

Lying in the disturbingly large bed, I started to worry about my mother. She was small and tired, wandering around that big casino, drunk by now and more vulnerable than ever. I imagined her being dragged behind a vacated gift shop by some frustrated craps loser, maybe a tough wise-guy type who didn't appreciate Mom's prick-teasing routines. I couldn't shake the image so I jumped out of bed and snapped on the TV. I watched the second half of Johnny Carson and began to fall asleep during his interview with Buddy Ebsen. Big laughs all around at a lame joke about Spiro Agnew and skullcaps, Ed MacMahon doing his Santa Claus laugh, his sweaty ballooning body ready to burst through his shiny gray suit. My mother always called Ed Johnny's blow-up doll. Then a Club Med commercial came on: "A vacation is a world where there are no locks on the doors on the mind or the body." I decided not to wait for my mother.

I went outside on the patio and took a slow walk around the condos, looking into dark windows that revealed little besides my own reflection. There I saw a sneaky prowler, a scary, dark-clothed figure moving through the inky night. I pretended to be Clara; criminal activity didn't frighten her. Studying my reflection, I saw her round eyes and ghostly skin.

Stepping closer to the next window, I peered into the shadowy living room. All was still, the door leading to the bedroom was closed. I could make out a woman's handbag—a small, leather purse with a flimsy gold chain—and next to it, a set of keys, some magazines. Finally, my eyes settled on a simple black billfold.

The sliding door was open a crack; I slipped my fingers into the opening just as I noticed a bottle of Blue Nun on the patio table, two empty glasses, a full ashtray. The sightseers had been dancing under the moonlight, drinking the wine with the laughing nuns on the label. Idiots. Nuns don't laugh. In fact, nuns were bitter and crusty-skinned and possibly subversive. With one swift motion I slid open the door and wriggled in.

Right away I became aware of a hickory smell and noticed smoldering embers in the fireplace. Tiptoeing, my arms slightly in front, my heart pulsing in my ears—a beat so loud I was certain it would wake everyone up. With each step forward there was a slightly audible creak. With each creak, I held my breath, finally reaching the table, then grabbed the wallet—which turned out to be a very small camera. Palming it, I shoved the camera into the front of my jeans. As I reached for the purse nearby, a voice came out of the dark air, a stern male voice: "Don't move." My body stiffened.

A hand was on my shoulder, heavy, causing my knees to bend. I had stopped breathing. The table lamp snapped on and I quickly looked away, outside, into the night.

"I thought I was in my room," I squeaked. "I must've come in the wrong door."

"You're just a kid. What the hell are you doing?" "I'm with my parents, in a room down a ways. I got lost." I was still looking outside, straining my neck, as if the intensity of my longing would transplant me. I saw myself outside the sliding glass window, deciding not to come in, skipping stones, breathing in the woodsy air. Instead there were strong male fingers pressing into my shoulder and neck. I had to pay attention.

"And I suppose you thought this was your purse?"

I tilted my head to look because I could no longer feel my arms; they could've been anywhere. Like my legs, they didn't seem attached to me. But there it was, my hand on the purse in a frozen grip. *Take your hand away, move your fucking hand,* but I couldn't. Out the corner of my eye, I saw a flash of clothing and a tiny sigh of relief escaped. At least he wore underwear. I looked down at the carpet, trying hard to think of something new to say but all that kept running through my mind was: *you're fucked you're fucked you're fucked.* Then I had an idea.

"Maybe I was sleepwalking. You shouldn't really wake me up."

"Oh, right," he grunted. That's when I finally dared to look at my captor. I had been staring at his spindly toes, curled into the carpet like overcooked spaghetti. I dreaded looking at the rest, imagining a lumpy body of old baggy flesh. When I glimpsed his face, I gasped. His eyes were two black stones, lidless, pried-open, hostile—his tanned, textured face seemed to crunch when he spoke.

"Do I look like a fool?"

I was trying to remember what dumb thing I'd just said.

"Well?" he insisted, digging his fingers further into my arm. I was moist with sweat.

My voice had abandoned me; I tried to force out sound but none materialized. I wondered if all my silent screams were stored someplace down deep with the uncried tears and evil thoughts—was there a capacity limit? *Sorry, the inn is full!* The old man squeezed my shoulder harder and I whimpered in pain. His boxer shorts were an Easter pink, dotted with tiny black golfers, his stomach spilling over like froth. He clicked off the lamp, plunging us back into the murk, then pushed me onto the balcony.

"The silent treatment, huh? Is this where you accidentally came in? Take off your shirt," he growled.

"What?" I shivered with disbelief, then tried to pull away but his grip held me firmly in place. Suddenly I got my voice back. "I'm really sorry, okay?" I pleaded. "I've learned my lesson now."

He freed up one of my shoulders to open the tiny handbag, its long gold chain making clinking noises. Handing me a twenty he said matter-of-factly, "Show me your tits and I won't turn you in. You can keep the Jackson."

Holding out the twenty, his hand was bony and delicate— crepe skin, polished nails. Spoiled, bored hands.

"You listening?" His toxic breath on my face caused me to flinch and I strained to get away from him.

"You better let me go," I threatened vaguely, crossing my arms.

"You picked the wrong room. I'm a judge," the old man countered. "You could go to juvenile hall, then prison. Breaking and entering is a serious crime."

Like I didn't know that. Then he yanked up my sweater and dragged his whiskery face along my chest, sanding it down.

"You might not get out until you're thirty. That's a long time."

"Hurry," I lamented.

I didn't want to go to jail. I didn't want to slow up the trip. My mother would kill me. I stared downward, following a crack in the cement that disappeared beneath the shrubbery, then saw the gleam of the Blue Nun and remembered the story of Saint Maria Goretti, a virgin and martyr who resisted the advances of a randy young man. He sneaked into her bedroom one night and raped her, then stabbed her repeatedly with a long sharp dagger until she split in two like an old piece of wood.

Just be quick, fucker. Hurry! The old judge's withered hand moved up the curve of my waist, then docked on my breast. Pressing closed my eyes, I bit down on my lip until it hurt. I felt fatherless, hopeless. I wondered why nobody was canonized anymore. Then I pictured our new apartment, a bird's nest balanced over the Pacific, the surf greeting the front door, sea mist hitting my face. The judge's heart was pounding, his breathing labored and rattled—the fucker was going to drop dead. I snatched the Jackson, shoved him backward, and bolted.

"That's it, you delinquent. Run! Get the hell out of here," he shouted.

And I did, wild and fast through the connecting patios, grasping the camera, spewing obscenities. Inside the room, I locked the window behind me, ran to the bathroom and wiped down my chest, scrubbed off any of the lech's residue. Hot tears plopped onto my socks. Then I climbed into bed, hiding the loot under my pillow.

※ ※ ※ ※

Sunlight streamed in through the top of the huge window, practically blinding me. I squeezed my eyes shut tight, a curtain of red, then immediately felt a rush of panic. Clutching the camera I shot up and realized that my mother's bed had not been slept in. A chill traveled up my spine. The clock read 8:12.

I jumped out of bed, paced, tried to think. Mom had been raped, possibly killed or she'd fallen down drunk and slipped into the coldest lake in the world. Maybe she had run into the judge and they were plotting my prison term. She had decided to leave me here and was already in San Francisco, living the single life.

Suddenly feeling self-conscious, I searched the condo for a hidden camera, looking in closets, behind curtains and under the beds. After convincing myself there was no one observing me, I buried my new camera deep inside my suitcase. Would that perverted bastard come looking for me? He wouldn't dare. He was more a criminal than me. But would anyone believe me? Nervous and jumpy, I stormed around the living room humming—nothing specific, thinking how Clara wouldn't be afraid in this situation. Clara wouldn't even worry about Mom. "Maybe she's never coming back," she would say, thrilled.

Unable to stand the silence anymore, I flipped on the TV. An overweight man wearing rubber suspenders and orange ear-muffs, knee-deep in a gushing river, demonstrated a fly-fishing technique, casting his rod over and over. "You need to anticipate their every move; outsmart the rascals," he lectured with a wink. I turned down the volume.

The ringing phone caused me to flinch. I put a hand to my heart, fearing the worst—pieces of Mom were found floating in the lake—Sasquatch! I grabbed the receiver.

"Hello?"

"Jeannie, sweetie, you're up." Mom's voice was jaunty, full of merriment. I let out a long sigh. She couldn't be too far away.

"Hon, you're not going to believe what happened, but I ran into an old friend of a friend. We got to talking and I must've fallen asleep on the sofa."

She was using the phony accent, but I didn't mind. She could pretend she was Chinese for all I cared—she was alive and we could leave this place.

"Jeannie, hon. Are you there? What are you doing?"

"Watching a show about some pissant fish."

"Honey, I'm sorry. I'll be right there, then we'll go out for a nice brunch somewhere. We'll have steak and eggs."

Mom laughed for no reason, then *he* chimed in. Cackle-cackle. "I just went out like a log." "That's *light*, Daisy," *he* corrected. "Went out like a *light*."

"Okay, Ma. Just *hurry*," I insisted, slamming down the phone, in front of a man she was trying to impress. I had never hung up on her before, but she deserved it—she needed to suffer a little. She had an obligation to comfort me, not frighten me. Christ, I could've been killed last night or, even worse, thrown into jail with homicidal Paul Bunyans. I hated Mom again. I bounced the phone on my thighs, realizing I could probably guilt-trip Mom into buying me a new pair of blue jeans, an expensive pair, with fancy stitching, using up the last of our cash, forcing her to somehow find some more. I decided to call my dad. Clara must be with him by now; she had been released from juvenile hall the day before.

I lit up one of my mother's butts and blew out perfect rings of smoke, watching them dissolve and float up to the ceiling. The taste of menthol reminded me of the numbing gel I'd once gotten from a dentist. I had liked the taste and requested more until I felt nothing at all.

Knowing Clara was going to be angry, I gripped the phone and gritted my teeth.

Clara answered the phone after half a ring: "You fucking bitch!" she shrieked, somehow expecting the call.

"How dare you and that whore take off without me! Dad said you were going to California! Is that true? Where are you? How far did you get?"

"Hey, Clara, calm down. Damn. Take it easy."

"No way! Turn around and come get me. Now! Or send me a ticket. First class!"

"Clara, listen. You were too fucked up to take along. Okay? I wanted you to come. So did Mom. But we have to get settled first, then we'll bring you out."

"That's bullshit." There was a cold silence. Then calmer: "Where are you?"

"Well, we're here. In California."

The admission excited me. Then I heard a loud crack, like Clara had slammed the phone against the wall. She started to yell again.

"Fuck, Jeannie, you can't leave me here! Please talk to Mom. She'll listen to you. Dad is going make me go to a Catholic school and to fucking church. They won't let me leave the house," she whined. "They pray every night and sing Hosannah's together after dinner. I live in the goddamn basement."

She went on complaining for a while, but I thought maybe it was a good situation. Maybe my mother was right—that you actually could force someone off drugs by keeping them locked up, on their knees and in church.

I looked out the frosted windows and noticed four people on the tennis courts—dressed in white, two tanned older couples with graying hair. I recognized the judge right away; he was playing tennis like nothing had happened—like he molested girls every day. I wondered how many other secrets he kept from his family. I bet that bastard wasn't even a judge, but a car salesman—a glad-handing, tongue wagging con artist. Why else would he have to keep his hands so clean and groomed?

Both women wore matching flying-saucer-shaped hats that

they clutched as they played. They ran around like idiots after the ball, falling all over themselves to keep their hats on. I hated them.

"Listen, Clara," I said. "I just called to make sure you were all right. I have to go."

"Dad says Mom doesn't give a shit about us," Clara said, her voice sounded small and desperate. But I didn't think this was true about my mother—at least, regarding me.

I pulled another lengthy butt from the ashtray and held it between my fingers, considering a response. But Clara started in on how much she hated Molly, our stepmother. I kind of liked her—or at least for the five minutes I had talked to her at my father's wedding. She was friendly and plump, the Old Lady in the Shoe, only with a few more bucks, and not as dowdy.

"I'll have to wear that school uniform," Clara snarled. "I'll kill myself first. I hate that fucking vest. Tell Mom I'm off drugs for good. I'm over Mo. Come on, Jeannie. Help me out a little."

Mafia Mo was her junkie boyfriend, the ex-con. Like my mother, I was against their romance, but secretly I thought Mo was kind of cute.

"Dad says California is filled with Satan worshipers. That succubus roam freely out there and serpents writhe! Jeannie? Are you there!" She was yelling at me.

"I'll call you when we get to San Francisco," I blurted. Although Clara was still yammering I cut her off, then realized I had just hung up on two family members in a row. I pictured Clara slamming the phone down, biting at her lip, looking frantically for a place to smoke.

I was relieved Clara hadn't come with us. A headache was spurting up behind my left eye, hot and bubbly lava. I lay down on the bed and clamped down on the pain with my fists.

My mother was wearing a tank top and cutoffs, her hair was stacked high with a mess of topaz stickpins, like someone shoved a sparkler in her bun. She stood at the check-out desk, smiling and chatting up the attractive, young receptionist. I was off in the corner of the lobby, flipping through a rack of postcards, desperately hoping I wouldn't run into my gray-haired rapist. I spun the rack slowly, glancing at so many places I would never see—spiraling horse trails, icy mountain peaks, big orange suns disappearing into oceans. I had forgotten all about exploiting my mother's guilt to get some blue jeans; I didn't care anymore. I just wanted to get out of Lake Tahoe.

"Jeannie, honey, come over here. Would you please?"

I detected accusation in Mom's voice. The accent was gone and her good mood had faded along with it. She was leaning against the counter, our bags at her sandaled feet, her face lost behind oversized sunglasses. She was waving our room bill in my face.

"What is this, young lady? I've been arguing with this lovely girl about how I hadn't made a single call, yet here it is. Can you explain that?"

She waited for an answer. I considered denying it, flat-out lying, then I remembered we'd be paying with a good-for-nothing check anyway. My mother's dark, mascara-laden eyes peeked over the top of her sunglasses, challenging me.

"God, Mom. What difference does it make? I mean, really." There was enough rebellion in my voice to surprise even me.

Mom's eyes widened, her angry glare causing me to take a step backward. For a moment, I thought she might smack me or pull my hair. Suddenly she relaxed, rolled her shoulders, loosening them like a boxer before a fight. She smiled, laughed—another show for the checkout girl.

"Of course, what difference *does* it make?" she concluded. "After all, isn't that what vacations are for, spending money?" I examined the counter girl for any sign of suspicion. She smiled blandly, pen in hand, waiting for the worthless check that my mother signed with a flourish. Now I stared openly at the unknowing clerk. Her shimmery, blonde hair was perfectly straight, with an enviable Cher-like middle part. She was golden and pretty. I turned away from her and pulled back my own stringy hair into a pony tail, using a rubber band that I had been wearing on my wrist for so long that it had cut a red stripe into my skin.

Mom and I walked to the parking lot without speaking. She was taking her time, and I was trying to speed her up. Weighed down by my suitcase, I glanced around in all directions, searching for gray hair or big hats.

"We're going to have *such* fun," my mother chirped, all smiles again. "We'll wake up to the sound of fog horns and seagulls. Oh,

Jeannie, let's be happy finally. I promise never to stay out all night."

She put an arm around me and squeezed me like a piece of fruit. I said nothing.

"Okay, I made a mistake. I fell asleep. It happens. But I'll never go out again if it upsets you like this. I'll never talk to another man as long as I live. Okay, Jeannie Beannie? Please just don't call your father anymore."

"Let's get away from here, Mom. I need to eat."

"Great. We'll go find eggs Benedict. How does that sound?"

She started playing with my hair, twirling it around her finger as we walked.

"Oh Jean, wait until you meet Donald," she mused. "We must've talked for ten straight hours. I haven't had this kind of feeling for a man in years. Maybe never. He's absolutely gorgeous. Reminds me a little of Richard Widmark." She looked at me and cocked her head. "You remember him?"

"I saw him once on *Lucy*."

We reached the grimed-covered Cadillac, its windshield a blanket of dead insects.

"Anyway, he's an architect . . . lives in the city. By the way, that's what locals call San Francisco. The City. Never call it Frisco. Never, never. So he's gorgeous, rich, and divorced. Can you imagine?"

"Sounds like you hit the jackpot, Ma."

She laughed crazily at this.

"This guy liked me for sure. I really blew him away. He has a kid, a boy—your age actually. Arthur or Evan or something. So we had that in common. Wow. We cross the border and our luck changes. Needed a little jump start is all. See how that works?"

After loading our bags in the trunk, my mother balked at getting back in the car. It was now filled to capacity with debris—sticky soda bottles, fast food wrappers, cigarette butts, splintering styrofoam cups. The Caddy had certainly lost its glamour. My mother wouldn't budge until we cleaned it out.

I worked fast, heaving out the trash, smearing ashes and other crud into the stained and singed carpet.

"So, what did Thor have to say anyway," my mother asked trying to sound casual.

"He wasn't there," I replied, wiping my sooty fingers on my

jeans. "But I talked to Clara. She sounded okay—drug-free, anyway. They've enrolled her in Catholic school."

"Good. That's what she needs. And it's about time he's done something for you girls."

Mom lit a cigarette and wiped off the dashboard with a used Kleenex. I pealed gummy Lifesavers off the floorboards, trying to stay hidden. "You don't know what I had to go through to get him to agree to take her. He wanted me to send him money! Huh! Can you believe that? Do you have any idea what that man owes both of you girls in back child support? Do you think the court system helps! Huh! They give you bricks of yellow cheese and powdered milk!"

She carried the trash to a flower planter and dumped it, still talking, a cigarette bouncing between her lips. "Just because he married that phony saint with the fat ass and joined a god damn cult, he's supposed to be good now."

We piled into the car.

"You don't think he's really changed, do you?"

I shook my head and offered a snort of disdain, but privately I thought he might've changed. It was possible.

"It's good he's finally in church. He needs to repent! All the shitty things he did to me, I'm sure his conscience can't take it anymore. Did you know he tried to kill me?"

I stared out the window and wondered if the gray-haired man was a churchgoer.

"You know, honey, by the way, you should've talked to that counter girl. Pretty thing, wasn't she? Maybe all of eighteen. You could work at Lake Tahoe during summers. Knowing someone like her is like money in the bank, Jeannie. The kinds of friendships that accrue interest. You shouldn't be so hostile toward people."

"Yeah, Mom." But I knew they would never hire me. I didn't have what they were looking for. That girl was decent—had been raised that way—an impossible thing to fake.

We sped along a freeway with gigantic redwoods on either side of us, icicles dangling off their branches like ornaments.

"I wanted to teach you kids to sing, take you to art museums and classical music concerts," my mother complained. "But no . . . not over his dead body, he said. Thor's idea of culture was to go to the international section of the airport and watch the stupid jumbo jets land."

I smiled involuntarily, remembering good times at the airport. But to please her, I feigned disgust. Then Mom repeated the story about the time Thor bunted her down the basement stairs in an attempt to snap her neck—*death by severed spina*. I had heard this story so many times that it had become part of my childhood mythology. This was followed by the tale when Thor struggled to asphyxiate Mom with a handful of pungent, winter socks—*death by smothering*. Finally—*death through mutilation*—my personal favorite, the Saturday morning Dad chased Mom around the front yard with his much-coveted John Deere lawnmower. Mom claims she outran the mower and flagged down a passing motorist who allegedly threatened to run down the John Deere with his more powerful Mustang, putting the kibosh on the entire incident. Whether these stories were true no longer mattered; we were revisiting legends.

"Did you know that the very thought of Campbell's Chicken Noodle Soup can send me into a clinical depression?" Mom reminded. "I cooked that crap up every day for twelve years for *Thor's* lunch. Orange Tang! Wonderbread! Spam! A few of his favorite foods! Well, they don't eat from cans in California. I can tell you that much!"

All these conversations ended the same way. It was finally time for my line.

"Well, it's sure good we left then."

"You bet your sweet ass it is." Then she punched me in the thigh and tee-heed victoriously.

CHAPTER EIGHT

＊＊ ＊＊ ＊＊ ＊＊

To make our arrival in San Francisco official, my mother insisted on driving across the Golden Gate Bridge. To Mom, the bridge represented a starting line, the point on the map where our real lives would begin. I kind of expected a gun to go off. As we approached the blood-orange portal, something was bothering me.

"Mom, what's a succubus?"

"A whore. Why?" My mother rummaged in her bag for a cigarette.

"Dad said the only thing we're going to find in California is the devil."

"That ass," Mom smirked, rolling her eyes. "Well, let's hope the prince of darkness is cute." She chuckled.

I laughed along, yet I felt haunted. Just because you cross a state line doesn't mean years of bad luck are erased. So far I had seen plenty of demons and evil serpents. My father had been right and we hadn't even reached our new apartment yet. Still, maybe dreams could come true at any time. Maybe it was that simple.

Vegetation was stacked so high in the back seat that my mother couldn't possibly see anything out the rearview mirror. To complement the Nebraska corn, she had collected a few dozen purple onions, feathery stems of pampas grass, spiky pine cones, and yellow broccoli-like flowers that she called corn lilies— stolen nature intended to decorate our new apartment, but it was already starting to rot and stink.

"Look up, look up!" Mom yelled, excited that the towering grids had disappeared into the clouds—we were suspended in mid-air! The muffled sounds of the moving traffic, the high-low groan of the foghorns, and the misty air made everything feel out-of-focus. I inhaled the smell of ocean and could taste the salt on my tongue. I thought of Bill, and a wave of sexual memory rolled over me, causing my face to flush.

"You are looking at the tallest bridge towers in the world," my mother announced, her voice rising with excitement. "We really are high up, honey. It's hard to tell with all the fog. But it's pretty high. People commit suicide from here all the time. Just jump right off. Something like eight hundred people so far. Grim, isn't it?"

Gripping the door handle, I was quietly terrified at the notion of traveling over such heights. The bridge didn't seem very stable to me; it might have even been wobbling. "Did you know this was the second longest bridge in the world?"

I wanted my mother to stop talking and concentrate on her driving, so I ignored her, looked out my window, and watched the orange railing whip past me. Clusters of pedestrians were out on the walkway, huddled in heavy jackets, faces hidden behind scarves and hoods—possibly contemplating their lives, considering the big plunge.

Below, hundreds of sailboats drifted aimlessly, littered across the bay like confetti, unawares. *Was that a rescue net?*

"I happen to know what the longest bridge is. Would you like to know?"

"Mom, just drive."

"Oh, relax."

She leaned toward me and looked out my window. "No one survives the jump. It's like hitting cement. Anyway, it's the Bridge of Sighs in Venice."

"Mom, come on! Just drive."

I pushed her back to her own side, then had my first big look of San Francisco.

"Wow!" I gasped, my stomach aflutter. A fistful of buildings sculpted from polished marble.

"We've arrived," my mother declared. "Does this look like hell to you?"

We both had dumb smiles on our faces as we looped around, fought our way through the web of fog, and headed back toward Marin County. We marveled at the fancy homes that sat precariously on cliffs, their fates uncertain. An endless greenery of shrubs and hedges layered the land, embroidered with radiant flowers, bringing an exaggerated beauty to the place. The plant life was unruly, rowdy, a floral revolt—unlike anything I'd seen in Michigan.

"Where's Sausalito?" I asked. "Where's our apartment?"

My mother was chain-smoking, keyed-up, pushing the button to lower all four windows.

"Look, see those silvery-looking things? Those are sword ferns . . . and those tiny red berries, that's the California huckleberry. Pretty sure it's poisonous. Smell that sweet air," she cooed. "The spirited waft from the vineyards."

We zipped under a huge concrete rainbow arch, the entrance to a long tunnel, and my mother started honking and yelling. "Oh, my god! I haven't been through this tunnel in years!" She pressed down on the horn like a maniac, then reached over to tickle me. I slapped her hand away.

"Laugh, Jeannie, laugh!"

"Mom, stop with the honking! God." I shrunk down in the seat and tried to ignore her delirium, hoping it would pass quickly.

All along the freeway, Mom happily pointed out hot tourist spots—trendy beaches, splashy towns.

"Stinson is where all the kids go. You'll be surfing in no time. The sand is like sugar. You'll see," she said, as though she were divulging a secret.

We pulled off the freeway a few miles later into a Howard Johnson's. The familiar orange-and-blue box crouched under the freeway like a hideous troll. Gilded fog was replaced with metallic overcast. Gone were the pretty trees and showy homes. It was as if we had stepped back into Michigan. Traffic roared over our heads.

"What are we doing *here*, Mom?"

My mother leaned back in her seat and rolled her head, making disturbing cracking sounds with her neck.

"I have to get my bearings—figure some things out. I promise we'll be in our new place tout de suite."

I lay on the musty, lumpy motel bed, breathing in diesel
fumes, watching a rerun of *The Mod Squad*. At one time Peggy
Lipton had been the envy of my life. I would gape at the TV spell-
bound as clever Peggy escaped the clutches of evildoers, running
gazelle-like into the arms of cute Pete. I prayed to be Peggy—wil-
lowy, weary—heavy eyelids explaining it all. Now, cowering in
the shadows waiting for capable Link to save her, Peggy looked
pitiful—scrawny and man-dependent. But I watched anyway
until she and Link were out of danger—until they met up with
Pete (who I still thought was cute) and strolled triumphantly into
the setting sun.

※　※　※　※

My mother came back late that night, waking me by waving
an official-looking piece of paper in my face. It was the lease to
our new apartment. She pranced around the room, reenacting the
scenario, how she had managed to talk the landlady into leasing
her a one-bedroom with an ocean view.

"I pulled another fucking trick out of my magic bag is what I
did," she boasted.

I quickly realized that we had never had an apartment waiting. There was no balcony on a cliff, or waves pounding against
the front door; Mom had been winging it minute by minute—
there was no *Taj Mahal!*

"This woman, Mrs. Palise is her name," my mother reported,
wired on caffeine. "She and I went on and on like we were old
friends. I told her that I had lived in San Francisco as a teenager
and it's taken me twenty years to get back. I was a fellow native.
She recognized that in me. Oh, we're so lucky, Jeannie. We did
it."

I forced a smile, then lay back down on the bed. All those lost
days when I could've been worrying harder.

Mom continued about how she was going to make a fortune
working in yacht sales, open her own art gallery and finally be
discovered as a great neo-classical twentieth century painter.

"Mom, what about my school?" I interrupted.

"What about it? You're as good as in."

She picked up the phone and ordered strawberry pancakes with extra butter and syrup while pulling off her clothes. Wearing a T-shirt and underpants, she sat down next to me and began curling strands of my hair around her finger.

"After we get settled, we'll start jogging around Marin. Everyone runs out here. By next year I'll get these veins removed. Look, honey. Look at my incredible legs."

Mom held up her right leg for inspection. This was a routine. "That's one thing I know for certain. I have great fucking legs."

"We never had a stupid apartment on the beach, did we?"

She held her leg up farther and twisted, highlighting the back of her thigh.

"But look, honey. This is scaring me. It's gross." She squeezed and pulled near the top of her thigh, an area of spongy, dimpled skin.

"This *never* goes away. I'll never be able to have sex with the lights on again," she sighed. "Just remember, the closer to the bone, the sweeter the meat."

"Mom!"

"See, you get that curdled-milk look when you get older, especially when you have kids. They completely ruin your body. Not to mention your entire life."

The doorbell buzzed and Mom leapt out of bed, her T-shirt barely covering the top of her thighs. She bent around the door in an effort to hide her body, grabbed the food tray, and slammed the door without offering a tip.

"God, did you see that boy? Handsome. People are just prettier out here. Maybe we should order something else. But he's more your age, so you should answer it next time."

"Mom, shut up."

"Look, Jeannie, I *had* the apartment. We were just a day late and a dollar short. But everything's fine now. It's not exactly on the beach, but it sure beats Detroit."

The last half of *Hawaii Five-O* filled the room while Mom devoured the pancakes. We both loved Jack Lord, how he took command of a perilous situation with his calm, reassuring voice. I wondered if we had been watching *Hawaii Five-O* instead of *Play Misty for Me*, would we be in Hawaii now instead of

California? Instead of Clint Eastwood, my mother just as easily could've been chasing down Jack Lord. "Book'em, Dan-o" was the last thing I remember hearing before drifting off to sleep.

❖ ❖ ❖ ❖

My mother made a vow not to write any more bad checks as part of her "crossing the bridge and starting over" plan. With a grand gesture she tossed her checkbook into a waste bin behind HoJos, and for a brief moment I felt such relief it bordered on euphoria. We were no longer criminals but law-abiding citizens embarking on a new life. No one knew us in Marin. The locals would assume we were decent and honest. But, as we were about to drive away, Mom ran back to the dumpster and practically fell in while trying to retrieve the checks. "Just in case," she explained, only mildly embarrassed.

We drove through Sausalito, our new home. Like Tahoe, it was well groomed and quaint, though more puffed-up. Haute couture boutiques, hoity-toity restaurants, candle and gift shops, a hand-made taffy factory—"the boulevard of bonbon's," we nicknamed it. My mother spotted the perfect location for her art gallery, a vacant storefront alongside a shadowy, nameless bar.

"I'll put *Horses on Fire* right in front," she said. "I think it's my best piece."

I agreed. Why not? I could even picture the fiery painting suspended in the front window, beneath it a simple hand-written sign: Daisy's. Classy. Sometimes I could do this—get caught up in the dream, the make-believe world of the tickled-pink—a Doris Day world.

We reached the end of the village and entered a residential area where houses and apartments sat stacked on grassy hills, overlooking houseboats and tackle shops.

Beyond the greenery, there were tennis courts, schools, and church steeples. No one used aluminum siding or red brick. There were no swing sets planted on front lawns or clunky four-door sedans parked in driveways. In fact, all of the cars were foreign, dinky affairs. Our Cadillac stood out like a great white shark cruising among smaller, more delicate fish.

I was mostly struck by the cleanliness of it all, the lack of litter, the calm—and such a courteous place. Spit shined fire engines idled proudly in front of the station as if on display, decorative wooden trash bins could pass for flower pots, signs that said "Kindly pick up your dog droppings!" and "No need to speed!" lined the manicured streets. There were no parking meters. Pedestrians looking pleased with themselves glided along the sidewalk, walking their coifed dogs, armed with pooper-scoopers. Even the 7-Eleven was custom-built with redwood decking and begonia-stuffed window ledges. I noted the comfortable bus stops—smooth, polished benches (were they made from marble?) and fancy cloth awnings.

Just as we were about to leave town and enter the freeway onramp, Mom made a sharp left and swerved up a steep gravel road. We drove through a tunnel of eucalyptus trees; the smell of spicy birch filled the air. "This is nice, Mom," I said, excited. As we wound to the top, the trees thinned out—concrete and black tar soon took center stage. Dozens of raggedy apartment buildings fought for a small space, each with congested parking lots and one measly tree. Constructed from wood and glass, the buildings were falling apart, the wood splintering like tree bark. Latticework balconies teemed with bulky vines, macramé baskets, ratty patio furniture, rusted bicycles. A few supported laundry lines, bleached sheets, towels, men's underwear. Clorox stung the air, babies cried, televisions blared. Not far beyond the few trees, the freeway roared. Every now and then we'd hear the muffled blast of a truck horn or the screech of tires.

"Well, this is it. Home sweet home." My mother primped in the rearview mirror, plastering on blue eye shadow and tangerine lipstick.

"Mom, these are projects!"

She turned to me, her face set in a business look—eyes squinted, mouth tight, one eyebrow arched. I saw my reflection in her eyes, a dark huddled mass, a shadow.

"There are no projects in California," she warned. Then, adjusting her bra, "Now, Jeannie. I forgot to mention it but this is an adults-only place."

My body slumped in the seat. "Mom," I whined. "God. I can't do this again."

"Okay, fine," she said, crossing her arms. "We'll sleep in the car. No problem. I'm getting used to it. You have no idea, young lady, what I had to go through to get this place. Nobody else, and

I mean nobody, would rent to me, especially with a kid. So let's be grateful."

I sighed and sunk further into the seat, realizing that the car had lost its new-leather smell. We had sniffed it all up.

"So, if anyone asks, you're my niece, visiting from Michigan," Mom insisted. "I already told Mrs. Palise that you're staying with me for a while because your mother is in the hospital recovering from colon cancer."

"Jesus, Mom. What happens when they notice that I never leave?"

"We can't worry about that right now. I don't plan on staying here forever. Besides, I don't have another scheme left in me right now."

She jumped out of the car, hauled out an overnight case, some corn lilies, and an armful of canvases. I followed her across the road, clutching my blue suitcase. Tree droppings crunched underfoot like brittle bones. I took in a breath, then stopped.

"Mom, what's that weird smell?" At first I thought it was diesel fuel from the freeway, but then realized it was much stronger, like sulfur, a rotten egg smell.

"It's nothing, honey. Some kind of sewage system. There's a canal that runs under the hill. The landlady assured me that the sea breezes blow it right over us."

"Oh, right," I muttered. The smell was now working its way down my throat, causing me to cough. "We're living on top of a shit pile."

My mother turned to me, rage in her eyes.

"Don't you start on me. This was the best I could do and still keep you in the fucking Taj Mahal school district." She pivoted and strode into the building.

A cloud of tiny black flies rose up from nowhere, swarming around my head like a giant hair net. I gasped and swatted, trying to keep them out of my eyes and mouth. "Fuck this," I lamented, longing to be back in Michigan. But dutifully, I followed my mother up three flights of stairs. This would be the second time we lived on the third floor, the fifth or sixth time I wasn't supposed to be there. There was a weirdly comforting consistency to it all.

The apartment was a spacious one bedroom, and to my relief, clean, even plush. Everything from the carpet to the bath tile was soft in color. "Like an eggshell," Mom whispered, tiptoeing like the place might crack open. Windows ran the length of one wall, the balcony had sunbathing possibilities. Although the apartment smelled of lemon wax and ammonia, the rank sulfur odor persisted.

"It's not bad, huh?" Mom said with forced cheer.

I dumped my suitcase and joined her on the balcony. Not exactly an ocean view, but through the buildings we caught glimpses of Sausalito and a spec of blue. *Shit and traffic*, I thought. My mother lit a cigarette, and I saw a trace of sadness in her eyes. She was doing her best; I felt like an ingrate.

Previous occupants had left two wilted ferns in small woven baskets. They sat dying of thirst on the edge of the balcony.

"Mom, we'll make it nice. We can get some deodorizer and stuff." I began picking the dead brown leaves off the plants.

"It will have to do. A bit jejune I suppose." She shook her head. "That smell didn't seem as bad last night. Christ, it's positively scatological. Well, we won't be here forever."

We slept on the floor that night, using wadded-up clothing for bedding. Despite the chilly weather, the smell and the traffic noise, my mother insisted on keeping the windows open.

At night the noise from the freeway became even more intrusive. "Pretend it's the surf," Mom suggested before she began her loud snoring.

❖ ❖ ❖ ❖

I awoke to a chorus of hysterical birds squawking outside the window—an unmusical sound full of misery. I jumped up and ran out on the balcony, expecting to see dozens of crows or vultures flapping about in all directions, afraid for their lives, fleeing from the horrid smell. But after searching the trees, I saw only one, a fast red flash. Soon it was quiet, and I wondered if I had imagined the whole thing.

My body was brittle and sore, my mouth a toilet bowl. I needed to bathe, eat, drink lots of coffee. But mostly I needed to curse out my mother, demand that she get organized. I would never adjust to California. For my escape, I would need some cash, a job. But first I needed breakfast. I wandered through the empty apartment—Mom had already begun arranging the pampas grass in various corners. The corn lilies were shoved inside empty shampoo bottles; pinecones, scattered aimlessly over the carpet. The *Reluctant Uterus* leaned against one wall, the other paintings rested nearby. We shared a look of empathy. My stomach growled loud and long—someone was frying bacon. On the inside of a matchbook was a note from Mom explaining that she had gone to San Francisco to return the car, then on to the grocery store. It was signed with x's and o's and tiny hearts. I sighed and wondered how long it would be before she returned, how long before I could eat. What if she liked the Cadillac owner? This could take all day.

In vain, I searched the empty refrigerator, the bare cupboards too. It was a futile effort, but it kept my mind off hunger. All the shelves had been lined with white contact paper, carefully cut and applied without an air bubble or an uneven line. I ran my hand over the smooth paper, which ran precisely to the edge and disappeared into perfect seams. Someone had done a great job— a previous tenant who had cared about such things. Papering a shelf never even occurred to us.

I leaned against the counter and gave the kitchen the finger. We would never have a real home. The smell of bacon grease caused me to salivate—I pictured the fatty strips dancing in the fry pan. In a kind of trance, I floated across the hall and knocked on my neighbor's door. Apartment 7. *Lucky seven.* People in California shared a special touchy kind of love; surely they would feed me. Shaky now with hunger, I knocked again, harder. "Answer the fucking door," I gurgled.

The door blew open and I stepped back, my neighbor's glare was that bright. Tall and blazing as a street lamp, she sported long, thick braids, had eyes the color of storm clouds, and wore nothing but a stamp of an apron that barely covered her crotch. I was eye level with her high-pitched bosoms, a deer trapped in blinding headlights. They really packed a wallop.

"Vhat!" she demanded to know, holding up a wooden spoon. She was foreign and glamorous like a Gabor sister.

"Um," I bleated, now having forgotten why I was there. My Viking-esque neighbor covered her breasts with an arm.

"Can I velp you" she asked.

"I'm hungry," I blurted.

I stood there feeling ridiculous, slack-jawed, weighed down

by ugly corduroy pants and a black wool sweater, homely and pale. I boldly continued.

"My aunt and I just drove in from Tahoe and we haven't shopped yet and I wondered if we could borrow some bread," I explained without letting out a breath. But my golden neighbor only shook her head movie star-style.

"Look, darlink," she said rolling her r's. "I no eat no carbo-hy(throat clearing sound)drates. Sorry." She slammed the door in my face, her coconut oil aroma washing over me.

Humiliated and stunned, I backed up into the apartment. "I no eat no carbohydrates." *Of course not. What beautiful person does?* A great shame boiled up inside, burning my skin. There had been contempt in my neighbor's eyes for someone who ate bread, someone too coarse to understand the fundamentals of California nutrition.

"I should've just begged for the goddamn bacon," I muttered. And then I was confused. Angry. I shouted into the hall "It's okay to eat bacon, but not okay to eat bread? That's stupid! Bacon is even more fattening! I bet you eat out of a can!" I decided it was a cultural issue. But what the hell was she? Cuban? Were Vikings Cuban? "I no eat no carbohydrates." I kept repeated her accent, hissing the C. Then it occurred to me that everyone I had seen in California glistened. Gas station attendants, shopkeepers, even toll booth operators. I stood out—too damn white. My blonde neighbor despised the pasty tourist in me—or maybe she just didn't like teenagers.

I lay down so I wouldn't pass out and dove into a food fantasy —an endless buffet of crispy chicken, corn dogs, and cream pies.

A soft knock on the door ruined my daydream but maybe it was the exotic blonde, making a peace offering with some crispy pork. "Have some vacon," she would hiss. But it could also be the landlady, checking out our story. I ignored two more bangs, this time loud and hard.

"Any buddy in there?" barked a man's voice. Maybe it was that Donald guy from Tahoe. I jumped up and flung open the door.

"Hey. Cappy Betti. How's it hanging?" He stuck out his hand and I shook it. "You must be da dotta."

Hiding behind mirrored sunglasses and wearing a nonde-script black suit coat, he looked like maybe he was an FBI agent.

I held out my wrists waiting for the handcuffs—the felonious-check interrogation—but he ignored the gesture, winked at me, and came into the apartment. "So, how was da ca? Was she a smooth sail?"

"Oh," I sighed with relief. "You're the Cadillac guy. Yeah. It was cool."

Cappy was a little guy, balding, and walked with a dumb swagger. He wore white golf shoes with black, feathery decorations spilling over their surface. His jeans were K-Mart junk, creased and too short.

"You know, your Ma, Daisy, she was supposed ta bring da ca ta me, but den she calls da morning and says she couldn't read da map. Now what da fuck is dat?"

His voice was high-pitched, girlish. My mother would've never dated this guy. She probably figured out everything about him by phone so she didn't even bother to return the car. Maybe he'd forget about it—Mom could get thinking this way. The car felt like ours anyway.

"She makes me come all da way over da freakin' bridge. Cab cost me fifty bucks. She can find her way across da country, right, but can't find my freakin' hotel."

He snapped his fingers a few times, then put his hands on his hips.

"She's makin' me late for my freakin' yoga class. Guru Bob hates to wait."

The sap wore a noisy red shirt that was unbuttoned on the top, but revealed no chest hair. He had little hands and big white teeth—Sammy Davis Jr. only Caucasian, and without the glass eye.

"Sorry. Want to see the view?"

"Yeah, what da fuck. So, dis is Sausalito, huh? Right on. Never been over here. What's that weird smell?"

I ignored the question and pointed toward the spec of blue.

"You guys settling in, eh? Your ma get a job? She mentioned something over the phone about selling boats.

"Hey . . . here she is." The Cadillac raced up the windy hill, then skidded to a stop, bumping up against a parking curb. Cappy clearly didn't like that.

"What da hell's she doing?"

"Wait here," I said firmly, then headed out the door to warn

Mom. We hadn't properly cleaned out the car. The guy was already pissed about the expensive cab ride, not to mention messing up his day. I sensed a real disaster brewing.

I flew down the steps and soon realized Cappy was right on my heels. I stopped. "Can you just wait a sec?"

"Hey." He threw his hands up and tilted his head like I was holding a gun on him. We stared at each other for a moment, then continued outside, and met my mother. She was struggling with three Safeway bags. As I took them from her I attempted to warn her with my eyes. "Mom, this is Cappy Betti, the Cadillac guy."

"You don't say. What a surprise," Mom replied coolly. "You sure got here fast." Flashing him her biggest smile while adjusting her bra, she stuck out her hand, but Cappy walked right past her to get a good look at his car. He peered at the tires and ran his palm over the fender feeling for dents. Finally, he looked inside.

"What da fuck is this? What is dis stuff on da carpet? Is that a freakin' tear? What did you fucking do, sleep in da thing?"

The tirade was under way. Cappy loudly detailed the dark brown stains in the carpet, two separate tears on the dashboard, one blown speaker. Then he turned on the ignition and blasted the air.

"Your smoke is in da goddamn air conditioner unit! I'll never get da bad smells out a da ca! I'll sue you, you fuckin' idiot."

I backed off a few steps; Cappy's face turned radish-red and was puffing out like it might explode. This man was not stable, but my mother walked toward him.

"How dare you talk to me that way?" Mom's voice was full of indignation.

"I want a goddamn explanation!" he screamed, clambering out of the car and planting his weak hands on his girly hips.

"An explanation? Who the hell do you think you're talking to, mister?"

He walked right up to Mom. They were the exact same height. My heart was pounding like mad. I looked around for some kind of weapon, in case he got violent then spotted a rake—a good strong one made from heavy iron. My mother crossed her arms and backed up a step.

"Look, Cappy," she reasoned. "Let's not argue. Just give me the money you owe me and go back to the city."

He spat on the ground and shook his head violently.

"Is dis how you treat udda people's property, Daisy?"

"Hey, you fucking Napoleon, I got it here, didn't I? What's your damn problem?"

"You know lady, it's people like you keepin' dis planet on a steady decline. You really should've stayed in Detroit, cause that's where da likes of you belong." He worked up more phlegm, then added, "I ain't givin' you shit." He let loose of the spit wad and it landed near my mother's feet.

Her mouth dropped open. "Oh . . . is that right? Well fuck you, you little wop."

My mother grabbed a toilet bowl plunger from her shopping bag and took a swing at him. "I smote you, ya prick!" He ducked and grabbed her wrists. She kneed him in the groin. Cappy pulled away, squealing like a hog. I looked on, gripping the rake, poised for attack.

"You crazy bitch. I could take you ta court."

"You owe me two hundred and twenty bucks, and I want the money," my mother shrieked. She had her hands all over him, searching for his wallet.

"Go ta hell." Cappy pushed her off and hobbled over to the Cadillac, then jumped in and locked all the doors. My mother pounded on the window.

"Give me my money, you thief!"

He fired up the engine and jerked forward a few feet then cracked open his window. "You know, I was actually looking forward ta meetin' you. I thought you were goin' ta be young and pretty. I might a even buyed you a nice dinner somewhere. But forget it! You're nothing but a low-class ho. And you're old!" The window zoomed.

"*Old*! Fuck you!" Mom wailed. "As if I'd ever go out with you! And what kind of name is Cappy anyway!"

With super-human strength, she yanked a fichus sapling from its roots and heaved it at Cappy's back window. *Thud.* Mom had gone too far! We both froze, anticipating his reaction, but then as if he suddenly had better things to do, Cappy roared away and disappeared down the hill, fichus tree and all.

"Goddamn him. We needed that money." My mother adjusted her hair and took a deep breath. We picked up the groceries and hauled ourselves up the stairs.

"That creep had some nerve. Thought I might a buyed you a nice dinna. Right. Asshole. You're the type of woman that keeps the planet in a steady decline. I mean really. Fucker has some nerve."

We ate scrambled eggs off recently purchased plastic plates as Mom red-penciled the want ads. I was on my fourth piece of toast, sucking up spoonfuls of butter like ice cream.

"Was actually pissed off because of a small fucking tear in the seat," my mother grumbled. "He examined it like it was the last Cadillac on earth, for Christ's sake. He was definitely suffering from that short-man, mushroom-penis complex. Probably would've done anything to get out of paying me. Tightwad."

A cigarette burned between my mother's fingers, the smoke spiraled up until it dispersed into a gaseous cloud.

"Honey, do you remember a speaker blowing?"

"No," I lied. I had cranked the speakers each time my mother disappeared into a bathroom, until finally they both had fried. Pulling a can of gardenia-scented room deodorizer from a shopping bag, I pointed it toward the ceiling and sprayed; the mist fell down on me like sweet sticky rain. I pulled out other purchases—hair dye, a gallon of white wine.

"Oh well. C'est la vie. At least his fucking car got us here."

"I bet he listens to Sammy Davis," I said. "That Candy Man song."

"What, honey?"

"Nothing."

Every now and then she would "Hmm" and bite into the eraser on the pencil. She contemplated being a woodcutter, a gal Friday, a shoe clerk—no ads for yacht salesperson, but Mom talked plenty about the job anyway, dreamy-like. "I'd take the prospective buyers through the yacht, show them the special details that good boats have—the galley kitchens, fine balsawood counter-tops, Murphy beds. Commission is where it's at. I know I could sell. I have that charisma, the great salesmanship that self-help books blab about."

I leaned against the kitchen counter, eating butter, sizing up Mom. A feeling of good will passed over me, even a small sense of hope. We still had a chance; we could still make it.

"I think I saw a movie star today," I said.

"What? You're kidding! Who? Where?" My mother put down

her pencil and took a long drag off her cigarette, squinting at me through the smoke.

"The lady across the hall," I whispered. "She was sunbathing. Naked." I looked toward the balcony like she might still be out there.

My mother shrugged. "That's California for you. Free as birds."

"Free maybe, but what a bitch," I said under my breath.

"Well, who was it?" My mother took a bite of her eggs before jamming her cigarette into the yolk.

"You know that Spanish lady," I asked, "that blonde Charo lady that goes on Johnny Carson?"

"You mean the hoo-che-koo girl?"

"Yeah," I said. "Someone like her. Or a Gabor sister. Not sure which."

"Jeannie, did you talk to her?" My mother raised a suspicious eyebrow.

"No," I lied. "I just saw her out on the balcony."

"Honey, the last thing these people want is to be watched. Now, try and keep from spying on her. Okay?"

"Mom, it's not like I'm going to follow her around all day."

"I can't believe a movie star-type girl would be living in the low-rent district of Sausalito," Mom concluded. "I'm sure it wasn't Charo. Unless maybe that's all she does is go on Johnny Carson. That can't pay very much, after all. I've heard stories about how cheap Carson is. Like really cheap, a miser. Maybe in everyday life Charo's just a bank teller or a prostitute."

Mom twirled her pencil, concentrated again on the ads. Feeling nauseated from the butter, I began to wash the dishes, using shampoo as soap.

"Well, anyway, I know of a really big movie star who lives not too far from here," Mom confided. Smug. "In fact, I think she lives right here in this town."

"C'mon, Mom, who? Who?"

"Vivian Vance." She practically sang the name.

"Ethel?" I dropped a plate into the sink and spun around. My mother nodded yes and smirked.

"Stick with me kid, and you'll see some real stars."

"Where, Mom? Where does she live?"

"Well, I'm not exactly sure. But I know she grocery shops at the Gracious Gourmet in Tiburon and that she wears some kind of disguise. We'll keep an eye out. Maybe we'll get lucky. Christ, maybe I'll sell her a yacht. You know what they say—— California . . . land of swimming pools and movie stars." She looked at me quizzically. "Who said that?"

"Jed Clampett, Mom."

"Really?"

I picked up the plate I had dropped and saw it was cracked down the middle. It was plastic! Making sure this went unnoticed, I gingerly dried the damaged plate before setting it on the counter.

The sun began its descent, filtering through latticework creating honeycomb patterns on the wall. When I snapped off the overhead fluorescent light, our reflections bounced back at us from the windows. Dimly lit and from a distance, Mom and I looked normal—even enviable. My mother in her skirt and bra, relaxing with the paper—me, the helpful daughter attending to the chores—discussing fashion, politics, maybe boys. I smiled and gesticulated dramatically with my arms as if making a point, then for affect, threw back my head and laughed *haughtily*. Strutting in front of the window, I imagined we were two fabulous blue-blooded gals from New England, leaving behind our concerned families, striking out on our own, giving California a try—WASPs, slumming in Sausalito.

"What the hell are you doing?" my mother asked, firing up another smoke. I stretched, yawned, and bowed to the balcony, putting a graceful end to the performance.

"Becoming a Californian," I replied, giving my mother the usual pat on the shoulder, then added a little squeeze to top it off. She touched my hand with hers and I wandered off, my perfect image tagging along.

CHAPTER NINE

MY MOTHER DID NOT GET A JOB SELLING SWANKY BOATS, BUT INSTEAD was hired as a hostess at a restaurant called Valhalla's, owned by the famous ex-prostitute and socialite Sally Stanford. Her restaurant sat on the edge of the bay, supported by rickety stilts sunk into the mushy bay floor. Towering walls of glass reflected San Francisco, the Bay, and Alcatraz. Chinese lanterns and moth-chasers hung over the crowded, almost rowdy patio. Valhalla's was the trendy in-spot of Sausalito, filled with can't-wait-for-happy-hour professionals wearing white deck shoes and berets, drinking Irish coffees and wine spritzers. I assumed everyone came to catch a glimpse of Sally, the famous madam of the ports, but she was rarely there and usually arrived unannounced. She was mysterious, even subterranean, almost invisible to the diners, spending most of her time in the kitchen hurling commands with her pointy red fingernails without uttering a word.

Sometimes I'd sit on her velvety sofa drinking Tab, and watch for Sally to exit the kitchen like an ocean wave, dressed in white silk and pearls, hair swept up tight as an ice cube. She exuded authority and behind it, some cruelty. Once she smiled at me and then winked, and I loved her for it. The whole gesture somehow suggested that my mother was a fool but I had a chance. Hoping for a promotion to waitress, Mom brought Sally gifts—scented candles, pet rocks, pampas grass. But Sally never responded. My mother began to call Sally names under her breath—"skinflint" and "Fuhrer."

A few weeks after arriving in Sausalito, my mother and I had fallen into a pattern. After walking down the long, winding hill from our apartment, we rode separate buses, Mom heading south into the city to look for work, ending up at Valhalla's at night. I would go north to my school, a few miles away, which I grew to detest within a week.

Mount Tam High was a bulky and elaborate structure, mission-like, surrounded with big, ruffly trees—petticoats and dust. Stuffy classrooms were filled with sycophantic teenagers with names like Briar and Clarissa. Most of them were blonde, tanned, and talked in slow exaggerated sentences that had musical lifts at the end. A statement such as "Welcome to Tam High" sounded like an accusation. Everyone smiled. Instead of jumping up at the sound of the bell and stampeding to the bathrooms for a quick smoke, these students leisurely gathered up books, wandered outside, talked in small groups, their faces pointed toward the sun like morning glories. Appalled, I sat hunched in the back row wanting to scream out words like "vagina!" and "ejaculate!"—or poke out my eye and lob it onto the teacher's neatly organized desk. Instead, waiting patiently for the bell to ring, I controlled myself—forced my wobbly reality to keep still. After class, I searched in vain for the "bad" kids—the ones who got high, hitchhiked to the beach, hated school—the ones from broken homes. But there weren't any such groups so I stopped going to school.

Folded inside a Mill Valley bus stop, under a clump of ash trees that shimmered like a canopy of silver coins, I wrote letters to Lara. For once the truth—my unhappiness, loneliness. I told her how my mother was working in a bar, this time for a prostitute, how we had no money, lived over a shit heap. I mentioned Buck and the judge. I admitted that my mother could be arrested at any time for all those phony checks, and I could be orphaned—*convince your kind parents to take me in,* I begged. I hid the letters in my suitcase without mailing them, tucked beneath my stolen camera. Something stopped me from taking the camera out and snapping pictures—I guess I had no interest in keeping track of where I was.

By the end of three weeks, I had written Lara seventeen unmailed letters and gained ten pounds. While sitting at my bus stop, I inhaled stolen convenience foods—pizza squares and chocolate bars. Hungry all the time, I ate uncontrollably and chalked up this new appetite to being in a higher altitude, until it occurred to me that we were at sea level. Then I blamed it on my depression.

Sometimes I looked for employment. Eating soggy French fries and filling out an application at a Chevron gas station, I counted all the Porsches that rolled in, all driven by single men. Businessmen, probably attorneys or character actors. *Forget the bad kids,* I thought. What I needed was a rich man. Better yet a celebrity. Maybe I would meet Van Morrison or that bald guy from *Kung Fu.* I handed my application to an oily, scruffy mechanic named Snoopy.

"You left the work experience part blank."

"I know how to pump gas, okay?" I offered him a fry and he took it. I filled out applications in motels, fast food joints, and boutiques. No one called. I couldn't figure out how to escape Marin County.

My mother promised to take me clothes shopping in San Francisco as soon as she cashed her first check. But payday came and went without discussion, much less a shopping spree. Mom seemed as miserable as I was; neither of us wanted to acknowledge it, both of us needing to pretend. Mom was often gone all day and into the evening, though she made good on her word not to stay out all night. Instead she brought men home and I would hear them in the living room, slapping skin, rolling around, clinking wine glasses. I would barricade myself beneath blankets and pray the men would be gone by morning. Mostly they were.

On one such night, Mom urgently woke me before dawn. She was cocooned in her good Laura Ashley sheet, drinking wine, clutching the telephone.

"Sorry to bother you, Jeannie. I know you love your sleep but I've been thinking." She was drunk—her eyes looked scratched and bloody. "I've decided to kill myself. I've thought it through very hard. My heart simply cannot sustain one more disappointment. Come look at the sunrise."

The sky was washed in soft shades of pink like one of her baby-ass canvases. My mother had threatened suicide before but never at such an unreasonable hour. Wadded-up tissue littered the balcony, along with cigarette butts, empty wine bottles, and a book of Shakespeare's love sonnets. Mom blew mucous and tears into tissue, then convulsed into sobs. The pattern repeated itself—wail, moan, blow. I guessed she'd been doing it this way for a while.

"Mom. It'll work out. Calm down. Whatever happened to that Donald from Tahoe?"

This caused her to sob louder, then she grabbed the telephone and began dialing. *How could all those tears be about some man?* It seemed impossible.

"Oh, right. Fuck him. Tell him this," my mother wailed into the phone. "Tell him he's no friend of mine. I want nothing to do with him. In fact, he can lose my fucking number! You got that? The name is Daisy. D-A-I-S-Y. He has my number!" She slammed down the phone.

"Who was that, Mom?"

She ignored me and started punching more numbers, then dropped the phone, and bawled. She was in a sinkhole for sure.

"Who ever made up the phrase good grief. There is nothing good about it. Jeannie! Look at this beautiful sunrise. God, it's perfect crimson. Don't worry. Someone will take pity on you. Your very own benefactor. Someone more capable than me."

She stood up and teetered as though on ice skates, gripping the ledge for support.

"Mom, why don't you lie down inside?" I suggested.

"I can't breathe in there. I need so much air. Jeannie, who always used to say that? Good grief."

"Charlie Brown. I have to get ready for school, Mom."

"My head will be in the oven when you return. I considered the balcony but it's not a sure thing and the bridge is too far a walk. I think that prick's in Japan by now."

She drained her wine glass and then suddenly her face lit up. "You like that school, don't you? Knew you would. At least that's working out. Try to stay in Marin after my death."

"Yeah, Mom."

She sat down, titled her head back, and closed her eyes. "Could you imagine if I ever did get married? My side of the church would be virtually empty." She started to snore almost immediately.

We never discussed suicide or the men in her life again. But after that day my mother always seemed to have extra cash on hand. I didn't question this and figured she was helping herself to their wallets, making it all somehow worth her while. I stole a few bucks myself.

After a long weekend of tearing out the kitchen shelf paper and spying on our possibly famous nude sunbather, I found my way to the mental health section of the school library. If the author's picture exuded joy, I checked out the book.

Sprawled under the trees at the bus stop, I tried to study my way into bliss; it seemed a simple solution. But as I came across concepts like "You were born to receive," "You are a perfect child of God," I became overwhelmed, my mind drifting into fantasy—locked inside an empty, padded cell, a tiny slit my only means of light. Wearing nothing but a straitjacket, wild, stringy hair flattened against bloated, pink flesh, I was a sea monster, *a succubus!*

At some point, I realized these self-help books were written for people with lesser problems, like acne or heavy periods. I took up chain-smoking and began grappling with my negative thoughts on my own—wrestling them down to the ground, sitting on them like buoys. I jerked my body around like I was taking an electric shock and waved the busses on when they stopped for me.

"Give it time. Give it a chance," my mother would say. Then lecture—"Be nicer to people. Don't be so sour and judgmental. Christ, you're just like your father. Smile, laugh, get some sun. You look sick. You're in California, for Christ's sake, cheer the fuck up. How dare you not be happy?"

So that's what I started to do—sink buoys at my bus stop and smile, practice friendly body language. As I spread open my arms to suggest a world hug, as if on cue, Marlin Factor was delivered to me in his flashy silver Porsche—a toaster on wheels. He leaned his head out the window, a turquoise peace sign dangled from one ear.

"Need a lift?"

"Sure," I agreed and slid onto the slippery wine-colored seat, deliberately keeping my legs uncrossed. Marlin's hair was pulled into a chunky ponytail, big dimples barely visible behind a full beard. His eyes were red and mysterious. They peered over John Lennon glasses, like two rising suns.

"Name is Marlin Factor. Where are you off to?" he asked.

"Wow, like benefactor?" He winked. I could tell by looking at him that he had seen a lot of action, been to Woodstock, maybe Viet Nam! He had swallowed the universe—the real McCoy. Bill's image faded quickly from memory. My face flushed, my skin grew damp. I drew in a deep breath and tried to muster up some nonchalance, but instead inhaled a lung-full of strong marijuana fumes and began coughing spastically. Marlin placed a protective hand on my back until it passed—his manly print would remain for the rest of the day.

"Well, I don't have anywhere to go," I confessed. "I'm a truant and have no friends or family. I just moved here from Michigan." The engine roared behind us as he pulled onto the main drag, Marlin negotiating the traffic with expertise. The Porsche was an early model, creaky as an old staircase, but well cared for. Marlin was someone who cared.

"Oh, yeah? No kidding!" He said this with such enthusiasm I thought he must be from Michigan too. "I've never been there. You ever been to the top of the hill?"

"I haven't been anywhere," I said.

We climbed up the side of the mountain, hedged in by giant sequoias, nature's debris trailing behind us like a wedding veil. Shouting to be heard over the engine, Marlin told me he was an anarchist and also blew glass.

"Oh," I replied, thinking he must do something in architecture —building houses, putting them up on stilts.

"Do you know Donald from Tahoe?"

Marlin touched a miniature glass winged horse that hung from the rearview mirror. "I'm good at Pegasus and satyrs," he said, adding that his best work was displayed in a fashionable shop on Bridgeway. His biggest sellers were grinning unicorns and the Golden Gate Bridge. Oh. Touristy things. Figurines. I pictured Marlin blowing up a bubble of glass until it magically took shape, like a street mime twisting poodles from balloons.

Marlin was talky, animated, possibly tripping. He went on about politics mostly, a subject I usually avoided, a class I liked to skip. I let my gaze follow his freckled arm down to the strong hand that shifted the car into high gear. I felt stoned.

"Someone should do a stage production about Emma Goldman," he shouted. "Maybe even a motion picture! Emma was misunderstood.Underestimated! Underappreciated! She tried to assassinate a president, took on the Soviet fucking government *and* she was hot."

"Wow," I enthused, feeling like a complete loser. I certainly hadn't heard of this Emma girl, had nothing to add and was scurvy in comparison. My growing sense of inadequacy sat on me like a lumbering, overfed dog that refused to budge. I struggled for breath.

"So, Marlin, do you water ski or polo ski or something?"

The car smelled faintly of mildew, a dirty fish tank. A wadded-up black rubber wetsuit was shoved into the small space behind us. Marlin seemed not to hear me.

"Better yet, a musical . . . someone like Patty Lupone!" Marlin went on with great excitement. "Hey! Ann Margaret!" he shouted. We kept plowing up the woodsy road, Marlin's attention all caught up in the Broadway fantasy. I was trying hard to think of Broadway stars, but went blank. I wondered if Marlo Thomas qualified.

"Who else? Who else?" he asked with some impatience.

I felt caught. I needed to come up with some names to add to the conversation—actresses, songs, shows. I was such a loser.

"Goldie Hawn," I shouted. "Diana Ross!"

Marlin glared at me, his red eyes glowing—exploding stars. He lifted an approving eyebrow. My cheeks burned and I thought we were going to have sex for sure. Maybe even later that day.

"Yeah, why not?" he shrugged. "Play it black. I can see Diana saying, quote, Government is the scourge of man, unquote. And she can sing!"

He affectionately squeezed my thigh; my heart skipped a beat. I automatically sucked in my stomach and suddenly became aware of my floppy breasts, my newly fat self, too-tight jeans. All this fat would scare Marlin away and ruin everything. Crossing my arms, I tried to keep his attention above the chin. Then I thought about my chin, how even it was beginning to double up and bloat out—a tree frog! I did a silent prayer, hoping Marlin liked his girls round and fleshy. Maybe Emma was large.

"What did Emma look like?" I asked.

As we neared the top of the mountain, I was almost deaf from altitude—my head stuffed inside a glass jar. My jaw cracked and popped when I swallowed and yawned. Marlin ignored my question and started to sing along with the radio—an unfamiliar song about mercury poisoning and ergonomics. He belted out the lyrics with bravado—a trait I was certain only came with age and extensive travel experience. I knew Marlin could teach me great things. Between shifting gears, he put his hand on my thigh like that's where it belonged. My body tingled with the possibilities of love.

High above Marin, we took a long walk along a grassy knoll overlooking the ocean. The sea was white and frothy, blending at the horizon with the overcast sky; thick fog embraced the hills like enormous white gloves. We were the couple crowning a wedding cake, clutching and smiling. By the end of the walk, we were holding hands.

"I haven't been with a young lady as sweet as you in a long time," Marlin whispered. "And I must admit, it's quite a pleasure." If he tried to make love to me, I wouldn't resist. I let my head fall against his chest and breathed in patchouli oil and peach nectar. Marlin didn't say much as he drove me home. He even kept the radio low.

We idled in his car at the bottom of the Ebb Tide apartment complex, finishing a joint.

"Tomorrow?" I ventured. "Sure." He winked in a good way, like we were peers. I stumbled out of the car, feeling dizzy and numb, walking backwards, waving. "By the way, I surf," he called out. "Maybe I'll take you sometime."

"Great!" I yelled, woozy with love. He had referred to a future, *our* future. He included me in his plans.

My luck was changing. My mother had been right.

The next morning I spent two hours in the school library boning up on anarchy, Bolshevism and mobocracy. Though somewhat disturbed by what I read, I was nonetheless diligent in my research. I even found a small biography on Emma Goldman—but no picture. I looked for Diana Ross' stage credits but couldn't find any.

I considered going to Government Studies class, but anxious to see Marlin again, I instead went to the bus stop and waited. This time I had brought my camera. Wearing my mother's best silk blouse, I imagined myself being thin and light, a girl a man could easily carry.

We sat on the wet edge of a jetty that overlooked Alcatraz Island.

"Did you ever see *Birdman of Alcatraz?*" I asked. "That weird movie where the convict had this thing for birds? God, Burt Lancaster must have frozen his butt off. Did you see that, Marlin, where he had to swim so far?"

The sun hid stubbornly behind gray skies, and Marlin put a bearish, flannelled arm around me as I shivered. I wore Clara's leather jacket but it was no match against the damp winds.

"They probably used a stunt double for the swimming scenes," he said, looking into the Bay. He seemed to be deep in thought. I wanted to engage him in conversation, the morning's research still fresh in my mind—a theory emerging. "But I also saw him in *The Swimmer* and that was him for sure. He was so cool, just swimming from pool to pool without permission, *ungoverned,* going into strangers' yards and stuff. You know, completely *lawless.* Did you see that, Marlin?"

He held my stolen camera up to his handsome face. Click, click. I posed in front of Alcatraz, forcing a smile. My face was icy cold and felt as though it might crack.

"That movie was all about the failure of the American dream," he said, his voice tinged with anger, "buying into that bullshit fantasy."

I didn't know how to react to this tone of voice. Marlin was a true scholar, an intellect, impatient with stupid people from the midwest. I was no match for him but I had to make an effort.

"I agree with you exactly, Marlin," I said. *Look pensive.* "I saw that film when I was seven, and I knew then we were all being hoodwinked. That the whole world is just one big *jerry-built* structure about to collapse."

Marlin pulled me against his chest and hugged so tight my boobs ached—my performance had worked. Later we drove to his house, but he didn't invite me in.

"You wait here," he instructed, then glided toward the cottage-type house and disappeared behind the front door. The two small windows on either side of the front door had their shades pulled down like eyelids—a sleepy house. I was familiar with this

Mill Valley neighborhood because my mother and I had frequented the local Weinerschnitzel.

A squared-off section of dirt lay next to his house, a vegetable garden or marijuana patch. *How sophisticated.* I was anxious for us to make love, to get our relationship jump-started. I would move in, finish school, read his philosophy books. He would buy me fashionable clothing, teach me to drive, enroll me in the community college. Together we would march in picket lines, publish political essays.

Marlin climbed back into the car, handing me a joint and a wool scarf. "You can keep this," he said.

I hugged the scratchy thing like an old doll, then wrapped it around my neck. It was red plaid and smelled like sawdust. I touched Marlin's strong arm.

"Marlin, in case you're wondering, I'm ready to, you know, to sleep together." My heart pounded and rocked around in my chest like a church bell as I waited for him to grab me and unlock all of his pent-up passion. Instead he smiled and winked. "I know," he said, firing up the joint.

We spent the next few hours together taking pictures in San Francisco of twisted Lombard Street, the cable cars, and the Golden Gate Bridge. We snapped pictures of seals flapping about on rocks and of a mime sleeping against a dried-up fountain. Marlin lectured, "The fish rots from the head down. Next thing you know they'll be giving pardons to the Manson family, Toni and Tenille will get the keys to the kingdom, Hugh Hefner will run for office!"

"The *Playboy* guy!" I shouted, happy to know something.

"Inflation is up eight point seven percent, veteran's mortgage is eight point five. There is eight point two percent unemployment . . ."

My mind drifted to Mom, dressed in her bunny costume, rabbit ears and fluffy tail, practicing the Bunny dip, the crouch and the stance while balancing a laundry basket on her head.

"The GNP plus eight. Eight point four percent of all people display some kind of need for solidarity. See what I'm getting at here?"

"I think so, Marlin."

All this political talk made me dizzy, but then so did jazz, his second favorite topic—the musical doodles of the collective psyche he would say then shove in a tape of local musicians, Spike Pluck and Brass Wax.

During Marlin's jazzfests I would imagine what the inside of his slumbering house looked like—burning incense, beanbag chairs, glass figurines dangling from light fixtures. I saw myself lying disheveled on his cozy bed, flushed and limp from our lovemaking, Marlin looking on with an artistic eye, sculpting my languid form out of molten glass.

But once again we ended up idling at the bottom of Ebb Tide apartment complex.

Marlin reached over and tightened my new wool scarf. I smiled, hoping to cover my disappointment.

"You're going to have so many boyfriends," he offered, shaking his head. What the hell did that mean?

"Don't you want to be one of them?"

He smiled and cocked his head to one side. "Maybe I'll see you tomorrow."

Oh, no. Maybe? He was already sick of me—longed for his grown-up friends. I developed a tight, steel-plate feeling in my stomach, but forced myself to keep smiling.

"You're just so . . . little." He ran his hand along my cheek in a parental fashion.

"Little? I'm not *that* young. Jesus. It's not like I'm a virgin or anything." Thinking fast, I fished the camera out of my purse. "Do you know how to get this film out? Where can I get it developed?"

"I'll take care of it."

"Thanks." I grabbed his hand and squeezed, unwilling to let go. I still had a chance; he would have to see me at least once more. I had to get lofty; there was no time to spare. Squeezing Marlin's hand as he tried to pull away, I heard my mother's voice and thought I was dreaming. But no such luck! Heading toward us wearing a red mini-dress, white high-heeled boots and a wool muffler, she looked like a deranged Santa's helper. I sank into the leather and prayed she'd keep walking.

"Honey! Jeannie baby, open up. Who's your friend?" She rapped on the window.

"Oh, God." I jumped out of the car and nudged her back a bit trying to block Marlin from her view.

"Oh, just a guy from school. He gave me a ride."

"Bye, Marlin," I called over my shoulder. *Pull away!*

My mother peered into the passenger window, then opened the door and climbed in.

"Marilyn," she grunted. "What kind of name is Marilyn for a guy?"

"Marlin, actually," I heard him say.

I turned away from them and crossed my arms against my chest to protect the gaping hole that was surely forming there. I felt sick. It was early evening; the moon hung full and low in the navy sky.

"Marlin? As in the fish? You look a little old to be going to high school, sailor," she said, shooting for a Mae West accent. Then she added, "Nice car." I was mortified.

Mom lit a cigarette and blew the smoke into his face.

"Mom, aren't you going to be late for work?" I called out to the night air.

Marlin said something that I couldn't understand. Then it happened.

"Well, Marlin the fish," she snorted. "You are aware that she's not quite sixteen. As in jailbait."

I wilted with humiliation. It was over. I had lied earlier and told Marlin I was eighteen, a senior.

For a moment there was silence. Had there been such a thing as a tear in the universe, a doorway to a black hole, I would've stepped through. But I just stood still.

"I don't mind you giving her a ride to and from school," Mom continued, "but if you so much as lay one hand on her I'll cut your fucking balls off and throw them into the bay. Understood?" Then she laughed. Then he was laughing too. I was shocked. I peeked inside the car and noticed Mom was holding onto the sleeve of Marlin's fringe jacket.

She leaned into the seat, adjusted her top, and started her interrogation.

How long had he lived in Marin? Did he sail? Was he a Democrat? My mother leaned out of her window, hauling me toward her. "He's going to give me a ride to work, honey. Save me from getting on that damn bus." Then she whispered, "Isn't he a little old for you? I mean really, Jeannie." She gave me one of her condescending looks then pulled me even closer and tried to kiss me. I jerked away and caught a quick glimpse of Marlin through the windshield. He winked and waved. I watched his car disappear down the road, my mother's arm resting on her opened window.

"Come back, Marlin. My mother's out of her mind. Please come back!" I pleaded to no one. As I trudged up the hill, I felt as though I was carrying extra baggage, like sandbags had been strapped to my body. I heaved myself up the stairs and at the top it occurred to me that I was pregnant. Just like that, I knew. Emma Goldman had been an advocate of birth control and I didn't know what that was. Not really.

I stared at my bloated image in the medicine cabinet mirror after taking my clothes off. I was swollen and plump from my face to my ankles. How had I not noticed? The weight of my sudden realization caused me to slump down on the edge of the tub, its cold porcelain biting into the backs of my thighs. I could not remember my last period. Legs asleep, heavy and tingly, iron things I had to drag around, I waded through the dark apartment with the desperation of someone just sentenced to death, my inflated image reflecting from the windows, unrelenting. I turned on the lights and tried to figure out what to do.

I thought of Debbie Kaner, one of my friends back in Birmingham who had gotten knocked up by her math tutor. Half of the algebra class chipped in for the abortion, then Lara and I drove her to the clinic, a small, windowless dive in Detroit. The whole deal was over in two hours, then we celebrated with fries from Burger King. Debbie revealed it was less painless than having her braces removed—plus they rewarded her with grape juice, gingersnaps and a year's supply of birth control pills.

Perhaps this pregnancy was a message—return to Michigan to undo what had been done. Plain and simple. My thoughts raced. I would call Lara in the morning and arrange to stay at her house. I would spend Christmas with the Wiesmans. Or Chanukah, or whatever.

I peeped over the neighbor's balcony. Of course, she was out, glamming it up, laughing, and enjoying her life, perhaps with some moody European man. I supposed life was a constant backstage pass when you were gorgeous. Then here I was, having had sex once and gotten pregnant—my wheel of fortune, perhaps an inherited fate. Only my mother could truly appreciate such an incredible injustice, but I feared the disappointment to her would be too huge. In fact, I would *never* tell her.

I fixed my gaze on the full, grinning moon and felt like the entire sky was laughing at me. There was Polaris, the romantic point of light that used to belong to Bill and me. It held no meaning now—a pinprick. Bill had never written or called. I sighed, went inside, and buried myself beneath blankets and clothes.

※　※　※　※

Though it was futile, the next morning I went to the bus stop and waited for Marlin. After an hour, having nowhere to go, I sat in class, attentive and even curious, answering questions and talking to a few fellow students. Knowing I was leaving somehow made them more likable. I told Clarissa about *The Swimmer* and suggested to Briar that he lose the Birkenstocks. Both were interested in what I had to say. Maybe I had been too hard on them.

※　※　※　※

"Lara, I'm pregnant," I whispered. "It's Bill's. My mom can't know."

"Oh, *fuck*," Lara said. "This is unbelievable! From that one time? Wow!" She was really shocked, then calmed quickly. "Don't worry, Jeannie. We'll get it taken care of. At least you didn't get crabs!"

For being wealthy and spoiled, Lara was surprisingly generous. But the one thing Lara didn't have was actual cash. Her parents gave her a small allowance each week and a gas credit card.

We made fast plans. Lara would pick me up from the airport, and store me in her away-at-college sister's room. Her parents would tolerate my visit since it would end Lara's constant whine to visit California.

I needed money. After I thoroughly cleaned the apartment, I prepared an elaborate meal for Mom—onion and avocado burgers.

"If I have to spend Christmas here I will kill myself, for real," I planned to say. "People like Marlin are bad for me!" Mom would lay out the cash.

There was a knock at the door. For an impossible moment I thought it might be Marlin coming to claim his love. I floated to the door Sandra Dee style and swung it open with a flashy smile. An older woman stood glaring, hands on hips, long silver hair hanging loose around her shoulders. She had a musty nun smell.

"Is your mother home?" she asked, lips pursed. Here eyes were motionless, gray pebbles. "Well?" she asked, tapping her foot.

I knew it was a trick question but I answered anyway.

"No, she's not."

"May I come in?"

I stepped aside and let her pass. She wore extra-wide bell-bottoms and a pleated, flowery smock—a folksy love-in outfit. It was Mrs. Palise, the landlady. A large button on her collar read, LET YOUR LOVE SHINE. Maybe she had a heart—would let us off the hook. Looking around the empty apartment she said, "You know, your mother lied about having children. She told me she couldn't tolerate kids." She smiled at me in a genuinely nice way.

I wasn't sure how to react to this so I coughed. Sighing, Mrs. Palise's face slid into a sneer, eyes filling with so much hate it chilled the air. I glanced down at her fingernails and expected to see long bloody daggers, but instead they were nubby, crusted with dirt—a gardener's hands. Lonely and cheerless, she called herself a feminist but secretly hated woman like Mom who still enjoyed wearing short skirts. A hippie but not liberal. A fake.

"And then there is the bounced rent check," the witch announced. She pulled the check out of her smock pocket and waved it in the air. It had been officially stamped many times and was torn and ragged, all used up.

"Oh. Sorry." I sucked in a breath and mustered up some courage. "Look, if it matters, I'm leaving in a couple of days. My mother's got a good job. She can cover the check."

Mrs. Palise crossed her arms and tilted her head disapprovingly. She was obviously gauging me, deciding. I pulled in my bloat-bag stomach, grateful to be wearing an oversized sweater.

"I let this apartment to your mother because she dropped Donald Whitmore's name. He's a prominent architect in this area. He and his wife, Sky, are important social activists. In fact we all belong to the same yacht club. Marin is quite a small place after you've been here a while."

"Yeah, well, he's a louse if you ask me," I said under my breath. She continued on about Donald and Sky but I had stopped listening. Sadly Mom still fantasized that Donald would come for her one day—keys in hand to one of the Victorian homes that crowded the hilly landscape. The comparison to Marlin was not lost on me. We were really pathetic, my mother and I. We would never have good lives.

I needed to go to bat for Mom, tell off this old shrew, but what would I say? *She fucked him and you didn't, you ugly bitch!*

"Anyway, when I asked Donald about Daisy, he said he'd never heard of her. So, for me, honey, that is just one too many lies."

"Are you going to evict us?"

She stared at me with those unmoving eyes, sighed. I couldn't stand it anymore.

"Look, Mrs. Palise, how do you know that Donald isn't lying? Just because he's a man and has money doesn't mean that he doesn't lie. My mother can't be the only liar in the world. Christ, it's the holidays. Don't evict her. She'll get you the money. There's probably just been a bank error. It happens."

She shook her head, rolled her eyes, and kept pursing her bloodless lips.

"I'm leaving anyway," I said. "Give her a break. Come on. Christ, you old wombat. You're just a big phony feminist. You must have a heart of stone!" Mrs. Palise strode toward the door, tsk-tsking all the way.

"Just have your mother call me," she said. "People like her never consider consequences, do they?" Her parting words were a punch in the stomach. I followed her into the hall.

"This place stinks like shit anyway! You should be paying people to live here! Plus it's filled with whores like Charo!" I hollered gesturing to the golden beauty's door.

I wiped some sweat off my forehead, then closed myself back inside the apartment. This was our fastest eviction to date and Clara wasn't even with us. I dug a cigarette butt out from the garbage and slumped against the kitchen wall.

❖ ❖ ❖ ❖

"I just miss Lara," I explained to Mom. The suicide threat was unnecessary, plus neither one of us gave it much credibility. Mom gave me plane fare and promised to wire more after Christmas.

The day before leaving, I bussed through the fog's morning creep until reaching Marlin's house. Shades pulled, lights low, I knocked softly. Somewhere incense burned. Marlin opened the door in his underwear. "Hi," I chirped, like I was spitting up a cricket.

"One second," he said.

He came out wearing a bathrobe and cowboy boots. We sat on the porch, both of us with our arms crossed over our knees.

"I'm sorry about my Mom, Marlin. She's had a real hard life."

"Don't worry about it," he said. "Parents can be a real trip."

I had nothing else to say. I had hoped he might invite me in for a lovers' breakfast, but we only sat in silence. The front door creaked open, we turned to see the silhouette of a woman—a pregnant woman. Marlin saluted and she disappeared.

"That your wife?"

"Yeah, Mika. She's pretty cool."

I nodded my head for a long time, until I had to put my hand on my chin to keep it still. The information was not entirely shocking. Why wouldn't he have a wife? It was perfectly reasonable. He would soon be a dad. She probably played the saxophone.

"Why were you hanging out with me, Marlin?" I mumbled into my knees.

"You seemed a little lost. Thought you could use a friend. That wasn't the first time I saw you sitting at the bus stop."

"Oh." He tousled my hair.

"You're going to go through more changes than the I Ching before you hit twenty."

"I'm pregnant," I said.

He nodded. "That's tough. Your mom know?"

All of the houses across the street were boxy one-story affairs like Marlin's. I spotted a scarecrow in someone's backyard made out of an old raincoat stuffed with yellowing newspaper, wearing a fedora, surrounded by garden gnomes.

"I can't tell her. I'm going back to Michigan to have an abortion. I'm not in love with the father anymore. I have a best friend, Lara. Plus there's my dad and sister."

"That's a good thing, Jeannie. You need someone to take care of you. You deserve better than your mom."

He patted my knee and I let him think that someone cared—

a real parent standing by, armed with comfort and goodness—a magical figure.

"Call me, Jeannie, if you get into a jam." He took my hand into his and squeezed hard.

"I mean that," he said, smiling, revealing his friendly dimple.

"You know what's weird, Marlin? Yesterday in school I sat in science class and really listened and I figured out what I want to be—a marine biologist. I'd love to study what's inside the ocean, discover new species, dig way beneath all that seaweed and gunk. Then I thought, your name is Marlin. Isn't that weird?"

"Yeah. Weird," Marlin agreed. "See, everything comes around in a circle. In fact, everything is a circle. Did you ever notice that? Oh yeah," he said as if remembering something, then hoisted up and went into the house. I pictured myself in diving gear somewhere near Honolulu drifting among the showy fish, spear in hand, poking at the bottom feeders. *Move it along, fellas, I have important work to do here.* My new marine biology goal gave me a sense of purpose, a real destination.

Gazing at Marlin's oval Porsche, I thought of his O-shaped glasses, the peace sign dangling from his ear. We would never sleep together. He had become an uncle—my cloudburst of love was merely a smoke ring.

Marlin returned with a thick envelope of photographs. I jumped up, and he hugged me, my arms loose at my sides. Mika stepped onto the porch, swollen belly in the lead, dressed in overalls and fuzzy slippers. She was Asian with cropped black hair, a friendly smile.

"I've heard some nice things about you, Jeannie," she said, extending a hand. Though the handshake was awkward, I didn't want to let go. Her grip was delicate but strong.

"Thanks."

Marlin shoved some money into the back pocket of my jeans. With reluctance, I walked down the steps and away from the house. I wanted to stay, to become their adopted daughter. *I'm great with babies. I could learn to garden. I could roll your joints.*

"You're a pretty good shot, Jeannie," Marlin said. "You're always welcome here." Tucking the envelope under my arm, I ambled toward the sunlit fog swirling around Weinerschnitzel.

"Just remember," he shouted through cupped hands, "Always question authority and never eat anything bigger than your head!" Mika gave me the peace sign and their laughter echoed in the haze.

Bussing it back to Ebb Tide, I filtered through the photographs, pulling out the ones featuring the judge and his moronic wife, ripping them up and leaving the pieces on the bus floor. In most of the shots, they wore their tennis whites, waving at the damn camera, showing bleached dentures, appearing drunk. Shot after shot of the same pose, probably on the same damn day. I decided to keep one because the background on these photographs were nearly postcard perfect, the lake aquamarine and flawless.

I anxiously searched through the photographs for one of Marlin, one I could maybe frame, show off to friends, stash inside my blue suitcase, but then realized we hadn't taken any of him. All the remaining pictures were of me, clumsy and self-conscious, a walrus posing all over the city. I hated the pictures and considered ripping them up as well, but Marlin had framed these shots, designed them with his funny red eye and except for the scarf and some cash, that is all I had to remember him by. I shoved the snapshots into my bag.

CHAPTER TEN

❖ ❖ ❖ ❖

WITHOUT EXCEPTION, I'D UNDERGO CRIMINAL TRANSFORMATION entering Lara's house—the Weisman manor—with each step my appearance grew more ragged, tattered, derelict. I half-expected a butler to announce, with great disdain, the arrival of the urchin, the tramp. Lara's home was nestled in an exclusive Birmingham subdivision called Maple Leaf Estates. Majestic and grand, the home was planted, throne-like, on a large piece of sloping lawn. Now draped with snow and outlined with razor sharp icicles, the house seemed even more foreboding.

"You sure this is cool, Lara?" I asked, clutching onto her rabbit fur jacket. I had an overwhelming urge to run, dive into a snow bank.

"Come on. Stop acting like you're some kind of loser. My parents love you."

I allowed Lara to tow me inside, then acted casual, pretending not to be impressed by the glittering chandeliers, the spiral staircase, the marble flooring. I swaggered right past the red velvet ropes partitioning off museum-like rooms called "sitting parlors" that boasted priceless furniture intended only for viewing.

It may have been Lara's mother, Red, who triggered in me a choking sense of worthlessness every time I visited. Her laserbeam glare burned right through my skin. She recognized the depravity in me, and it was only the great love she had for her daughter that forced her to put up with me. Lara must have sensed her mother's apprehensions, because she would regularly tell Red how smart I was, how well I did in school. I would return the compliments with a weak smile, waiting for the moment to pass, telling myself that Lara's sales pitch was enough for me to slide by on.

"Jeannie, lovely to see you," Red welcomed, penetrating me with her Arctic stare. Red's real name was Carol, but she insisted on keeping her hair Lucille Ball-red, though it looked seriously fake.

"Jeannie wants me to be her roommate at Sausalito State. She's going to be a scuba diver!" Lara announced. "Cool, huh. So, can I?"

"Sausalito State?" Red questioned. "Let's just get through the holiday visit, Lara."

Letting go of Lara's jacket, I could still feel Red's eyes drilling holes into my back as I attempted to conceal the clump of rabbit fur stuck to my sweaty palm. Lara and I traipsed down the long hallway to her oldest sister's bedroom. Mindy was away at a real college in the east studying medicine.

Lara was jumping around on clunky platforms, embarrassing me with stupid questions about California boys. "Do they talk with an accent? Do they all play guitar? Walk barefoot on the water?"

I tossed my suitcase onto Mindy's yellow polka-dot bedspread, my eyes burning with exhaustion, then carefully placed my ass on the edge of the bed, not wanting to make wrinkles in the coverlet. The entire room gave off a yellow hue, as though the Weismans had leased a bit of the sun, then hung it in the corner of their precious Mindy's room. The wallpaper mixed bright yellow daffodils with tiny brown chipmunks peeking out from behind their petals; lemon-colored shutters framed a bay window that took up most of one wall. The view overlooked the country club golf course, dusted white with snow. In the spring, Red and Sy would spend entire afternoons on the putting green, drinking tea and putting around.

Like the rest of the house, Mindy's room was impossibly clean, as if vulnerable to inspection at any moment.

"Unpack and stuff," Lara said. "I'll go try to get the car."

Lara clomped down the hall, ranting on about this fantasy college on the Bay. "Jeannie would be a great influence on me," Lara whined.

"You've got to think about your future, Lara," her father bellowed from another part of the house.

"Oh, but Daddy, I don't want to be a doctor. I want to be a fashion model."

Still feeling watched, I noticed the glistening eyes of Mark Spitz, all seven swimming medals roped around his neck. The imposing poster hung on the wall above the bed where a crucifix might belong. Scraps of tape were stuck elsewhere suggesting other posters long gone. Mark had staying power. I wondered how Red had let these scrappy remnants remain, how their maid had missed them. I panicked, thinking somehow I would be blamed, then made a mental note to peel the tape clean after everyone was asleep.

Eyes stared at me from all corners of the room. Stuffed animals and doleful dolls sat in bunches on the window ledge, porcelain dancers tiptoed on top of music boxes—keepsakes, their eyes sad, tiny gems. Mindy was the smart one, the leader. Lara was expected to follow her lead, study medicine like their father, Sy.

I snooped through Mindy's mirror-door closet, pretending to look for a place to hang clothes I didn't own. The garment bar was loaded heavy with silk shirts, gabardine slacks, matching sweater sets, designer dresses, and rows of colorful shoes—most of them in their original boxes. The closet smelled like fresh pine, Lake Tahoe. I sighed.

"So. How do you like living on the Coast?" Red stood in the doorway, her arms folded beneath her big, spikey boobs. I felt caught and quickly turned away from the closet. The entire room grew dark, as if all that yellow light had suddenly been sponged up by her towering figure.

"Well," was all I could say, my face hot with shame, sweat beading up around my hairline.

"Tell me what your Mom's up to."

My brain went dead, just flat-lined. I had nothing substantial to offer Red, the perfect housewife and mother—exemplary role model for all birthing females. My body felt twisted and yanked—an old strip of macramé rope.

Lara burst through the doorway, stuffing dollars into her purse.

"Ma, you guys can talk later. Jeannie and I want to hang out," Lara said, dangling the car keys from one hand. "We're going to the mall."

Red drew in a dramatic breath, her chest expanding, her ivory-white neck crane-lifting that blazing hair toward the ceiling.

"Just slow down, young lady. You can't afford any more speeding tickets." Red impaled me with her squinted eyes as if to say, *don't fuck with me, kid. I'm onto you.*

"We mean that, Lara. Take the lead out of your foot!" her father called out. His voice boomed with fake authority. Lara and I usually giggled when Sy ventured to be parental; he was almost too silly to have an effect and his lines seemed rehearsed.

"Where's that California pooky?" Sy's call for me delivered a much-needed sense of relief. Sy was a likable, pear-shaped sort who loved to tease and tell lame jokes. Though a doctor by profession, he was a salesman at heart—everything a pitch. He called us his little pookies.

Sauntering down the hall wearing a cucumber green one-piece leisure suit, he was well into a Groucho Marx impersonation.

"Jeez, missy. You've put on a little weight, huh. What are ya, pregnant?" This threw me—I actually backed into a wall, bumping my head. Of course he would know; he would sense my pregnancy, smell it out. This was his job. "Huh? Huh?" he was waiting for an answer and I considered a full confession, but Red came to my rescue.

"Really, Sy. Stop acting like such an idiot. You should never mention a woman's weight. That is in *such* poor taste."

"So, she's a little fat," Lara intervened. "Big deal." She gave me a knowing look, we both snickered.

"Speaking of the culinary, get back soon or you'll miss a great dinner," Sy said, wink-wink. "I made your favorite, Lara."

Lara rolled her eyes and I let myself relax again. Sy didn't know, Red didn't know. I was still welcome here. We were getting along tickety-boo.

"Oh, Daddy. Okay what?"

Flicking an invisible cigar, in Groucho-speak he said, "We're having wok-fried placenta and ovary burgers."

Grabbing my stomach, I forced out a ha-ha while Lara and Red groaned.

"Really, Sy," Red muttered, wandering down the hall, her cashmere crackling with static. My ha-ha swelled into fat laughter, a needed release. Maybe this wouldn't be so bad—Sy would make this visit bearable, Red would eventually grow to love me. Hadn't she just defended me? Sy grabbed my arm, gave me a tilted, goofy smile, then produced a fat, silver coin out of thin air.

"Now, there's a girl who can appreciate me, even if she is a little zaftig," he told Lara. "There's a girl that wouldn't make fun of her old *macher* because every now and then he sells a watermelon on the side to buy nice things for his family."

He snapped his fingers, pressed the half dollar into my palm, and followed Red's trail down the hall. Sometimes I had no idea what Sy was talking about.

Lara said, "Don't mind him. He's nuts, loves to *kibbitz*." I had heard the obscure watermelon reference before but remained in the dark on the subject and decided it was an inside pip among the Jewish community.

Lara and I barreled down Woodward, snowflakes popping against the windshield like spit balls.

"So he just didn't call you back or write or anything?" Lara asked.

I was sunken into the leather seat, struggling to get warm beneath Lara's suede poncho, but it was like wearing a lead teepee.

"Maybe he split town," I said. "Maybe he's actually in Colorado."

"He's around," Lara said. "I saw him on Woodward. He's just a jerk. I mean, you were really in love with Bill."

"Well, that was a long time ago. Bill's nothing compared to the guys in California."

"Right."

I had told Lara about Marlin, sort of. I described him as a rich artist who owned an airplane and planned to run for mayor. I went on to say that he had proposed, but of course I had to turn him down due to my age. My lies were getting a bit out of control—really swelling up and I knew I had to stop them. I planned to do so as soon as my life improved.

"Bill's a dead end," Lara agreed. "You're better off. I mean that Marlin sounds amazing. Here it is."

Lara parked the Cutlass in front of Bill's house. My stomach clenched with fear but I needed abortion money.

We marched up to the small, two-story aluminum-sided home, and knocked with purpose. A Christmas wreath crafted from crudely painted macaroni shells hung crooked on the front door. No answer. Bill lived with his mother, who worked nights in a pinball factory. Lara and I huddled together under the heavy suede blanket, our cold-as-metal cheeks pressed together, braving our way into the backyard. Snow poured like rock salt, sheathing the world in ice. Bill lived in the basement; the window was frozen shut and needed a few kicks and thrusts before budging. We managed to squeeze through, landing on the cement floor with resounding thuds.

After checking for damage, we gingerly rose to our feet. "No one's here. They would've heard us by now. Anyway, it's just Bill. Bill the fucker. Right?"

The room was dark and dusty like charcoal ash, the air humid and rank. We tiptoed around, knocking over an occasional beer bottle. Lara found a light chain in a utility room that turned on a small, dirty bulb.

Laundry hung on thick ropes stretching across the room. A few pair of blue jeans, a half dozen pastel-colored dresses as big as sheets and two sets of thermal long johns hung next to each other like old friends. I had never known Bill to wear long underwear, but then I had only known him during the summer months.

"Well, it sure looks like he still lives here," I observed.

A bruised mattress lay on the cement, with an old and rusty electric blanket wadded up in the middle. Bill's clothing sat in piles along the wall; one sock, stiff with age, topped a short pyramid of Bud cans. An empty Mad Dog wine bottle sat on the dresser, melted candle wax dripped down its sides leading to a hard red puddle at its base. Fistfuls of change were scattered all around. Just above the bed, stuck onto the ceiling, was a life-size poster of a droopy-eyed Janis Joplin smirking down at us, holding a bottle of Southern Comfort.

"Hey. What do we got here?" Lara said, holding up an opened

box of tampons lined up like fresh cigarettes in a pack. "Told you he was a jerk," she said, extracting a tampon and holding it between two fingers like she was about to light it.

"Maybe they're his ma's," I said.

"Oh, puke!" Lara dropped the box.

With a sudden surge of anger I tossed around discolored T-shirts, wadded-up Jockey shorts, a Zippo lighter, tiny hard balls of tinfoil. Lara picked up a blackened bong pipe and inspected it for dope, but found only a few seeds.

"What are we looking for, anyway?" Lara asked me.

"I don't know. Money or a joint maybe." We heard something upstairs and both froze—statues. Trying to suppress laughter, Lara wobbled in place on one foot.

"Can you guess what I am," she asked.

"One-legged Indian?"

"Hah, hah."

The footsteps passed right over our heads, slow and heavy like Frankenstein. We half expected to see a giant foot crash through. Creak, creak, then whump—whatever it was settled down. The familiar theme of *The Mary Tyler Moore* show traveled down the stairs: "You're gonna to make it after all."

"It's his mom," I whispered. "She's real big." We unfroze ourselves, then grabbed each other's arms, and made our way back to the window. "We'll cut into the next yard, then sneak around to the car," whispered Lara. "She might be looking out the window."

We slipped out the window, ran through Bill's backyard and then into another, whooshing past snow-covered bushes, causing small avalanches along the way. Laughing so hard, we fell twice, the snowy world frosted and unreal.

"Let's break into another house. This is great," Lara suggested.

"No, come on," I said, hanging onto her arm. "I think I got four bucks."

Lara and I sat hunched in uncomfortable chrome chairs at the Weisman's kitchen table, eating poppy seed bagels caked with cream cheese. Except for the steady hum of the refrigerator, the house was unnaturally quiet.

"Maybe we'll just ask my dad to do it in his spare time."

"Yeah, right."

"At least I can supply you with birth-control pills," she offered.

My abortion appointment was getting closer and I was still all the money short.

One small light shone from above the stove. Lara tiptoed through the kitchen trying to avoid the creaky spots in the floor. Wearing black-and-white checked pajamas, Lara was both glamorous and color coordinated, matching the black-and-white tiled floor. In an effort to break the hopeless mood, she recounted her latest sexual escapades. During her recital, I noticed the Weismans had a specially marked compartment for everything from breadsticks to toothpicks.

"Then I gave the drummer a blow job," she bragged, while carelessly plopping our toasted bagels onto the table. I watched in horror as little black poppy seeds scattered across the table and onto the floor. Hoping to prevent more from spilling, I body-hugged the table, but the persistent seeds bounced across the smooth floor and under the cupboards.

"Oh, God," I said, agonized.

"Jeannie, what is your problem?"

"I just don't want to make a mess."

Lara grinned then clamped down into her bagel, flinging the seeds across the room. I leaned back, trying to relax, but kept picturing a sleepy-eyed, barefoot Red getting teeny seeds caught between her toes and blaming me.

"Do you want to hear this story or not?"

"The poppy seeds are everywhere, Lara."

"You're cuckoo. Anyway . . ."

I considered grabbing a sponge and corralling every last seed, but finally gave up and assumed the role of a disrespectful teenager, oblivious to the slop left behind.

"We ended up in the Motel Six behind the Palladium."

"With that guard?"

"Jeannie, no. With the band. They gave me their drumsticks!"

"Cool," I said, genuinely impressed.

I lay in Mindy's plump bed and gazed into the smooth, clean ceiling, recalling the many bumpy and flaky ceilings I had fixated on over the years in cheap apartments, motels, basements, attics. Nubby ceilings revolted me, brought up images of fresh vomit. I sniffed up closet pine and saw Mom arguing with a saleslady in a high-end department store. My mother was hoping to purchase Clara and me fashionable dresses for an upcoming Christmas pageant. It would be our first Christmas without my father, our first at a new school. Mom was holding up twin lace-trimmed pinafores, but the clerk would not allow the purchase—refused Mom's welfare coupons. Instead the snooty clerk pointed her toward the bargain basement, calling out, "Check the remnants, the irregulars. That's what you need." Clara and I hid behind brassiere racks, anxiously watching my mother be humiliated—and for no reason. We found the pinafores hideous; plus, we had no intention of going to the mawkish Christmas pageant.

"Go to hell," my mother snapped, tearing at the coupons. She signaled us, and we all marched defiantly out the front door. Clara flipped the crusty lady the bird.

Fluffed up in Mindy's bed, I kept seeing Mom's disappointed face over and over and longed to speak with her, be with her, have her get me through this abortion. I hadn't expected this—I hadn't expected to miss my mother at all.

❖ ❖ ❖ ❖

"Dad," I whispered.

"Who's that?" His voice was full of unfinished sleep. It was six A.M.

"Me. Jeannie."

"Who?"

A few hours later Lara, drowsy and disoriented, dropped me off in front of a family medical clinic.

"Well, he owes you this at least," she said. The windowless brick building was crammed between a pet store and a dry cleaner.

"Just remember," Lara added, "Debbie Kaner said it was no big deal. Even Maude had an abortion." I had missed the episode. Lara grabbed my head and held it to her chest. "I love you," she said. "We'll get French fries after."

I sauntered through the dimly lit lobby allowing my eyes to adjust. The dark silhouette of my father was pressed against a

back wall, where he sat in an orange plastic chair. I recognized
the wavy outline of his hair, his greasy Dick Tracy curls.

"Jeannie?" Dad stood up, laughing nervously. The waiting
room was empty except for an older black woman wearing an
oversized woolly bathrobe and holding the Bible. "Hello, darlin,"
she kept repeating. "Hello there, baby."

Dad trudged toward me in his lanky way, wearing a baggy
gray suit, pens clipped to his shirt pocket—a regular dad heading to the office.

"You look a little pale there, *Porkchop*." He crunched his forehead up, looking genuinely worried.

"Please don't call me that. Okay?"

I couldn't look at him and instead studied his newly polished
loafers—no pennies. Dad gave me a one-armed hug, tucking me
under his armpit. He had a clean smell of snow and minty soap.

"You need to give the lady at that desk some money," I blurted, anxious for him to leave. "They only take cash." Dad put on
his serious *money-transaction* face and peeled off some bills. A
tired woman wrapped in dead mink accepted the bills, mentioned something about the second trimester and gave him forms
to sign.

Over the phone, Dad hadn't seemed very surprised to hear
from me. He was relieved to know I was staying with the
Weismans and didn't ask to know more. I was showing him pictures of Tahoe.

"This is where we stayed. This is the actual lake."

My father leaned forward, resting his elbows on his knees, his
hands clasped, forefingers forming a steeple—a position I had
seen countless times when we went to ball games, coaching the
teams from the sidelines. I proudly held the pictures up to the
light, but he paid little attention. I expected him to be impressed
by their postcard-like quality.

"Who's that old guy?"

"Oh. Friend of Mom's."

I immediately regretted having mentioned Mom. Looking
defeated, shaking his head, sighing, he said, "This is all your
mother's fault. You know that, don't you? California, for Christ's
sakes. A state for lunatics."

He nudged me expecting agreement. Instead I coughed into

my hand, then pretended to swallow down something foul. I wasn't in the mood to start defending my mother.

"Dad, thanks for your help, but I should go in now. I think they need to ask me questions and take tests and stuff."

His eyes welled up. I had never seen my father cry.

"Dad, please. It's okay."

"You know, Jeannie, I never stop thinking about you. I pray all the time that you are okay. Your mother's not right. Never been right. You can stay with me and Molly. We'll take care of you."

"Mom's okay, Dad. Really. Don't worry about this."

He stood up, adjusting his suit, glancing at the Bible-thumper, soliciting sympathies.

"Praise Jesus," she said wearily.

"Oh, God doeseth work in mysterious ways," my father preached. "Jesus doth love you, Jeannie." He put his hands on my shoulders and applied pressure. "He's the big daddy in charge now."

"Praise Jesus," the woman repeated, lifting her Bible to the ceiling. Then, "Hello there, baby."

Dad hauled in some air, then exhaled, closing his eyes, and finally let me go. Taking giant strides to the door, he turned to me.

"Hey, do you have any plans for Christmas? Molly wanted me to invite you over. I'm sure Clara would love to see you."

"Thanks. Bye, Dad." He sort of saluted, then left.

I needed to talk to Mom; the ache hit me so deep that my knees buckled and I fell against one of the plastic chairs. I gripped the plastic like it was the one thing preventing me from being sucked into my own black hole, a one-way funnel to nowhere. A thick-waisted nurse led me into another dimly lit room. She smelled of rubbing alcohol and her shoes made squishing noises.

A freckle-faced girl my age was slumped in a vinyl chair, leaning up against fake wood paneling. Wrapped in a blue paper dress and matching booties, she picked at her frosted nail polish, small white nubs—baby's teeth. A pastel watercolor of generic ballerinas hung on a wall—cheap like the paneling, but the dancers had rosy, hopeful expressions.

"You better ask for a lot of drugs," the girl grunted. "Man, are they tight with the stuff. Last time I had to pitch a fucking fit. This your first time?"

"Yeah."

"Can't this dump afford some fucking heat?" she yelled into the hall, lighting a match.

The nurse returned, armed with fistfuls of pamphlets and anatomical objects. The freckled girl popped the lit match in her mouth. Holding up a timeworn plastic uterus missing an ovary, the nurse launched into her rehearsed speech. Dragging the pencil along the uterus, indicating the travel path of the fetus, she explained the procedure and like an airplane attendant, held up various objects to accentuate a point. "Insertion will allow dilation . . ." Her nametag read 'Nurse Copless.'

"Menstruation!" the freckled girl shouted. "Who the fuck thought up that word anyway? And what's with *menstrual cycle*? Is that supposed be a combination between mistress and damsel?" We both giggled. Nurse Copless pressed on.

"This is a common surgical practice technically known as suction . . ."

"Just call it a Hoover!" the girl interrupted. "When do I get my fucking drugs?"

Wearing the scratchy paper dress and sitting on the edge of a frigid table in a small sunless room, I wondered where the aborted contents ended up. The walls were cold and white like the inside of an icebox. My feet dangled below me—pulpy, inhuman things. I had no sorrow and had so far been proud of my indifference. But glimpsing the steel stirrups, the shiny receiving dish latched onto the table, I wondered if the thing already had eyes, or fingers. Just how big was it? I panicked. *Fried placenta.*

I jumped off the table and paced around the small room, warmth slowly returning to my toes. What did the clinic do with the remains? Where does all human waste go? How come I didn't know anything? I imagined an immense network of underground pipes chugging along all the by-products of human blunder.

A surgical nurse walked in, smiling, her mouth painted red and plumped out—phony wax lips. She had the coloring and texture of a russet potato; an older, sturdy woman whom I immediately liked. I grabbed her arm, which was warm like a furnace.

"Listen, how big is this thing, this fetus?" I asked.

She gently pulled away and busied herself lifting instruments out of drawers, shuffling Q-tips and tongue depressors, humming a fast version of "Silent Night Holy Night." I guessed she was used to girls like me.

"Oh, they're not even developed," she said. "Really just a mass of tissue. They certainly ain't no soul yet." I sighed in relief. A cigarette butt, a hairball.

"Where does the stuff actually go?"

The hefty nurse made me lie back, then wrapped the blood pressure belt around my arm, and pumped, tapping her foot to the beat of my pulse.

"Peaches, that's a good question . . . I think everything ends up in some refinery and then they make some kind of fertilizer out of it."

"Oh," I replied, partly pacified.

My nurse's nametag read Laveyda, she wore gold hoop earrings as big as handcuffs, and around their rims were little red stones. I could count them during the procedure. I was grateful for something to do.

"Laveyda?"

"Yes, angel face."

"I want to keep the contents."

"What's that, girl?"

"Whatever falls into that bowl. Could you get me a jar or something? I need to have it. I really do. I want to decide where it goes."

She smoothed back my hair with her practiced hands, then twisted it in bunches until it fit into a paper cap. "That's completely against medical regulation. You don't really want to be carrying all that around with you (pronounced *which-u*)."

My arms were being strapped to the table.

"Why are you doing that, Laveyda? I won't go anywhere. I promise."

"It's all just procedure."

God, I hated that word. Heart pounding, my entire rib cage vibrated with each beat. I was locked down, helpless.

"Please, let me keep the fetus." I forced out a tear.

Laveyda dabbed my forehead. "It's going to be okay, baby," she whispered, her breath moving over me like warm summer air. The door swung open and in rushed the doctor, an older man, graying, with thick glasses.

"Hey, Jeannie. I'm Doctor Goodrich. How are we doing?" I was suddenly terrified, weepy.

"She wants to keep the fetus," Laveyda reported. They looked at each other. *Be on my side, Laveyda. Help me out here.* She put her wrist in my hand and I squeezed.

"Don't be afraid to dig in," she encouraged.

The doctor rushed around the room asking questions—where had I gone for summer vacation, what I liked to study in school, dumb-ass stuff that he asked all the girls.

"Could I take the remains with me?" Tears fell freely.

The medical duo spoke in hushed tones then the horrors began. Without warning, Laveyda stuck a long needle into my arm. I watched the fluid disappear inside me.

"Don't let him be mad, Laveyda. Don't let him hurt me!"

I heard the clicking of tools, the rattling of jars. Goodrich shoved open my legs while Laveyda pinned down my shoulders. I grappled and struggled to get up—a freestyle wrestling match with my big nurse who unfairly outweighed me, thinking there must be a better way. *Maude went through this!* Exhausted, I went limp; Laveyda's welcomed wrist was back in my hand. The engine sparked, an anemic engine like a sewing machine, stopped, then fired up again, louder, more like a lawnmower. Exactly like a lawnmower, a machine with sharp, spinning blades. I imagined Dr. Goodrich struggling with the cord, like my father igniting the John Deere.

"Everyone back up. She's going to connect," Dad would shout, tugging on the cord, red-faced from strain. "Get back! Don't want to put out an eye."

Sweating and shivering, I sensed I was being ruined, sterilized. "Laveyda. Aren't I supposed to be asleep?" I screeched. All at once, the doctor connected and the housecleaning began.

I dug my nails further into Laveyda's skin, then a warmth enveloped me, the drugs had kicked in and I no longer cared. *Let's just get on with it. Move it along, Goodrich.* I thought of all the people I had ever known in the world and just as I was being plunged into a deep sleep, I realized not one of them had ever lost an eye. Except, of course, the odd celebrity.

I woke up leaning against a pillow on a hard child's bed wearing a sanitary napkin the size of a bicycle seat. A paper cup filled with grape juice sat on a tray next to the bed.

Gazing around the room, I released sigh after sigh of pure and utter relief. Freckles was across from me, looking dazed, staring up at nothing. I searched the room for the plate of cookies. I had been looking forward to them.

"Hello, ladies!" Laveyda emerged like a tidal wave from behind swinging doors, looking larger than before, carrying a plate of gingerbread men. Freckles and I looked at the smiling cookies and exchanged smirks of disbelief. We ate them anyway.

"Did I pass out, Laveyda? What time is it?"

She pulled the medical clinic take-home bag from under my bed. "You fainted some from the drugs, but that's good. You need to rest for a while longer, sugar." She rifled through the plastic sack, then gave me a knowing look before pulling out a small jar wrapped in masking tape. I shook the jar, surprised by its density. I expected the contents to be a tiny loose thing—a grasshopper, but instead it was like compressed dirt.

"Thanks, but I changed my mind. You can keep it."

"That's a good girl. Now I don't wanna be seeing you again. You got that?" Laveyda scooped up the jar, patted Freckles on the head, and disappeared behind swinging doors.

"Well, that was exciting," I reported to Lara. We idled in the alley behind an A&P grocery store. We had driven a few blocks from the clinic hoping to forget we had ever been there. Snow was melting around us into piles of slush, revealing streaks of dirt and road debris.

Lara was meticulously running wet eyeliner over my lids. "My dad wants to take us to Style Center tonight and do some Christmas shopping, then take us to the Lobster House for fresh fish." I felt something slick run across my eyebrow.

"Lara, is that really necessary? I never wear makeup on my eyebrows."

"Well, you just look like shit," she sighed, disappointed in her efforts to make me look presentable.

"You should wear your sunglasses as much as possible. Maybe Monday we'll go to my bye-bye thighs class. You've got to get back into shape, girl. Close this eye."

She painted on more liner, then blew, her bubble gum breath making me queasy.

"So what's in the bag? Party favors?" I sorted through sanitary napkins and belts, a dozen packets of birth control pills, gauze and tape and some extra aspirin.

"Gauze and tape. What the hell is that for?" Lara asked.

"Maybe I'm supposed to tape myself closed for a while." We lit up cigarettes as Lara blended foundation into my forehead.

"Did I tell you I'm getting my nose done?"

"Wow. When?"

"This summer," Lara said. "I can't fucking wait."

"What about the Indian look?"

"Fuck it. I'm over it. I want to model and you can't look Jewish."

She blended foundation into my hairline, behind my ears, down my neck, then rubbed rouge into my cheeks.

"There." She smiled, satisfied with her work, handing me a mirror. I gasped at the results.

"I look like a corpse!"

"You look fucking great. Let's go spend some of Sy's money."

Maybe I looked sophisticated and didn't realize it. A young A&P worker wearing a blood-smeared apron was hauling boxes into a dumpster. I willed him to look at me, to test the makeup. He squinted and leaned forward. Just as I was about to smile, he gave me the finger.

CHAPTER ELEVEN

MOM WAS GONE, MISSING. ONE WEEK HAD PASSED SINCE THE ABORTION. She had not forwarded the money for my return plane ticket and the Weismans were expecting me to leave after Christmas.

"Daisy blew away with the wind, honey," Sally had said wearily. "Just stopped coming to work."

I celebrated an evening of Chanukah with the Weismans, lighting candles and exchanging gifts. I felt like a heel for not buying them anything, especially after receiving an expensive pair of cashmere mittens. A moody candelabra cast shadows on everyone's face as we ate foods I wasn't familiar with—kashka, kosher veal, matzo paste.

"You feeling okay?" Red asked. I realized that I had been slumped over the table, clutching onto my stomach as though trying to keep it from falling away—rendered weak from pelvic cramps. Releasing a shallow breath, I quickly brought my arms up to the table, rested my elbows, trying to look interested in the meal. Grabbing my fork, I forced myself to eat some veal but envisioned a slaughtered calf and nearly gagged.

"I'm sorry. It's not your cooking, Mrs. Weisman. Maybe I've had too many candycanes this season."

"That's fine, doll," Sy said. "Hope you have room for cake.

We're having a chocolate A-bomb," he teased. I forged a smile and kept it there. Fresh coffee was brewing and its heavy bitter smell filled the room, making me feel even more nauseated. Though I guzzled the stuff, I never knew whether I actually liked the taste.

My cramps had progressively gotten worse and I wondered if this was normal or if something had gone wrong. I considered asking for Sy's professional opinion but I feared being banished forever.

"Jeannie's got a visitor this month," Lara said matter-of-factly. The Weismans shook their heads in sympathetic unison. Lara was brilliant sometimes.

"Give her some Midol, honey," Red suggested.

"Why didn't you tell us she was feeling bad?" Sy added with real concern. "She didn't have to sit through supper."

Lara led me away from the table like a cripple and I felt a genuine, weepy affection for her parents. "Thanks for dinner," I said, woozy with gratitude and pain.

"You're welcome, Pookie. Keep those legs propped up," he said with a wink.

❖ ❖ ❖ ❖

I decided to take up my father's offer and have Christmas dinner with him and his family. It would be good to see Clara plus I needed a back-up plan in case my mother was lost forever. Maybe my father wasn't that bad. Perhaps my harsh judgment was too influenced by my mother.

Herbie, my step*brother*, a term I could not accept given we had no relationship, picked me up in a wood-paneled Olds station wagon. Herbie was an anguished-looking sixteen-year-old, pimply and scabby, fingernails bitten down to the quick—streaks of blood across the nubs. Maybe *step-bother* was the more appropriate term.

"So, what's it like in California?" he asked.

"Lots of socks and sandals," I said, going for a chuckle.

"What's that mean?" Herbie asked with a sneer, his skinny upper torso practically draped over the steering wheel. I got a bad feeling looking at Herbie, as if he was collapsing under some great weight, perhaps my father's fist, pressing down on him like an anvil, keeping him bent over and crooked. My earlier memory of Herbie had been of a sunnier lad.

A Virgin Mary holy card hung from the rearview mirror, weeping blood.

We passed an occasional silo, a smattering of goats, red pickups. Waterford was a runty farm town, known mostly for its racetrack and fresh milk stands. The town also boasted the most amputees per capita in America and each year held a parade in their honor.

Pulling into the maze-division, my dad's newly built, clean, white tract home was one of dozens, a freshly pressed communion host. My father, his wife, Molly, and her flurry of children stood huddled on the snow swept porch, smiling and waving as we pulled up. Clara was not among them. Barefoot Dad danced around on his toes, arms folded, shoulders hunched. Clenching my teeth, face frozen with indifference, I shoved open the door.

"I hate your fuckin' father," Herbie rasped.

A jet roared overhead and all of us looked toward heaven, as though anticipating a crash, then watched as the plane passed by, leaving a swirly trail of chalky smoke across the empty blue sky. I remembered when my father and I held aloft A&W root beer mugs waiting for Halley's comet to pass, hoping to catch some magic cosmic dust.

I shuffled through the excited crowd; getting pinched and patted like the new family pet. "Glad you came," Molly cheered, drawing me into an awkward hug. Large chunks of her poofed-up hair had turned gray, but she was the same fat cheeked, jovial woman I had remembered. All of her children, like Herbie, had dark rings under their eyes, a similar worried expression, bitten-down cuticles. In a short amount of time, I realized my father had sobriquets for all of his stepchildren—Herbie whom he called *Scab*, followed by *Pig, Warts,* and *Squat* for the boys, and *Scratch, Skank* and *Flem* for the girls. Clara was still referred to as *Clap.* Despite his newfound religion, my father had, in fact, changed not at all and possibly had gotten worse, more vicious. As he regaled us with stories from earlier days, I noticed his physical connection to his stepchildren was charged with hostility—his backslap carried a wallop, a tousling of the hair could lead to a migraine. The kids were afraid of him, cowering, flinching. The stories touched on my childhood, but left me feeling empty and disconnected.

"How you feeling, Porkfat?" he whispered, crinkling his forehead, gesturing to my troubled stomach. "Our little secret," he winked.

"Good, Dad. I'm feeling just fine," I told him. "I asked you to not call me that anymore." He showed me to the basement door, tinny rock-and-roll music drifted up the stairs.

"Go say hi to Clap," my father said, nearly shoving me toward the dark cellar.

Clara sat crossed-legged on the cement floor in her silver-studded blue jeans, the studs glinting like tiny stars in an unlit corner. The room had an underground tunnel smell—wet clay and asphalt. Clara attempted a weak smile, her face hollowed and pale. She was scraping the contents of a cold-medicine capsule across a TV tray with a dull butter knife, the remaining Contac capsules wedged between her knees.

"Hey, girl. Heard you were coming. Slut." Clara regarded me with a flat stare; her long unwashed hair crawled down her back like a wounded animal.

"If you eat just the white ones, you can get a good buzz," she slurred, her eyes at half-mast. "I knew you'd come back," she added, tugging feebly at my jeans. There was a shave-and-a-hair-cut knock at the top of the stairs.

"We're going to eat soon, girls!" Molly's pleasant voice wafted down the stairs, along with the smell of roasted turkey and something lemony that made me salivate.

"Fuck you, bitch," Clara replied in a soft singsong tone, rolling her head toward me. "Want some?" She held the tray up to my face, the tiny white grains popping around like molecules under a microscope. She collected a few on the tip of her finger and spread them across her tongue.

"No, thanks."

"You're such a fucking bitch," she sputtered. "I knew you'd never make it out there, little Miss California."

Clara had clearly not gotten better. Being here had made her worse, putting up with this illusion of family. There was no love in this house. And now that tiny spark of light I had seen in Clara's face at Juvy was extinguished.

"How can you stand to be fucked up all the time, Clara?" I asked.

"How can you stand to be straight?"

I helped her to her feet and she adjusted her clothing, preparing to sit with the adults, fake it through another meal.

"Here we go," she said. "They never know. They're too stupid. Don't worry."

I took her frail hand, fingers as brittle as wax candles, and led her upstairs.

We all managed to squeeze ourselves around the holly-trimmed dinner table, decorated for the season with plastic place mats depicting the nativity scene, a baby Jesus smiling up at me. The stereo played "Hark the Herald Angels Sing" while the television broadcast marching bands and parades. We sat on hard, low chairs, elbow to elbow, my father carving up the trussed bird at one end, Molly slicing a candied ham at the other. Molly and her daughters were elegantly dressed, perfumed. Her sons made efforts with clip-on ties and hair gel. Christmas meant a lot to them, they troubled themselves to make it right. They deserved better than my father. I tried not to think about it.

Instead, following suit, I dove into the mile-high potatoes, overcooked carrots, and gelled cranberry sauce that was being spun around on the lazy Susan. We grabbed, pawed, raked, gouged, butchered, and dissected. Orange pop bottles and wobbly stacks of Wonder bread dotted the table landscape. Ketchup poured.

"How's your mom?" Molly asked, her kind face filled with a maternal sympathy.

Clara scoffed, then rolled her eyes as if to say, *Right, like you really give a shit.*

"She's fine," I said. I believed Molly did care and if my father wasn't around I might've opened up to her. But I knew better than to discuss my mother.

"You two adjusting to California?"

"I guess."

Then our conversation ended, got lost in the din of seven kids talking at once—a recent football win, a fistfight at school, the latest game show.

Molly put her hand over mine. "You're always welcome here, Jeannie."

"Like she would ever fucking want to live here," Clara hissed, then spat some chewed-up turkey onto her plate.

My father abruptly stood up and everyone froze, stopped chewing. The Christmas album limped along in the background—glory this and glory that. I had the feeling that if it were not for my presence, Dad would've smacked Clara, perhaps throwing her down the stairs and back into her cave.

"It's okay, Jack," Molly said, her voice still bright. "It's Christmas. Everyone is on edge." My father settled back down and tried to lighten up the mood by tossing Brussels sprouts into the air, attempting to catch them with his open mouth.

"How did I end up with so many kids, huh, Scab?" he laughed, then swatted Herbie across the head. I could tell by the way Herbie dodged that this was a familiar gesture. I winced.

"God has blessed us over and over, hasn't he?" Molly said, then went on about how if most people just had a good hot lunch every day there would be less crime in the world.

I noticed that most of the children were wearing braces, headgear, and other complicated apparatuses. The oldest daughter (Scratch?) sat quietly beside my father, looking worried and serious. Her thin, dark hair drooped down her face like wilted flower petals. I had an impulse to tell Molly to get up and run, flee, find a safe haven but instead I decided to save Clara. I would take her to California with me. I had to.

"Your mother was never right," Dad said out of the blue. "The woman was always a loon."

"At least she's with all the other loons in California," the youngest boy added.

"That's right, Warts," Dad agreed.

My stomach tightened, I jumped up from the table and announced, "I'd like to go for a walk with Clara."

"Yeah!" Clara blurted. She rose up and wobbled back and forth, unstable as a bowling pin.

The kids were silent again and everyone looked to the head of the table to see how my father would handle this. Apparently, Clara was rarely allowed to leave the basement.

"We'll be fine," I said, knowing he had no jurisdiction over me.

"Yeah," Clara said, pushing her thicket of hair away from her face.

"Let them go," Molly pleaded.

"Fine," Dad grunted.

Clara moved away from the table, her body drifting along as though boneless. Just as we were walking out the door, my father rushed over and pulled me close to him, his turkey breath in my face.

"We're just kiddin' back there. You know that, right."

"Yeah, Dad."

He grinned childishly, showing me a mouth full of old, tarnished fillings.

"Your Mom gotta boyfriend out there?"

"I have no idea, Dad."

Then he shrugged, gripped my shoulders and motioned me out the door.

"Molly's a looker, ain't she?" He held his hands in front of his chest, indicating her cup size.

"You girls stay out of trouble." I nodded and followed Clara down the ice-covered porch steps.

❦   ❦   ❦   ❦

We hitchhiked across miles of snow-covered flatland, slowly making our way to Detroit, smoking stale cigarettes in the back seats of Cadillacs, Dusters, and Firebirds.

"I know you had an abortion," Clara said. "Dad told everyone in the house."

Clara flicked ashes onto the vinyl seat and smeared them with her hand. I contemplated telling Clara that I couldn't find our mother, that I was on my own. I wondered if it was possible to form some kind of bond between us, if Clara could clean up, stay straight. We could be a team, keep moving, hitchhike all day and night until we found a good place to live.

"Clara, you should come with me. To San Francisco. We can start over, but you have to stay off drugs. It's the only way."

"Does Mom want me to come?"

"Yes," I lied. "But you have to stay straight. Mom can't help you anymore. You have to be able to handle that. There's no more second chances."

"I can do it. I promise. Just take me."

"Okay. Great. Where we going anyway?"

"Mo's. He just got out of prison. He's having a Christmas party."

Mo's house was in a pocket of faded brick two-stories in a run-down older section of Detroit. Below Eight Mile—not a good place to be. It wasn't far from the neighborhood we had grown up in, its edges were still bruised and scarred from the riots. As though noticing for the first time, I realized how ugly Detroit was—used up, defaced, barely showing any color at all. No wonder California was considered a magical place. Compared to Detroit, it was a radiant flower in perpetual bloom.

Clara talked our last ride, a hairy guy wearing an eye-patch, into taking us all the way to Mo's front door.

"Let me get that for you," she had offered, reaching over the front seat to caress his crotch. She was giving the driver a hand job, wearing my new cashmere Chanukah mittens."

"We're in a hurry," I yelled, sinking deeper in the leather. Another man, another penis, another free ride. What was I to learn from this? I made a silent vow to never become so cavalier with the penis.

"What's under the patch?" Clara asked the guy.

"Nothing. Nothing at all." He yanked off the eye patch in a jerky ta-da motion. I let out an audible gasp, leaning forward to see a centipede-type scar embossed onto where his left eye should be. I'd finally come across someone who *had* lost an eye! I wondered if that was some kind of sign. "See, I got nothing under there," he repeated. "Wow," Clara said, backing off to get a better look. "How do you cry out of that thing?"

"I never cry, baby." He grabbed her cashmered hand and placed it back on his crotch. I closed one eye and for the rest of the ride pretended to be half-blind. Clara's efforts paid off. The furry guy not only drove us all the way to Mo's, but gave Clara five dollars. She scrawled something illegible on the back of a matchbook, shoved it inside his pants zipper, then kicked open the passenger door. I leapt out of the car.

Clara strutted in front of me up to Mo's front door. Just before we went in, she pulled off one cashmere mitten and chucked it into the slushy driveway, gooey sperm and all.

A gleam of bright, polished chrome caught my eye. Along one side of the house was a long, neat row of motorcycles.

Mo flung open the door, wearing a black raincoat and industrial boots, smelling like singed hair. In fact his fingernails were charred at the ends, like he had been playing with matches all afternoon. He might have been the kind of boy who lit stray cats on fire. I didn't like Mo much because my mother hated him, but sometimes I wanted to squeeze him like a stuffed toy. He leveled off at my chin, had shiny, black button eyes and a frazzled mop of hair. His skin had a yellowish quality to it, and his whole effect caused a strange sensory overload like I was looking into the sun.

"Hey, Babe," he said to Clara. "I see you brought along Miss California." He talked in a sugary whisper, like he was telling you dirty secrets. People had to bend toward him to accommodate.

"Hey," I said, looking past him into a weird collage of people milling about the dark house. It was his grandmother's home filled with timeworn heavy furniture patterned with oversized daisies and giant green leaves. Lampshades shaped like half-opened umbrellas sat on skinny-legged end tables, the tabletops blanketed with faded doilies.

Mo and my sister wrapped themselves around each other and ambled toward the bathroom.

"You want an eggnog or some reds, my little L.A. woman?" Mo's voice came out from under the bathroom door, high and squeaky like the door hinge.

"I was never in L.A," I called out.

Partygoers were nodding out on the sofa, some walked around like zombies in search of their graves. I wandered into Mo's cave-like bedroom where I sat on the edge of his single bed and smoked a cigarette.

I snapped on a pre-Jurassic TV and watched the Christmas day parade; pretty cheerleaders making a big stink with their batons.

A thick section of yellowing newspaper advertising Timme Fake Furs was taped to the only window, blotting out the afternoon light. A gangly woman in platforms, her body draped in fur, was smiling in that fake game show way. She looked cold and hungry but I knew she was rich and spoiled, a pampered model. She had designer clothes, interesting appointments, and charm to spare. Men worshipped her. I poked a hole through her forehead. Paper-thin sunrays shot across the stuffy room highlighting dust that seemed to settle everywhere; the ratty dresser, the windowsill, the back of my throat.

Clara slowly poured herself out of the bathroom, her body liquid from heroin, her face a handful of putty. Mo was still stumbling around, maybe looking for the way out.

She sat down next to me and patted my thigh. "I love you Jeannie," she slurred. "I can't wait to get to California." She slumped against me. "We're practically fucking twins. Right?"

"Mo," I called. "Can you drive us home? Back to Waterford?"

He managed a laugh from the bathroom. "No fucking way."

There was a sudden bang, then a thud that made the walls vibrate. I froze, adrenaline shooting through me, nailing me to the ground. Male voices boomed and echoed. *Fuck you. Cocksucker. Pigshit.* Whams, crashes and bangs, a full-blown ground war was happening in the next room. Bodies hurled, glass shattered. Clara collapsed on the floor then crawled under the bed. Mo was in front of me and led us into a closet. We crouched beneath racks of clothes; long heavy fabrics caked with dust. Mo pulled the door closed, the whites of his eyes the only points of light.

"Don't make a sound," he whispered. "It's a vendetta. Evening up the score."

Then Mo's hand was caressing the inside of my thigh, his lips brushing against my ear. "I've always wanted to get you alone in the dark," he whispered. I yanked him closer to me and held on to his greasy head, excited, terrified, and flattered, thinking I'm hiding from bad guys, maybe the Hell's Angels, hiding out with a dark, sexy Italian who wanted me, a small-time Mafioso who probably had a gun hidden in his pants. He would protect me.

"I always liked you, little sister," he coaxed, his hand had moved to my breast. "They won't hurt us," he whispered, leaning into me. "I want to fuck you, Jeannie." Mo's puffy lips covered mine, his breath sweet. His kiss made me feel small and floaty and I allowed it, disappearing into black space. Our breathing got heavy and aggressive. I bit into his lips and pulled his scruffy body even closer to me, the darkness robbing me of any good sense.

I could hear people shuffling in the other room, groaning and cussing, calming down.

"We can't do this," I whispered.

"Just fuck me," Mo purred. "We'll be quick." He was really

gripping my ass, holding me down, his small body wedged between my legs.

"Get off," I said, pushing him away, fighting for air.

"Cunt," Mo grunted, then sprung up and was gone.

The sudden light hurt my eyes. Trembling, I pulled myself up by the old musty housecoats.

"Stupid fucks," Clara yelled from the living room. I wandered cautiously into the next room where Clara stood on the sofa, screaming and wiping blood from her face. Several collapsed men, their faces battered, bloodied cheeks lying against a thick dog-haired carpet, surrounded her. They wore leather jackets, steel-toed boots looking like junked-out cars, gutted and immobile. The room was a shambles, blood streaked the walls, stained the doilies. Then I noticed Clara held a gun. She lifted the weapon into the air, waved it around, wobbling on those boneless legs. I had no idea what to do, how to handle the situation. What was she doing? How high was she?

"I got everything under control," she yelled. Everyone ignored her. Was it possible they were all dead? My heart raced. Mo sat next to her, daydreaming.

"Put that down, Clara," I pleaded, motioning her with my hands like some idiot cop from a bad TV drama.

"Don't tell me what to do, Jeannie, because you don't know anything. Right, Mo. Tell her," Clara shouted.

Mo calmly surveyed the damage with his blinky eyes, shaking his head, considering his next move.

"She doesn't care about me," Clara whined, pouting. "Treats me like I'm some piece of trash. Miss Perfect who gets to do whatever she wants."

Clara pointed the gun at me and I lost all feeling in my legs, fell against a chair, accidentally kicking a man in the head. It was alive after all and he grabbed me by the ankle, a grip so tight I felt it clear to the bone. "Suck my dick," he told me.

Holding Clara in my gaze, my heart moved its way into my ears. Clara gripped the gun with both hands, aimed, and pulled the trigger, an ear-splitting crack that caused me to fall to my knees. My heart stopped beating. I had no pulse. Did she hit me? I saw my mother holding me in her arms, crying, lamenting. "What was she doing here?" she would have demanded. "My one good daughter. She was meant for something better!"

No one moved as the bullet zipped right over my head, piercing through the front window, making an impossibly small hole without shattering any glass.

Tears spontaneously sprung from my eyes as I slowly came back to life. Mo tackled Clara to the ground, grabbed the gun, and slapped her.

"You ruined my fucking high," he yelled. "Everybody get the fuck out of my house," he ordered.

All at once, the broken men rose up, dusted themselves off, and peacefully filed out the front door. Seizing the opportunity, I pried Clara away from Mo and followed the bikers out the door.

We staggered down the snowy street, her sluggish body leaning heavily on me.

"We'll find Jimmy Page and surf," her voice trailed off. "Mo loves me, Jeannie. We're gettin' married," she said, attempting a smile. Her rubbery face looked bloodless, her lips blue. I pressed onward, the wind whipped against my face, burning my skin. Water from my eyes trickled down my cheeks. I had retrieved the cashmere mitten before we left, beating it against the brick house until it was pliable enough to put back on Clara's limp hand.

Perhaps Clara had been right, taking aim at me. I was an awful sister, inconsiderate, selfish, not to be trusted. I went to California without her, hogging Daisy all to myself. I had kissed her boyfriend without remorse. I had to get Clara back to Dad's. Maybe start over. Try again. Get her cleaned up.

I sighed heavily and thought about the bullet, how it banged through that window, making a beeline for the outdoors like it needed to be there. In the spring, some kid would find the bullet lying in the street, a gutter. Excited, he would show it off to his friends.

Clutching my arm, Clara slurred, "Remember how we used to run over bumblebees with that stupid red wagon, then try to pull out the stingers . . . remember, Jeannie? You would get so scared. You were so afraid of getting stung."

I parked Clara inside a bus stop on the main road—across from a Dunkin' Donuts. Rudolph's red nose flickered in the window. Although it seemed impossible, it was still Christmas day.

"Let me do all the talking when we get a ride," Clara mumbled, her head falling to one side. She dug around in her bag and pulled out the gun.

"Jesus, Clara. What are you doing with that?" I yanked it from her and shoved it into my bag.

"Next jerk we'll just blow his dick off," she slurred, then she was out, a torpid condition I recognized, limp and futile.

"Clara, Clara. Wake up!" I shouted, shaking her. But it was useless.

I darted across the intersection and rushed inside the warm shop, rich with the smell of freshly baked donuts.

The place was empty except for an overweight middle-aged woman wearing a tight uniform. Her face was pink and puffy like a bath bubble. She had taken off the pointed Dunkin' Donut hat which sat on the counter like a dunce cap no one wanted to claim.

"What can I getcha?" she asked, wiping errant crumbs from her mouth.

"I need an ambulance. Could you call one for me, please?" I gestured to Clara, who had fallen facedown onto the sidewalk. "She's had too much heroin. I can tell when she's gone too far."

"Wow. Should we call the police?"

"No."

"Your parents?"

"No. Please. She's really out of it."

She studied me, and then sighed. "Okay."

I sat at a wobbly vinyl table, face pressed to the window, my sister appeared dead, her tangled hair lying in oily slush—a child's broken body lying in the street. It was over for Clara. She was doomed.

"Tell them to hurry," I urged.

"They're on their way. "

The counter lady brought me a black coffee and a glazed donut.

"You know her?"

"Yeah. My sister. She lives with my dad. He's a jerk but better than Juvy." I wrote down my father's phone number and handed it to her. "You can give this to the emergency guys."

The setting sun cast an unsettling orange pall over the city; the murky streets seemed embalmed in moist decay.

"I had a nephew who was a methadone addict. He's in prison now. Where are your folks?"

I looked at the nice lady, feeling caught, unable to form a response. I drank some coffee. I seemed to have run out of lies.

The paramedics arrived, sirens wailing, lights twirling. They covered Clara with thick blankets, secured her with an oxygen mask, and hoisted her slack body onto a gurney.

"I'm going to go talk to those men for a sec. Give them your dad's number and such. You okay?"

"Yeah. Thanks. Thanks a lot."

I drained my coffee and watched until the ambulance lights faded away. Waving goodbye to the donut lady, I hit the pavement. I needed to find my way back to Lara's.

CHAPTER TWELVE

"WHAT IS IT, BOYFRIEND PROBLEMS?"

The voice was familiar, but I was too self-conscious to look at the driver. He had picked me up in his Lincoln a few miles back . . . a middle-aged guy in an expensive car. I figured he could be trouble so I never made eye-contact. Instead, I fixed my stare on the snow swept windshield, hugging my purse to my chest, trying to get warm. My fingers were hard and brittle from the cold. A relentless shiver gripped my spine.

"Could you please turn up the heat a little?" I asked.

The driver's smooth hairless hand reached in front of me and the hot air blasted outward, rolling over me like an electric blanket, the heat pressing its way through my clothes and beneath my skin. I needed my blood to boil. I was sniffling back hot tears, both from sorrow and fatigue; the despairing kind that burned the delicate area behind my eyes.

"Sure looks like boyfriend problems."

The question was so innocent and so far from the truth that I had to lock myself down to keep from erupting into a genuine pool of grief. To this normal guy I was just another unhappy teenager.

"Didn't get what you wanted for Christmas?"

God, he was persistent. Tears swelled, plopping down in fat

157

quarter-sized drops onto my lap. Even though my driver was way off base, his authentic concern gave me a much-needed sense of comfort. He handed me a plain white, neatly folded handkerchief that looked like an oversized Chicklet and I blotted up my tears, then dabbed at my lap. I was certain I recognized his gentle, storytelling voice. I looked over at him through watery eyes.

"You're Bobby Bonds!" I blurted, sitting up straight, swallowing back a tiny ball of excitement. "I used to watch you all the time on Channel Two. Wow! My mother had the biggest crush on you."

Then I noticed the stretched and waxy appearance of Bobby Bond's face—like someone had laid Saran Wrap over his skin, then pressed and pinched all of his features into place.

"That's me all right," he said.

I wiped the remaining tears from my face, then shoved the hankie in my pocket—a souvenir.

"I wish I was crying over a boyfriend."

We drove down Orchard Lake Boulevard, winding through the tree-lined road, passing plantation-style homes by the edge of the still, glassy lake. I had been up and down this road hundreds of times, to and from school. In fantasies I had lived in the stately homes, particularly the most exclusive ones hidden from the street, protected by complicated security systems and fierce attack dogs.

"Do you live in one of those mansions?" I asked. Bobby was wearing a tuxedo, an overcoat, a checkered scarf. He was probably returning from some hotshot Christmas party where snooty butlers wearing crisp white gloves served chilled champagne and fancy finger sandwiches from shiny silver platters. I could smell liquor on his breath. My mother had idolized this man for so long he almost seemed a relation. It seemed impossible that I was sitting this close to him.

"Do you know this?" Bobby increased the volume of the car stereo, which played an eight-track soundtrack of *Hair*—Mom's music, a grating song that belonged in church, not Broadway.

Bobby would occasionally close one eye to get a better view of the street, a pretty clear indication that he was tanked.

"Incredible piece of work," he mused.

Other movie soundtracks were scattered on the floorboard—*The Sting, Cabaret, The Poseidon Adventure*. I dug through my purse, grateful at least that we weren't listening to, say *Godspell*, and wondered if Bobby Bonds had missed his calling as an actor. Hoping to make a connection with him and being careful to not expose the gun, I pulled from my purse a photograph of my mother, a Polaroid somewhat faded with age that accentuated her best features—silky, evenly bleached hair, her face in a broad movie-star smile. Glamorous. I held it up close to Bobby's blood-shot eyes.

"That's my mom. She's away on business in San Francisco. She's a real beauty. Popular. Even prettier in person."

"Say now. Bet she is. I see where you inherited your nice looks." This made me feel warm and hopeful, like we could become friends.

"So, you live with your mom and dad in these parts then?"

"Just my mom. We like being on our own."

"Oh, here's the good part."

Bobby cranked up the music and accelerated, taking the curves in a sloppy manner, skidding over the icy pavement in a way that made me think of bad toboggan rides. I held on to my door and wondered just how drunk Bobby was. I suddenly recalled Bobby Bonds being labeled a tosspot, a boozer noted for being driven home by the local sheriffs. My mother had once denounced him as a wino and said he had a ridgy forehead like a Neanderthal, but still found him attractive and wouldn't exactly throw him out of bed. As he belted out the lyrics to "Aquarius," I glimpsed from the corner of my eye Bobby's hand inching toward my thigh, tarantula-like, a motion that, especially as a seasoned hitchhiker, I was now familiar with. The hope I had felt evaporated; it came out of me in one long slow breath like a deflating balloon and seemed to fog up the windows. He wanted something, old drunk Bobby—he realized I was a nobody from a nothing family—a Jane Doe, up for grabs. My throat clamped shut and apropos to nothing, I had this idea that if I were in charge of regulating my own breath, I'd probably be dead. Breathing suddenly seemed incredibly complicated, a chore both so delicate and complex that for a moment the very notion of it eclipsed any mental comprehension on my part.

Bobby was doing a finger dance on the seat, tapping out a beat along with the music. He squeezed my thigh as the song climaxed—"Let the sunshine in . . ." My head suddenly felt heavy with anger, my chest tight. I thought about the gun in my bag, imagined how it would look to Bonds as I pointed it at his famous face.

"Let me out, okay. I'm not exactly interested. And I hate your taste in music."

Bobby seemed lost in the lyrics, squeezing my thigh, hydroplaning around the curves, like it was normal.

"I could shoot you. Just pull out a gun and shoot you in the face. Plus, I don't care that you are all famous. I used to live in the same neighborhood as Vivian Vance."

"What? What's that? Relax, sugar." He started to rub my thigh. My anger grew, my chest heavy with it. Then my heart began to race at the idea of pulling out the gun. I thought I'd warn him one more time.

"I said I could shoot you if you don't stop. Didn't you hear me? My sister probably would've shot you long ago. Take your stupid hand off my thigh!"

"What does your sister look like?" Bobby asked, oblivious to his danger. I slipped the gun from my purse, gripped it with both hands pointing it right at his face. My heart banged around in my chest, I stopped breathing. Stars formed out of nowhere right before my eyes. The air was thick with the pungent odor of stale booze and sweat.

"Stop the car, you big fat child molester!"

The car skidded across the road and glanced off an embankment of snow. Bobby's head bashed into the steering wheel causing the horn to blow, then he straightened up.

"Hey, now. What the hell you doing?"

I fumbled to break away but the door was locked.

"Let me out!"

"Put that away you crazy kid! I wasn't going to do anything. Give me that goddamn thing!"

The tape ran out with a whistle and moan. I looked into Bobby's blotchy, moist face, his nose flaring, both of his hands locked onto the steering wheel. He looked tired and old and I saw my father in his sad, pained expression. I could tell he was harmless.

"No." My new found bravado sounded unfamiliar to me but I stayed with it. Guns make you entirely brave, I thought.

"You should've listened to me. It's not right what you were

doing. I just needed a ride. It was nice of you to pick up a hitch-hiker, but that doesn't mean you can touch me. I've had a really horrible day," I said.

Then it was silent around us except for our breathing, strangely synchronized. The windows were now completely fogged up, the outdoors a blur. As I held the gun on Bobby I felt like I could talk forever.

"I don't have a boyfriend, Bobby. There was no actual Christmas. I haven't had those for a long time. I barely have a father. I lost my mother in California. My sister's in ICU getting shot up with adrenaline, which she hates. She's crazy and wacked on drugs. She actually took a shot at me with a gun. Like, for real."

Bobby was still as he listened. I had an urge to tell him many things. I felt he needed to know for some reason.

"I have no place to live. I have all these step siblings that wear braces. They make me sad. I used to take ballet and was good at it. I had a real chance at things when I was little. My mom had such high hopes for me but now everything has changed and I can't figure anything out. I have really bad luck and I need to get back into school. Men like you are ruining everything."

Holding the gun with one hand, I dug a cigarette out of my bag and punched in the lighter. The newscaster looked on with sympathy, sober now.

"I could tell the station that you're a pervert and I bet all the mothers will stop watching your channel. My Mom used to say there was something wrong with you. She likes Clint Eastwood though and we left Michigan to find him, but that got us a big fat zero. Sometimes I believe in her dreams even though they seem crazy."

"Why don't you put that thing down? How can I help you? What can I do?"

"You should be a nicer person given all the good fortune you've had," I told him. I sighed and let the gun rest on my thigh. I wasn't going to shoot Bobby and we both knew that, but I couldn't let him off the hook either.

Bobby's face softened, he wore the expression I had seen so many nights on television—fireplace cozy, trustworthy.

"My mom used to say that in order to be a newsman you'd *have* to drink. All those horror stories to retell night after night. You know?"

"Well, your mom was just making excuses for me."

"If you give me money for plane fare I won't call the station. I won't tell them you're a pervert. I guess that's extortion but I'm desperate."

He tossed me his wallet. "Take what you need. You know, young lady, I can tell you've had some bad breaks. I bet with the right opportunities, I'm sure you could be a halfway decent kid."

"How would you know anything about being decent?" I pulled out a thick wad of twenties. Bobby was flush.

"I'm never coming back here," I said. "And I'm never going to hitchhike again."

"I have a daughter your age," Bobby said, glancing over at me.

"Yeah. That's pretty pathetic."

I lit the cigarette and blew the smoke into the steamy air. I felt cocky and in control. I had this premonition that my life would never be this bad again.

"I bet she knows what a weirdo you are and pretty soon she'll run away from home and end up just like me. I feel sorry for her." Bobby massaged his forehead above his eye and I thought he might cry. A traffic light swayed in the icy wind.

"You know," Bobby said, throwing back his shoulders like he was about to address an audience. "We fight monsters all day, which is the easy part. The difficulty comes in not becoming one," he added, proud to repeat this old saying and claim it as his own, then clicked open the door lock.

"So long Bobby Bonds." I shoved open the door and watched him drive off, red tails lights fishtailing in the fog.

I was stranded in familiar Keego Bay, miles from Lara's house. The small town was closed for the night, even the laundry mats and donut shops. The streets were deserted. I slipped the gun into a sewer grill and heard it click on the drop. Shoving the cash into my pants, I trudged down Orchard Lake Road until I found Sommers Lane, my old street. I found my way to the long, even row of condominiums, dark now, everyone asleep, heads filled with sugar and hope. I reached the back window of the old condo, which faced the row of parking stalls where I had first spotted my mother's new Cadillac, the shiny transport that was going to take us straight to heaven.

The window pried open easily, and I pulled myself inside, freezing, arthritic from the cold, my bones constructed from lead.

The condo was vacant, cleaned, painted and so quiet my heart-beat seemed to echo. No one had rented the place since we moved. I sank into a corner and looked hard at one wall where a mural had been, the sleeping angels, buried now in primer and thick, white paint. Gone.

And the smells were gone too. Perfumes, hair sprays, kitty litter, coffee, cigarettes. Instead I breathed in disinfectant, window cleaner and fresh paint. Even the carpet smelled of cleaning chemicals as I lay my face into the fuzzy pile, praying to god, or someone above me, for some kind of good fortune to come my way, some kind of end to this dead end.

CHAPTER THIRTEEN

⠮ ⠮ ⠮ ⠮

I SAT AT OUR OLD DINING ROOM TABLE, THE ONE MY FATHER HAD inherited from his parents, playing with the wadded-up chewing gum on its underside, drinking scalded Taster's Choice from one of my mother's chipped mugs that read "Playboy Club 1972." Leslie's coffee smelled like burnt oil, tasted like boiled Pepsi, but it quickly made me feel better, nearly normal. Perhaps all I needed was a good cup of coffee.

I was huddled beneath a scratchy pile of cheap, wool blankets but I still couldn't get warm. Leslie had rescued me at dawn when I stood shivering outside her back door. Without asking questions, she pulled me in from the cold and lay me on her raggedy sofa. Then she started boiling water, toasting bread, and telling me everything that had happened since my mother and I had left.

Her three blonde blank-faced children sat in a semi-circle in the living room watching *Sesame Street*, eyes wide, slack-jawed, transfixed by the images of Bert and Ernie, the Cookie Monster and the others whose names I had forgotten.

The house was cluttered with broken toys, smudged dishes and chewed-up plastic cups, soiled diapers and orphaned shoes, a few dying potted ferns, empty jars of fluffer-butter and opened boxes of pink snowballs. A tricycle sat on a folding chair. The effect was dizzying. Water dripped from the kitchen tap and a round bold-faced clock dangled above the stove from a thick black wire, its glass face cracked. The time, however, was correct.

Leslie had been talking to me for over an hour, once again, wearing me down with one her dramas. But I didn't mind. I was grateful to be in her home. Leslie knew me, knew my mom, even if just for a little while and I drank in that recognition along with her bad coffee.

One side of her face was slightly yellowed and bruised, she wore day-old false eye-lashes, suede platform shoes and one of my mother's faded denim work shirts that fell just below her knobby knees.

"Anyway, Brad must've come by a dozen times looking for Daisy. Remember that cop I was dating?" Leslie asked.

"Well, that ended with a bang, but anyway, he was always coming around. Not for me, but Daisy. It was Daisy this and Daisy that. Says there's a bunch of warrants out for her arrest."

I remembered Brad and could see his thread-like mustache, his loppy ears.

"Did you ever tell Brad about how your husband hits you?"

She laughed, rolled her eyes, and took a big slurp of coffee. "Like that does any good," she huffed. "I've got enough restraining orders to wallpaper the bottom of Keego Lake. That s.o.b. just pounds down the door anyway. You want to live with me? I can fix up the basement for you. You can go back to your old high school. I'll take you in as one of my own, you know, while Daisy gets adjusted. I'll give you a curfew, though. Something I know Daisy never did. You're still a kid, you know."

I nodded in agreement, staring into the plexiglass art piece of my mother's, the one she called *Damocles Sword* subtitled *Hanging Tomatoes*. It was a huge sheet of thick glass punctured with twenty or so red balls, like clown noses, strapped onto the glass with shiny aluminum wire. The piece dangled from the ceiling like a disco ball.

"A curfew would be good I suppose," I said, but my mind was already fixed on returning to California. I would find my mother and figure out a way to live in Sausalito. I wouldn't be so insistent on being happy. I would adjust. I drank down the coffee with a sudden and inexplicable thirst. It burned my tongue and left a ring of copper taste in my mouth.

"I can't," I said. "Thanks, though."

Leslie and I chatted and boiled water until I heard the familiar beep of Lara's car. She was surprised to learn I was hanging out with Leslie on Sommer's Lane, but was glad I had survived the night.

CHAPTER FOURTEEN

❖ ❖ ❖ ❖

BECAUSE I HAD BEEN LYING TO THE WEISMANS FOR SO LONG ABOUT Mom's impressive life, I nearly believed it myself, imagining her standing in the San Francisco terminal, waving and cheering, thrilled to see me, hugging a huge Macy's gift box.

Even though I knew this was an absurd picture, it got me through the last few hours I would have with the Weismans. It gave me a sense of purpose as we all packed our bags, showered, powdered our faces, and brushed out our hair. Somehow it kept me on the same level with their various excitements and enthusiasm. Even Lara, who knew the truth about my lost mother, kept embroidering the lie.

"Daddy, I really want to go to Jeannie's for spring break, okay? Instead of Aruba. Her mom's got this big apartment that looks out at the Golden Gate Bridge and Alcatraz. They put special holy lights right on the bridge. Her mom makes these incredible lamb-shaped breads and stuff like that. Come on, Daddy. I never get to celebrate Easter."

"We're Jewish, Lara. Quit being such a nudnick. We'll see. Sheesh."

Lara elbowed me, giggling, dousing me with perfume and powder. We indulged each other in this ongoing fantasy—the tinkling apartment, perched up high over the Bay—an intricate

Christmas ornament, Lara and me drinking espressos from porcelain cups, spotting the handsome sailors as they drifted by.

❖ ❖ ❖ ❖

"Just look for the Christians and you might avoid this stuff," Dad suggested. His tone was high and full of complaint. Clara was safe, for the moment, in her cave, still sleeping off the Christmas day drugs. She had spent a night in the hospital then it was back to Dad's, business as usual. "Keep in touch, Jeannie."

I knew my father was more or less incapable of any real kind of help—another pretend parent. But I went along with it, like he was a regular father and I was a standard daughter. I didn't tell him about Bobby Bonds or my missing mother.

"Okay, Dad. Well, I'll send a postcard or something."

His tone shifted to an easier, friendly lilt. "Just look for the Christians and you'll be okay."

I snuggled close to Lara in the back seat of her dad's Thunderbird, a sleek white animal that Sy called "Snowball."

Lara was wearing an oversized straw hat fresh from Bonwit-Teller, wristfuls of crazy bracelets and beads draped around her neck and ankles, her Neiman Marcus travel bag stuffed with fruity oils and girlie outfits. She was prepared for sunny beaches and hot sand. I sat next to her, breathing in her smells of coconut and starchy hair sprays, bundled in Clara's old leather coat, which I now considered mine, my blue suitcase clamped between my knees. Everything I owned was clamped between my knees.

"Let's write each other every day," Lara whispered. "And good luck finding her because I want to be able to visit." We clasped hands and squeezed tight.

"Did you have a nice time at your dad's, Jeannie?" Red asked, her voice still managing to pierce my heart.

"It was okay," I answered with phony glee.

"Glad to hear it," Red said, pulling some lint off her wool coat. Sy told jokes all the way to the airport and they even hugged me goodbye, though I knew they were relieved to be getting rid of me. The Weismans bought my act, or chose to not question my circumstances too deeply and for that I was appreciative. I focused on the task at hand—find Mom, a single woman now, carefree and most likely drunk, her big teeth flashing in some cavernous bar in Sausalito.

❖ ❖ ❖ ❖

The huge success of pet rocks was said to be a testimony to the individual's power over his environment. As I read this statement in an airplane magazine, I caught a shiny glint from the corner of my eye, like strands of Christmas tinsel that had been tossed onto the floor. But actually it was the steel casing of a leg brace; crippled legs that belonged to the small boy seated next to me. Secured beneath the complimentary blanket, he was intensely focused on a thick, academic looking book. Maybe he was ten. He snuck a glance at me.

I put down the magazine and pulled out my old army knife, then began cleaning my fingernails.

"Cool knife," he said, his voice a raspy whisper. We had just leveled off in the sky. Passengers jumped out of their seats, lit cigarettes, relieved we didn't crash.

"Thanks. It was a gift like an heirloom."

"Wow."

"Do you have a pet rock," I asked.

"No, but I have a Chia pet that has hair longer than mine." He ran his hand over his military style haircut to prove his point.

"Also, I can't walk anymore." He pointed to a wheelchair, folded and stuffed inside a tiny garment closet in front of us. The spokes were beribboned in festive greens and golds.

"That's mine."

"What's wrong with you?"

"I broke my neck diving into a pool but didn't know it was shallow. I was eight then."

I stared at him and imagined his fragile body collapsing against cement. He had tiny freckles across his nose and large ears that stuck straight out. He wore a red clip-on tie and smelled like Juicy Fruit gum. I felt bad for him but didn't really feel much like talking, but I wanted to be polite.

"Do you live in California?"

"Now I do. In Palo Alto. We used to live in Michigan."

"Me too."

"Where do you live now?"

"Somewhere in Marin County."

"You don't know where?" he asked with some awe.

"I'm an experienced drifter. Who knows, maybe I'll pitch a tent on Alcatraz." I smiled at the boy who was genuinely impressed. I decided to ask him about the textbook he was reading. It looked complicated and too grown-up for him.

"Do you understand that thing?"

"Sure. My mom is a professor and she teaches from it. It explains why people have anxiety and how they can use it. Did you know that anxiety can keep you creative and sharp?"

"No. I guess I should read that book sometime. What's your name?"

"Kevin."

"I'm Jeannie. Want to hold my knife?"

"Yeah!"

He ran his tiny fingers along the edge as I told him a lie about its history—how it had come from an Indian reservation in Arizona, perhaps from Pocahontas, and how it brings luck to anyone that owns it. I continued the story until Kevin fell asleep, one hand clutching the knife, the other my arm.

❖ ❖ ❖ ❖

Of course there was no one waiting for me in the San Francisco Airport, but the fantasy somehow had made its way into the hopeful part of my heart. I traipsed into the area reserved for families and loved ones, and actually looked for her, searching the excitement on people's faces for a clue. I may have even said, "Darn, where is she? It's just like Mom to be late." Kevin and I shared a wave as he was carted off by a group of grown-ups. There I was, talking to myself, the drifter. Perhaps I really would be pitching a tent. But then this charade gave way to a pitiful sadness.

Slouched in front of the white curb zone, I looked on as boxy buses, hotel limos, and imported cars rattled by. No one would be stopping for me. I put my hand out and waved into the traffic like a New Yorker and a taxi actually stopped. An orphan's pumpkin. With caution, I pulled open the door and tilted myself in. "Are you for me?"

The driver had a great swell of white hair that cascaded over the seat, and on top balanced a red beret, like a floatie.

"You got money?"

"Well, yeah."

"Then I'm your man."

Blue suitcase in the lead, I clumsily lay down across the shiny vinyl seat.

"Where we going?" the driver asked, his voice pleasant. I didn't answer because I wasn't sure.

"You okay?"

"Air sickness or maybe seasickness now that I'm on the coast and all."

"Christmas always brings out the blues," the driver sang with comforting melody, a tune that sounded both familiar and unfamiliar, his long, pointy fingernails tapping rhythms on the steering wheel—a night creature.

"Could you take me to Sausalito?"

"Got an address?"

"No. Just drop me off at the first bar you see." I hoisted myself vertical and leaned against the door, trying to look normal.

"That bad, huh?" The sun had dropped beneath a blanket of dense fog, its blazing orange light a ring of fire.

Despite the sea-foam hair, my cabby was young, sort of cute, his pale eyes as wide and ready as freshly popped corn. He had a friendly overbite and flushed cheeks, a face full of frolic—a Warner Brothers cartoon, someone who still farted for the fun of it.

"Been raining since Thanksgiving. How long you been away?" he asked. I relaxed and lit a cigarette.

"I can't remember," I said, cracking the window. Small, irritating raindrops speckled my cheek and shoulder while I massaged a blossoming headache in my temple, thinking hard. Where was I going? What if Mom wasn't in the random bar? I watched the meter, the red numbers ticking and climbing. The sky grew darker, the fog not as innocent- looking now, but gray and menacing like smoke from a hostile fire. My driver sang all the way across the bridge and into Marin and by the time we arrived in Sausalito my headache was gone.

"Are you into bubbling?" he asked as we glided over the bridge.

"Sometimes," I answered, having no idea what *bubbling* was, though he struck me as someone who would be a bubbler.

Perhaps in Marin it was a dance that involved hula hoops and beachballs, or maybe he was going to pull out a bong. Then a string of soapy bubbles traveled into the back seat, hovering in the air like fireflies, before one lit on my knee and popped.

"Cool," I said.

We pulled in front of the Trident restaurant, the first bar along Bridgeway. The place was deserted. As we idled, white mist rose up all around us.

"The fog here reminds me of cotton balls, you know, the ones in aspirin bottles," I said.

"I like that," my driver said, punching the meter off. "Cotton balls rising, levitating, climbing. Cotton from hell. So guess what? Some dude swan-dived off the bridge last night and the fucker lived! Now he's a celebrity, sees things from a different perspective."

"Wow. Why did he jump?"

"Taxes," Bing said, shaking his head, like he was totally disgusted by the idea of tax. "I think hemp should be legalized. Sometimes I think about jumping state, moving to Oregon. Know what I mean? But I'd miss my folks, plus I do like it here."

Bluish veins shaped like question marks bulged through my driver's manly hands, beckoning me with life's riddles.

"But this state can be tricky," he warned. "It's big-time conservative even though it pretends to be happy-go—schmappy, living the life of the proverbial Riley. You know?" he explained, his coloring unnaturally white as though dusted with chalk. I wondered whether he was an albino. I could almost see through his skin, to his nervous system.

"But, when you cut through the flummery, mostly what they care about in the city is material wealth, stocking the wine cellar, and, of course, the big thing, Tantric sex. How long and how often. Entire families are falling apart because suddenly this new ideal of having, like, a week-long orgasm cannot be achieved daily. Come on. Don't these people have jobs! Weird. At least on this side of the bridge, people just fuck the way they want to, everyone seems to be happy, and also they like to jog a lot. My parents live in Fairfax and they fuck like bunnies," he explained, twirling hair around his finger. "I can always tell when they're going to have sex because my dad keeps referring to some quote 'conversation' unquote he's needs to have with Mom," Bing mused. Then pointing a finger at me, "Hey. Cotton tails coming from hell, rotten cotton. That's so cool."

This guy was kooky, but I liked him. "Wow," I said. "Your parents sound nice."

"Thanks," he said, then gestured toward the restaurant. "Tourist trap. Shit tippers. I used to wait tables here. Now I'm studying agriculture during the day over at College of Marin. Oh. And I love fractions. I have the best math teacher." My driver shut off the engine and slouched into the seat.

"Really. I went through a bunch of cornfields in Nebraska last fall and wondered how they got into freezer bags and stuff. So you have to go to school for that?" I asked, genuinely interested.

"Yeah, pretty much." Then he told me how he once grew a banana squash the size of a Dachshund but I was reminded of my mother-finding chore.

"If this place is for tourists," I said, "she won't be in there." I pulled three twenties from my back pocket and handed him the crumpled bills, accidentally brushing the soft skin of his hand with my own.

"I thought all Californians had tans," I said slyly, trying to check for pink in his eyes without being obvious.

"I am tan. For me," he said, holding up a bleached arm for inspection. He held my gaze, I felt caught, then blushed, my pulse raced. His eyes were pale green, almost yellow like zucchini pulp. He was merely a sun dodger.

"Do you know a bar that would be for locals?" I asked, then looked at an invisible watch on my wrist, embarrassed by the charged air. I thought if I touched my driver again I would receive an electrical jolt, my hair would stand on end, stick to the window like a galvanic balloon.

"How local?" His voice dropped an octave. That made him cuter.

"Well . . . she's kind of been here all her life. I mean, she considered herself a local way before she moved here."

He cranked up the engine and pulled onto the two-lane boulevard, the quiet street that divided the small town. Glossy from rain, the storefronts looked slippery and colorful, reminding me of a children's pop-up book.

My driver's body swayed slightly to the motion of the windshield wipers, like a metronome. I wanted to touch his shoulder, risk the shock. We idled in front of a small, nondescript building.

"This place is so local it doesn't even have a name," he said, raising an eyebrow, our silent seduction continuing.

"Oh. Good."

Coolly handing him a five dollar tip, our hands touched again and a tingle shot up my arm and traveled to my toes.

"So, you want to go out sometime?" he asked, trying to be nonchalant, fussing with his hair again, flipping and twisting it into a ponytail, then letting it tumble. Some kind of nervous twitch. I wondered if he considered himself undesirable, a spastic outcast, perhaps teased as a child, called a milksop. He needed me. I hadn't realized my door was open, rain was soaking my jeans.

"Yeah," I said. "Sure. I'll go out. I don't have a phone number but I will eventually."

He scribbled something on a Weinerschnitzel napkin.

"I've eaten there," I exclaimed.

"Yeah? Great pups."

"Your name is Bing?" I asked. "As in Bing Crosby?"

"Yeah, yeah. Mom had a thing for him."

"Oh, my God," I said, relaxing back into the seat. "Me too. I mean I've got a famous name. My mom named me after Jean Harlow. I don't even know who she was, but my mom loved her. This is so weird."

For some reason I found this "coincidence" incredibly meaningful. I sat there, just staring at Bing, my new weird friend, then made an effort to step into the rain. He grabbed my hand and squeezed, charging my body with his warmth. I backed into the rain and smiled.

"Bye!" he called out, driving off, waving his arm around like a fluorescent tube.

CHAPTER FIFTEEN

STEPPING ACROSS PUDDLES, I HEARD THE SCRATCHY BRUSHING OF A snare drum. Twisting in the rainy breeze was a poster-sized wooden sign, splintered and unadorned, dangling from a piece of driftwood that was stuck like a finger in a dike into the side of the building. The sign swayed and creaked and read 55.

Pressing my face against the cold hard glass, I could see in the dark redness fishing nets, rusty anchors, an oil painting of a sunken pirate ship. A nautical place.

Impossibly, I could smell my mother's pungent perfume, corsage sweet and optimistic. Bar types came into focus, mostly men, a half a dozen or so, bearded, in boots and parkas, like a gathering of fishermen discussing the day's catch.

The band was made up of three: a lanky pianist hidden behind a wool cap, a smiling drummer, eyes in a dream-like flutter; and a stout violinist, the instrument tucked under his chin like a child's toy. They were playing a tortured version of "Que Sera Sera," the beat so unsteady the song might tip over.

The long L-shaped bar stretched out of view as though the place had no end. I quietly creaked open the door and slithered inside. Almost immediately, my eye caught a familiar flash of something gold—the glitter of her yellow hair. In one hand Mom held a wine glass, in the other a cigarette, a familiar halo of smoke hovering above her, balanced on a bar stool, one foot dangling. I recognized the high heel, it was a shoe she had once spray-painted black to match an expensive dress she had worn on a promising date.

Now she wore a different dress, something airy, saffron, and summery with thread-thin straps and a low neckline. She looked mushy and warm like a plate of steaming yams. She was laughing, so I presumed the rosy-cheeked, wind-burned men were telling her their high-seas adventures.

For a second I thought I caught my mother's eyes. Knotted with panic, I considered running, but stepped forward, closed my eyes, and waited for the sudden onslaught, the fuss. But nothing happened. The music and chatter doddered along, Mom's circle ignoring my presence. I had more to do. No one was going to meet me halfway. Fans twirled and chopped overhead, blenders whirred, glasses clinked, laughter vibrated beneath my feet.

I stared into the wide backs of the burly men, broad shouldered, covered in suedes and hooded flannels, shiny pile.

Teeth chattering, knees knocking, I looked back at the window, almost expecting to see myself standing there, pathetic, a voyeur with no life, all weird quirks and twitches. Someone who had spent entirely too much time alone.

I sighed and watched Mom's vampy variety show, a wisecrack, a knee slap, a group laugh. She was sort of looking my way, while delighting the men with her *bon mots*, then studied me, quizzically, like she couldn't quite place my face.

All the men's eyes were on me now, some windowed in thick glasses, others bloodshot—spider-veined faces of dulled expression.

"Jesus H. Christ," Mom whistled. "It's you. Holy shit." She broke free of the circle, her heels unsteadily clomping across the wood floor, fleshy warm arms scooping me up. Relief. But soon she was carrying on in her exaggerated way with the phony accented voice.

"This is my honey, the baby I nursed with my own bosoms! Look at her!" she squealed, holding me out like merchandise.

"Oh, my God, Jeannie, what are you doing here?"

Male voices, questions coming up from behind. Ooohs and aaahs, whoas and far outs. Then it was silent, like they wanted an answer, collectively, to satisfy my Mom. *How could she have asked this?*

"Looking for the Christians," I told them. Then everyone roared like I was really hilarious, a genuine cutup.

"Willow . . . bring this kid a drink. She's been doing some serious traveling. Make it a Shirley Temple . . . she's only sixteen. Did I tell you she was a stitch? Did I tell you she was gorgeous?"

I was fifteen, but that was okay. At least Mom had mentioned me to her friends.

She smacked some burly guy on the back and I wondered if they were fucking.

"Subtle, that's what she is. She gets that from me," she shouted, maintaining the phony accent.

Blown fuses, exploding circuits, bad toasters. I began to sweat with embarrassment, hot oil seeping out of me. Mom's hands were all over me again, long nails painted sweetheart pink, scraping along my skin. She deposited me on a fat cushiony chair that deflated and puffed, shooting up gauzy dust and stale body odor. The bartender Willow, a thin, pale woman with reedy limbs, handed me a red drink, the glass mug rimmed with waxy cherries. "Can't believe Daisy has a daughter your age," Willow said, shaking her head in disbelief, handing me a tin cup of goldfish crackers.

"I know, it's amazing. Even I feel too old to be her daughter," I replied. I wanted to ask Willow if she grew into her name or if she changed it after realizing she would grow up to be tall and lithe, but she whisked off to serve someone else.

My mother had gone back to her pals, rapidly adjusting to my presence. She was swaying to the music, coiling and twisting, moving from man to man, the well-defined muscles in her back catching the light. Torturing my candied cherries, I wondered who would be her closing time date. Body thumps and squeaky springs. Some of her audience began to clap to my mother's strange dance, her neck doing wide, ridiculous spirals as she snapped her fingers and tap-danced on those stupid heels. Did she do this every night? Didn't she have a job? Had she lost her mind completely? The burly man caught her, cupping her tiny breasts, breasts I knew she hated, often tried to disguise in fancy bras we could never really afford.

I ground away on the goldfish crackers. Maybe coming here hadn't been the best solution. I had heartburn and my ears rang. I bummed a cigarette from a chinless, balding man seated near me, a greeting card smile slapped on his face, a clapping seal. I lit up the Marlboro, a brand I didn't like but could get used to. I thanked the man for the smoke, wondering if he knew my mom. Was she considered an actual attraction at this bar, like the slumberous band? "Que Sera" had taken on surreal proportions, circus music for the seals.

Mom was recounting wild tales—her famous art gallery, romantic brushes with a few Kennedys. But no mention of the heroin addict chained like a rabid dog in my father's basement.

The men were getting closer, moving in for the kill, then she burst through them. "Good bye. Ta-ta!" she said, grabbing my hand, pulling me away, into the wet night air. She was laughing and teetering, these men meant nothing to her. As soon as she touched me, I started to vibrate from trapped tears, whirring through my chest like a swarm of bees.

"Wait till you see what I got, Sugarpie," she said, smiling, her eyes bright.

We slogged along the slick sidewalk, pelted by rain. My mother dangled keys from her hand, taking off her shoes, staggering like she had been shot full of lead.

"Have I got a dream job! Did you see that guy with the beard . . . well, that's only Harvard Price . . . one of the biggest architectural designers in the fucking city and I work for him," she said, leaning on me like I was a cane. "Only good thing I got out of that asshole Donald. My god, Jeannie, he designs those cylinder hotels . . . you know they go straight up forever, like rocket ships."

Mom gestured toward the sky, then looked at me, raising an eyebrow. "Well, you wouldn't know . . . they have them only in New York and Toronto . . . places you haven't been."

"Mom, where are we going?"

"Some day I'll be designing those hotels. You just watch. Price knows a talent when he sees one for Christ's sakes."

She sucked in a deep breath like she was about to dive into the deep end of a pool, then let it out all at once, paused as though trying to remember something, then continued on.

"Well. He asked me to go to Sonoma for the weekend. That's when you know it's getting serious. Oh, honey, it's all working out. You came at the perfect time."

Clothes drenched, my hair a soggy mop, *I came first* I kept thinking. *She left the bar.*

"For now I answer his phones—well not his, but the firm's."
She stopped, then started to laugh. "Can you imagine, Jeannie?
There I am in my good two-piece gabardine suit, sitting like a
jack ass, smiling and pressing buttons. 'And whom may I say is
calling?' Right? Then this odd man calls and says 'Mr.
Frankenstein calling for Mr. Price.' Can you imagine? So I said,
'As in like the Doctor?' and he said, "Yes, but it's Bob. Just Bob.'"

"That's funny, Mom. C'mon. It's cold."

"For some reason Price didn't think it was funny." She
searched the sky, puzzled, as though noticing the rain for the first
time, then turned to me.

"Honey, where the hell is your umbrella?" she asked, poking
the wet air with a finger. "Don't you know about Marin? It rains
a lot. Absolute cataracts!" She heaved a sigh and we resumed our
wet stroll.

"Wait till you see my apartment, Jeannie. I have an entire
family of deer that eat off the balcony. I feed them lettuce leaves.
Just wait."

We arrived at a small red convertible, its windows open, the
seats drenched.

"Honey! Look! I got my very own foreign car! A convertible!
Remember how I said that's all I ever really wanted? Things are
finally coming together. It only took thirty fucking years."

I climbed onto the puddled seat, shivering, my thin, water-
logged suitcase shredding, splintering.

"You still carrying that old thing? Jesus, Jeannie," Mom
slurred. "That one guy was cute, that blond, with the wire-rims.
Steve, I think. Hadn't seen him before. Says he worked in
Berkeley. Lives in the hills or something. In case Price is a wash.
Nice. Really nice. Do you remember him?"

We drove in the demoralizing downpour on the wrong side of
the road, cold air blasting at us from heat vents. My mother continued about her prospects.

"Mom, get over to the right, put on the wipers," I interrupted.

She sighed. "Haven't you heard anything I've said? God. Did
you come all the way here to put a damper on my life? Is that it?
Don't you be telling me how to drive, Jeannie. God, here we go
again. My stick-in-the-mud daughter. You haven't smiled once
since you saw me! Came all the way here, across cornfields and
forests just to give me a hard time."

We bumped up on the sidewalk, glancing off the curb. She wiped the inside of the window with her coat sleeve, squinting.

"Can you drive, honey? My vision isn't what it used to be. Do you know how to drive?" Then, as though she were seeing me for the first time—"Oh Jeannie, I've missed you so much." She slammed on the brakes and we skidded up an embankment, her arms all around me again, her sweet perfume stuck like glue in my throat. She started to cry, bawl.

"Honey . . . we're finally together. I'm living in Tiburon now and there's this great high school. It's so fantastic all the kids graduate and go directly to Yale. You're going to love it. Did I mention I went to a shrink, just once, and he told me I was so depressed I was happy," she sobbed. "Can you imagine that ass! But don't worry baby. It's nothing a drink can't fix. It's a blood sugar issue. I knew it would become a thing sooner or later. Keep an eye on your sugar intake, sweetie."

She sat upright, wiping her mascara-streaked face with her fringed shawl, stopping the tears. "Hey! Did you know that Tiburon means shark?"

She had my arm and was kissing it up and down, hugging it to her chest like a favorite blanket.

"Wait till you see the view. I see the whole fucking world. Oh, honey, I tried to find you so many times. There were so many goddamn Weismans in Birmingham. Christ."

Her waterworks of emotion made me want to jump out of the car and run off, but I held on, too afraid of losing her again. I'd put her on a leash, lock her indoors, dump the booze. I'd get her involved in my homework, read novels aloud, entertain. We'd bake, sew wimples. My mind was spinning! I was fatigued by the very idea. Off in the distance, I saw a yellow bubble move through the wet dark air like a misplaced star. It was Bing coming back for me.

"Mom, let's take a cab. You're going to kill us."

CHAPTER SIXTEEN

WE CONTINUED TO DRIVE THROUGH THE RAIN, NOW IN THE BACK SEAT of Bing's cab, sloshing along the slippery streets like a giant golash.

"Your name isn't really Bing, is it?" My mother was blowing smoke all over us, fumy vapors fogging up the windows.

"Yep. After the entertainer."

"What was your mother thinking? Bing Crosby. That fascist bastard. Are you aware that he beat his children, his wife? Huh," my mother huffed. "Bet you didn't. It's one of the best-kept secrets in Marin. You have to be in-the-know."

She hauled the nicotine into her lungs, alternately batting away smoke and drying her hair with the bottom of her dress. Bing and I exchanged a look in the mirror. I shrugged and he smiled.

"Jeannie. You'll thank me someday for what I've done. Getting you away from Thor. Damn, we've done pretty well on our own."

"Yeah, right. God, Mom, we've lived in the park, slept in cars, dressed in closets, we've starved. What are you talking about?" I griped, exasperated. "I'm a truant, I have no school books, no clothes. My boots are wet shoe boxes and I hate my hair."

"You have nice hair," Bing intervened.

183

Mom ignored me, peering into the night for inviting places to drink. "One day you'll thank me, honey," she mused. Then, "Good god. Let's go get a drink. Bing baby, take me to Sharkey's," she rallied. "I need a tall glass of vino."

"Finally, here we are, me and my baby. Jeannie is the most amazing girl. Bing, did I tell you she once recited 'Hello Dolly' from beginning to end when she was just five? She could play a mean violin. Remember? Bah bah black sheep, have you any wool?"

"Shut up, Mom. Just shut up. Can't we just go home? I traveled for hours, I'm tired and need a break. You are the worst mother on earth and I can't do this anymore."

"Sheesh. Aren't we touchy? Just calm down, Jeannie."

"You don't even know why I went to Michigan or what happens to me when you're not around."

"Jeannie, I trust you. I know you're okay, you can take care of yourself, always could."

I decided to tell Mom things, right there in front of Bing. He gave me some nerve.

"That's no excuse. Plus, it's just not true. I can't really take care of myself. For example, Mom, I had an abortion, I was almost molested more than once, and by a celebrity and I was nearly shot to death by my very own sister!"

I let the information soak in but Mom didn't miss a beat.

"You had sex? With who? What celebrity!"

"Bobby Bonds."

"You had sex with Bobby Bonds? He's fucking ancient!"

"We didn't have sex but maybe he was going to molest me."

"Jeannie, what are you talking about?"

"I had the sex with Bill."

I looked at Bing with guilt, like I was two-timing him, though I knew this was ridiculous. He taxied on, sending me comforting glances in rearview mirror.

"Oh, I knew it," Mom hissed. "Bill, that inbred idiot. Should have known. Didn't leave Michigan quick enough. Well now you know, Jeannie. Now you know where sex leads. I could've told you that! We need to discuss this, but in private. We'll talk about birth control and your future, all the fun stuff. Don't you know to take the pill?"

I rolled my eyes and sighed.

"The point is you're here. Let's get along, go have one more drink. Sing me a song, Bing. What was that song your father was famous for."

"Christ, Mom, he's not actually a Crosby."

"I did it my way," Mom crooned.

"Mom, please stop. Don't. That's Sinatra anyway."

"Jeannie thinks I'm nuts, don't you Baby? That I'm some kind of alcoholic. Well, I'm not. I can pass on a drink anytime, I just don't want to. I like to have a good time, but I know what's going on. Meanwhile, Sugarsnap, I need to keep up a certain joi de vivre."

She leaned over and kissed me on the top of my head.

"Yeah," Bing added. "I am what I am. It is what it is," he sang, trying to lighten the mood. Rain splashed against the windows like a car wash.

"Say. Who was it that said that?"

"Popeye, Mom," I told her.

We surged ahead toward a huge lit-up club, stopping in front of a bright neon sign that read Sharkey's. Crowds of people were huddled in bunches, webbed together by umbrellas. A flashing disco ball was reflected through the window.

"This is my stop. Bing knows where I live, honey. He'll take you home." She turned to me, "I'm doing the best I can." I believed her; she hugged me and teetered off to another party.

"You know my mom?"

"I'm the only cabby in town." Bing offered me a stick of gum and I took it. "Hey, like, you can stay with me if it gets rough. My parents don't drink. Maybe the *only* ones who don't."

We drove along Bridgeway. I got out my camera and took pictures of San Francisco, a glittering jewel in the distance, shuffling drunks back and forth, up and down. I got this sense everyone in Marin was little mad, off-kilter, but the community somehow held itself together, supported the chaos, nurtured its own. We taxied late into the night, until every last drunk was delivered. Bing and I *bubbled*, brainstormed, and cobbled together a plan, a blueprint for my new life in Marin. There was Bing's offer, his nice parents, I could call Marlin. My mother would take a secondary role, the eccentric aunt called upon to sign legal documents, provide family history, furnish me with a room—with a view—all the while reciting her fire-eating adventures, romantic shipwrecks, fairy-tale ambitions.

With this combined effort, I would find my way back into the familiar security of classrooms and bus stops. My mother couldn't make good on her promises, but perhaps I could. My happy ending would be another beginning, rugged but new. After all, here I was taking pictures, flapping around in the rain with a regular entertainer, the lights of Sausalito dancing all around us. We would drive until the rain stopped falling and the rising sun made its debut, a ribbon of light on the horizon. There had been some luck on my side, plenty. Not the sweepstakes kind of luck with bells, whistles, and pots of gold, but the kind of luck that kept you alive and afloat. Sensible luck, my brand. If this was the lowest, the worst the world had to offer, it suddenly didn't seem so bad. It didn't seem so bad at all. I pointed the camera at Bing, white hair flowing, blushing cheeks and red beret, his eyes shiny and bright. He was waving at me like it was all okay.

RHONDA TALBOT is a film executive. The graduate of countless writing workshops, her work has appeared in such periodicals as *Ground Zero* and heard at Spoken Interludes. One of her short stories was adapted into a short film that was accepted into the Sundance Film Festival, and later aired on MTV. She lives in Los Angeles with her husband and son.